APOLLO in Tweeds

BY
BARBARA HAMMOND

PublishAmerica
Baltimore

© 2005 by Barbara Hammond.
All rights reserved. No part of this book may be reproduced, stored in a retrieval system or transmitted in any form or by any means without the prior written permission of the publishers, except by a reviewer who may quote brief passages in a review to be printed in a newspaper, magazine or journal.

First printing

All characters in this publication are fictional and any resemblance to real persons, living or dead, is purely coincidental.

ISBN: 1-4137-6869-5
PUBLISHED BY PUBLISHAMERICA, LLLP
www.publishamerica.com
Baltimore

Printed in the United States of America

To George
Inspiration, friend and beloved husband

Chapter One

The crates were labelled 'fresh fish'. They stank and had enough old guts and scale smeared over them to fool the casual observer as to the fish, if not the freshness. Their contents, however, were very different.

The small fishing boat, pretentiously named *Herakles*, had cruised into the harbour of the Greek Island of Sigandros at first light along with the legitimate vessels. Well, mostly legitimate. There wasn't one that didn't have a case of duty-free cigarettes or booze discretely hidden under a tarpaulin.

Robert wrestled another case out of the hold and stacked it with the others on the quayside. It was not yet eight in the morning, but the August sun was already hot. In contrast to the short, dark-haired, olive-skinned fishermen, this young man was tall, fair and blue-eyed. He wore a baseball cap, long-sleeved shirt and full-length cotton trousers. Long ago he had learned to his cost that his skin was never going to take a tan and it was cover up or burn. The sunshine so prized by tourists to the Greek islands was his enemy.

As he turned back to the boat he saw Yánnis and Costas smoking in the wheelhouse. Lazy gits, he thought.

"Hey, come and give me a hand," he called in English.

"*Sindoma*," Yánnis replied in Greek, indicating they would help soon, and the pair waggled their fingers to indicate the motion they had no intention of making.

Robert reached for his bottle of mineral water, knocked it

with his trainer and sent it rolling, splashing its contents over the stones until it ended up in the scummy waters of the harbour.

He cut back a profanity. These characters should all be in gaol a dozen times over but they disliked blasphemy and were likely to reinforce their opinions with their fists. Whilst he could take care of himself, it was too bloody hot to start mixing it this early in the day.

It was time for a brew and a smoke. If the Greeks didn't like it they could do some of the sodding work themselves. In the tiny galley he extracted another bottle of water from a pack. It was lukewarm but welcome. He took a long swig then poured a few inches into a battered aluminium pan and set the water to boil on the tiny gas ring. When it was bubbling fiercely, he made a cup of instant coffee. These characters made enough money, why couldn't they afford some proper equipment, a few luxuries, like decent coffee? Answer, because then they would look more like the smugglers they were, rather than the innocent fishermen they were not.

Suddenly Robert longed for grey skies, gentle rain and the good strong tea of his native Scotland. He had been away from home too long. He looked out of the dirty windows of the galley as he lit another cigarette and drew smoke deep into his lungs.

These will kill you eventually, my boy, he thought. Still a short life but a merry one.

They were moored in the deep-water harbour of the little island of Sigandros. It was, in fact, the only harbour on the island. The rest of the coastline was made up of jagged rocks and steep cliffs. There wasn't even the usual tiny beach. On the other hand, the view of the harbour was as pretty as a professional postcard. Well, it was if you didn't look too closely.

In the early morning light, the sea was so deep a sapphire as to be almost black. Dark green forest of plane and pine interspersed with silvery olive trees came almost down to the line of the few white cottages that made up the village. Round the harbour were a few bars and tavernas with gaily striped awnings, tables and chairs flowing out onto the road.

Up on the cliff was the spectacular villa of that archaeologist guy, what's-his-face, which looked like one of the palaces of the ancient Greeks. Over it all was a sky as blue as an evangelist's dream of heaven. Everybody's ideal Greek island, simple and unspoiled.

Except the water was full of rubbish and untreated sewage. The picturesque houses had not seen whitewash since the second world war. Inside they were dismal, bare and dirty. Professor Whatever in his porticoed Erie ruled his little kingdom like a medieval baron. No one drew breath unless he said so. The islanders were all too scared he would take his excavations elsewhere and their major source of income would dry up. A few tourists would do everyone a power of good, except there was nothing to attract the tour companies to this miserable rock in the southern Aegean.

Tourists no, smugglers yes. Situated halfway between Milos and Ios, the deep-water harbour ensured that Sigandros was on one of the regular ferry runs from Piraeus. It was also near enough to Turkish waters to be a convenient staging post for less legitimate craft. There was a continuous run of cigarettes and booze out of Marmaris on the Turkish coast for onward despatch with more or less legitimate papers to Athens.

Robert threw the remains of his cigarette out of the window. He'd better get back to work before it became too hot to think. As he passed below the wheelhouse he heard his own name mentioned. He stopped and listened. His spoken Greek was highly accented and ungrammatical but he understood a great deal more than he let on.

"You don't trust that character Roberto, do you, Yánnis?" Costas asked.

"Doesn't matter if I do or I don't. He can't tell anyone, anything," the captain replied. "Let the lazy bastard do the donkey work with the crates. He'll leave as soon as we get back anyway."

"Why did you take him on?"

"Because Andreas got sick in Marmaris and we had to get another pair of hands at short notice, you fool."

"*Min aploneis to zonari*, hang onto your belt, I know that even Andreas couldn't work with a ruptured gut, but why this character?"

"He had a mate's certificate, he seemed okay with a bit of private enterprise, and his story about working his way back from New Zealand to Britain checked out as far as I could tell."

"So why don't you like him?"

"Nothing I can put my finger on. He's too bright, too nosy. He's done three trips now and he's onto the fact that there's something we're not telling him. He's not a bad kid, he does his share of the work even if he does speak Greek like a Turkish pig."

"Kid? He must be thirty if he's a day."

Robert had heard enough. He eased himself back into the hold and continued to shift crates as if he had heard nothing. He was not in immediate danger and he preferred to think things through when he could. Still, even thinking things out had not prevented him from landing in trouble on a regular basis.

He would just have to watch himself. They might be suspicious but they would not compromise their business just to get at him. Whatever he knew or suspected he knew, right now he could prove nothing. Nor did he want to. If the smugglers were content to leave him alone he was not going to stir up a hornet's nest. Yánnis was right; this would be his last voyage with the crew. He had other fish to fry. He would tell them that he was looking for a berth on some more legitimate freighter going north.

The strident sound of a car horn interrupted his meditations. A small white van with the logo of Athens University on the side was threading its way along the quayside between stacked crates and heaps of nets.

"Hello there!" A ginger-haired girl in the driver's seat waved to them. As the van pulled up alongside the boat she called, "Cook says she wants two cases of fish and please no octopus." Turning to Robert, she hissed in a stage whisper, "We've had so much sepia stew lately some of us are growing tentacles."

"Some of those women from Athens Uni. had tentacles before they arrived," muttered her passenger, a thin pimply youth with colourless hair in a lank ponytail. "Makes you think Lovecraft was right after all and some of us are related to the giant squid. Ouch, that hurt!" The driver had hit him with considerable force.

"Neanderthals aren't extinct either," she commented to no one in particular.

The cases for the dig had been marked with bright paper labels. There were six of the special cases. Yánnis suddenly decided to leave the shade of the wheelhouse. He grinned at the girl. "*Ya sas*, Kerasimou," he leered.

Ginger grinned back. "Kalimera Yánnis, how's the wife and six children?"

"You know you are my only love," Yánnis crooned.

The man stood 170 cm in his sea boots, had a gut on him like Father Christmas, plus a moustache to rival a walrus. He seemed to think, however, that he was irresistible to women. The odd thing was that many women—and not just the ugly ones—didn't seem averse to flirting back with the greasy wop.

"For you only my finest catch, and at a price that will deprive my children of bread." Yánnis waddled off and flung a couple of cases of the genuine article onto the quayside.

Meanwhile, the boy with the ponytail had slid out of the van and opened the rear doors. The six cases with the labels were loaded without comment together with the fish.

"See you in two weeks," the girl called as she manoeuvred expertly back down the quay.

"That Professor McKenzie, he's a one," Yánnis said appreciatively.

"What do you mean?" Costas asked, although he looked as if he knew.

"He's been excavating on the island for more than a dozen years now. Every year he chooses one of the students to be his special assistant. It's always the prettiest and most lively of the girls."

"I bet she gets plenty of extracurricular activities." Costas gave a dirty laugh. "See what having a good education does for you."

"Is Professor McKenzie the guy that owns the villa?" Robert asked. "It's pretty fancy for one of your average university types."

"Get back to work both of you," Yánnis growled. The moment of easy camaraderie was over. In rapid Greek Yánnis whispered to his mate, "Nosy, far too nosy, watch him."

Later that morning another closed van drove down the quay. This one was dark green, battered and looked as if it might have once belonged to the army. A taciturn bloke with one eye got out and was immediately invited into the cabin. Yánnis shouted to Robert and Costas to get lost and come back in a couple of hours.

As Robert walked down the quay, Costas followed like a dog on a string. It was obvious the mate was not going to let him out of his sight. Robert could have kicked himself for the stupid remark about the archaeologist. There was obviously some private enterprise going on there. Why couldn't he have kept his mouth shut? He could not care less if the dig supplemented its funds by moving a few cases of duty-free cigarettes.

"Look, it's nearly noon," Robert said as they reached the road. "Why don't we go down to Maria's and have an early lunch, my treat."

Costas looked relieved, he had not relished the thought of trying to trail the young Brit from bar to bar. Maria's was about the best of the waterfront inns; the beer was cool and her kitchen clean.

Costas scowl returned when he saw the red head and another girl already seated at a table. "Let's go somewhere else," he muttered.

"Don't be an idiot," Robert whispered back. "They've already seen us. We'll look even more like a couple of crooks if we slide off as if we have something to hide."

Indeed, Ginger was already waving enthusiastically. The two men pushed to the back of the taverna and joined the girls although Costas continued to look unhappy.

"What's the matter with you, Costas?" the girl said in passable Greek. "Think someone will tell your wife you're seeing another woman?"

"Doesn't matter if they do, my wife does what's she's told," he said truculently.

The girls seemed to find this irresistibly funny and burst into a fit of the giggles.

"Maria's married to your wife's cousin. She says Galina wields the meanest frying pan in the islands."

Even Costas had to smile at this. To change the subject Robert signalled Maria for fresh drinks for the girls and a couple of beers for himself and Costas. Then he ordered four dishes of Maria's famous stifatho stew.

"I'm Robert," he said, offering to shake hands.

"Margaret McDonald," the redhead replied. "I really don't care to be called Ginger." Her touch was warm, firm and impersonal. He then turned to the dark girl sitting with Ginger.

"Rena Theoharous," she whispered, stretching out her hand. It was thin and cold despite the heat of the day. For a moment her hand lay in his, limp and unresponsive, lacking in life; Robert squeezed it very gently.

"Are you with the archaeology group?" Robert asked.

"I'm in my first year at Athens University studying for a general arts degree." Her English was almost perfect with only a trace of accent. "Professor Solómos, the head of the archaeology department, persuaded me to come. He said it would be good experience. I contacted Margaret, we have been friends for some time."

"Yes, Rena convinced me that this was a good way to have a cheap holiday in the sun. She didn't tell me that the organisation was crap and grubbing in the dirt when the temperature is in the nineties is bloody hard work."

Robert turned to Rena. "Your English is excellent, where did you learn?"

"Thank you, I learned the basics at school of course, then I had a gap year between school and university. I spent it in Scotland going to classes during the day and working in a restaurant belonging to my relatives at night. That's where I first met Margaret."

"So what exactly are you doing?" Robert asked.

"Me personally?" Margaret asked. "I was supposed to be taking photographs and making sketches of the finds, I'm doing an arts course as well. Unfortunately, all that has come up so far seems to be seashells and fossilised lamb bones, so I do a bit of everything. I scrape away at the ground, make coffee, hold the theodolite, make coffee, carry away buckets of stone and of course I make the coffee."

"Seems very interesting," said Robert with mock sincerity, belied with a huge grin.

"Although it doesn't help," said Rena with disgust. "When Professor McKenzie, who is supposed to be in charge here, discovers that all the measurements made last year were taken away by the student who wrote them up and the boy is apparently excavating in Crete this year."

"Don't forget Philip," commented Margaret. "He's McKenzie's nephew and apparently a chip off the old peristyle. He's doing his thesis on the cult of Poseidon in the Aegean. As a direct descendent of God, he demands that the rest of us do his donkeywork, write his notes and show due deference at all times. The only thing he has not required so far is droit de Seigneur, but I suspect that will happen any time now."

"Lucky old us," Rena added dryly.

Costas was bored; he had finished his food. No one was paying much attention to him and he barely understood what the girls were taking about. "I go back to ship now," he said, standing up. "Robert, you return before tide turns or we go without you." He walked off demonstrating offended dignity with every step.

Robert exchanged glances with the girls. He was not sorry to be free of his watchdog for a little while. "Okay," he said when Costas had passed out of earshot. "That is what you are doing. What were you supposed to be doing?"

Margaret pointed to the promontory that formed one side of the sheltered harbour. "The site is just behind that headland. A group of French archaeologists started excavating there back in the 1860s. They uncovered a double door entrance, a central court, and an altar dedicated to Poseidon. Political troubles eventually intervened and the French packed up and went home.

"Professor McKenzie came across the records whilst working in the Louvre. He applied to the museum of antiquities in Athens and somehow got permission to excavate. These days the Greeks are very fussy about who heads up their excavations. The Elgin Marbles still rankle."

"So what makes McKenzie so special?" asked Robert.

"He was head of archaeological studies at Franchester at the time and a pretty big cheese in the academic world. He started working here during all the university holidays and as much of the term time as he could wrangle. He did most of the work at his own expense and that was important. The University of Athens is as strapped for cash as any other academic foundation. When the prof. retired, he moved here full time and built that poncy villa, supposedly with family money."

"Is that where you are staying?" Robert asked

"You must be joking!" the girls said in chorus. Margaret continued, "New students are graciously invited up to the villa for a drink when they first arrive. It is then pointed out to them that the house and grounds are out of bounds to all of the archaeological team unless specifically invited. The only one that rule doesn't apply to is, of course, the divine Phillip."

"All we've got is a scabby campsite a few hundred metres from the dig. It's like being back in the Girl Guides. The most serious digging any of us has done has been for the latrines," Margaret added. "The prof.'s cook Ékaterina prepares a decent evening meal for us, but we have to pick up the food at the kitchen door and take it back to our campsite. Unfortunately, the main course tends to be octopus rather too often because it's the cheapest thing in the market."

"I take it you won't be coming back next year," said Robert

"You can bet your sweet life on it," Margaret replied. "The thing that bothers me is why does the professor continue to excavate here? It's obvious even to a first-year student that the place is played out. All there was to be found has been found. The boundary walls have been located and the excavation has been taken back to the floor of the earliest building. Apart from some rubbish heaps there's nothing left. Yet each year a considerable team wastes their energies when there are plenty more worthwhile places without enough effort.

"I did some reading before I came away. Annonay and Guimet, the original French archaeologists, thought there might be some domestic ruins round the temple. The same way an English village clusters round a church. They also recorded some references from the wandering scholar, Philistophanes, who was around in the fifth century BC. He apparently mentioned a large and prosperous temple to Athena associated with this island.

"I did not have time to look up the references before I left home so I asked the professor about it. He dismissed the idea as gossip and folklore. When I said that there might be something in the stories he got quite shirty and said that anyone making unauthorised explorations in the hills and upsetting the villagers would be asked to leave the island."

"Villagers, what villagers?" Robert was surprised.

"You know that dusty track just behind the church?"

"Yes, I thought it just led up to the olive groves."

"There's a little hamlet up there too. Apparently the whole population hid in the hills when the island was subject to pirate raids in the eighteenth century. Now it's just a few very conservative families scratching a living producing olive oil and honey."

Robert looked at his watch. It was time to be making his way back. He bid adieu to the girls who seemed in no hurry to go back to their excavation. As he strolled along the harbour, he wondered idly about the contents of the boxes that the van would be bringing down to the boat from the villa that evening.

Yánnis was in a foul mood when Robert returned. It was almost a relief to hose out the hold rather than endure his glowering looks and muttered curses. Something had not gone well and for once both Yánnis and Costas were keeping very closed mouthed about it. The sun was just sinking behind the hills when the white van inched its way once more onto the quayside. There was just the one person and he drove with nowhere near the speed or panache of Ginger, no Margaret, Robert corrected himself mentally. The good-looking dark-haired boy who walked up to the boat with a decided strut could be no one else but the crown prince of the archaeological kingdom, Phillip.

In a calculated drawl, the youth indicated that Robert should unload the van. Robert seriously considered throwing the poser into the harbour, but as he would probably be the one who would have to fish him out, it was not worth the bother. Costas and Yánnis could both swim like fish. Robert knew that both men had earned money for their families as boys by diving for crabs and lobsters. However, the two seamen had very firm views on hierarchy, and Robert was definitely at the bottom, so lousy jobs were his by definition.

The boxes were lighter than Robert would have expected. Still, he was not complaining about that. Phillip, however, seemed very concerned that they were handled gently.

What a prat, thought Robert. He is almost going out of his way to indicate that the boxes hold contraband. Not a character I would want as a co-conspirator. He is probably so used to thinking of himself as the brightest bod around, that he no longer believes that anyone else has any brains.

Robert was down to the last box. Phillip, who had been whispering ostentatiously with Yánnis, climbed back into the driver's seat and started the engine. He must have left the van in gear because it suddenly lurched, sideswiping the box in Robert's hands and sending it spinning across the quay. It smashed open. Inside were about ten bubble-wrapped packages of irregular shape in a nest of vermiculite filling. The largest about the size of a double fist had not been covered very well. Through the gaps could plainly be seen white marble, carved in stylised waves. Identical to the classical Greek sculptures of a female hairdo Robert had seen in museums.

"You fool," Phillip screamed. "You stupid ignorant lout, you don't have...." Robert was never to learn what he lacked.

"*Isihia*, silence," growled Yánnis with such force that Phillip immediately shut his mouth. Yánnis opened a box of fish. Dumping the contents in the harbour, he and Costas transferred the fallen packages into it and swept up the scattered vermiculite until not one white bead was left on the stone paving. The work was done quickly and in silence. It was almost frightening. Robert had begun to think that neither of the Greeks could do anything at more than a snail's pace and without a constant grumbled accompaniment.

When the box was safely stowed, Robert was sent to the

galley. He heard Yánnis mutter to Phillip.

"Don't tell the professor, it will only worry him. I will take care of everything."

"*Endaksi*, okay," the youth replied, obviously relieved, and returned to the van.

Yánnis went immediately to the wheelhouse and started the ancient engines. He called sharply to Costas to release the mooring ropes.

Robert was very conscious that he had seen too much. He would have to be very plausible if he were going to see Marmaris again. He wondered what he could say to convince Yánnis that in his book smuggling out the odd artefact for a connoisseur was a lot less harmful than carrying heroine or crack cocaine.

Robert returned to the galley, lit the gas ring and filled a pan with water. Coffee would be a good idea. Perhaps he would offer a slug of brandy from his private store. He thought briefly of jumping ship. The professor would be even less impressed with him than Yánnis, and there were no police on the island. There wasn't even a post office. He would have to take his chance on the boat.

If he kept everyone happy, perhaps he could slip over the side as they passed one of the other islands. He would get out his money and papers at the first opportunity.

In the wheelhouse Yánnis sucked on a cigarette. Keeping his voice low, he said to the mate, "The little twerp did that on purpose. I've always thought he was more than a wandering tramp. He's a spy, they're onto us."

"Calm yourself, Yánnis. Even James Bond couldn't have known that Phillipi was such a bad driver. Roberto's just a fool, he can't know what he saw."

"I was watching his eyes, he knew all right."

"So he knows, what's the lazy bum going to do about it? Tell him to get lost once we're back in Marmaris, just like you planned. He'll drift off and we'll never hear any more about him."

"Once he's on shore the next thing we know he'll be in Athens spilling his guts to the university and collecting a nice fat reward. I'm going to sort him out, and I'm going to do it now."

"Captain, wait until we're clear of the island at least."

Yánnis was going purple. "Are you in with him too? I've seen you two cosying up in Maria's bar."

"You told me to keep an eye on him." Costas was getting jumpy. He had seen Yánnis work himself up like this before. It didn't happen often but when it did somebody ended up dead and he did not want it to be him. "Okay, Captain, anything you say, but keep it quiet, please. The islanders are all in the professor's pocket for sure, but it's no use looking for trouble."

Yánnis picked up his fish knife. The thin blade was 20cm long and as sharp as a razor. The captain wielded it as if it were an extension of his hand.

"It will be quiet as the grave." Yánnis laughed. It was not a pleasant sound.

Robert started to wonder what he would make for supper. He could not face fish again. Perhaps there were a couple of tins of bully beef left? An unexpected breeze on the back of his neck made him turn quickly. Yánnis was standing in the open doorway of the galley with a long fish knife in his hand, silent and deadly.

Without a word the little captain feinted to the left then struck low. That fighter's move gave Robert time to reach for the only weapon to hand. Robert swung the pan. A litre of boiling water hit the captain in the face. Robert then bashed the man over the head with the hot pan for good measure. Yánnis's scream was horrible. He dropped the knife and clutched at his head, moaning. Robert jumped over the kneeling figure, scrambled up the companion ladder and flung himself over the side, diving deep to avoid the deadly propeller.

Chapter Two

The radio burst into Mozart's clarinet concerto. Emma Johnston, Douglas thought automatically as the last of a sunlit dream cleared from his brain. Then a lurch of fear from his gut reminded him that he had more to worry about than who was the soloist on the morning music programme of classic FM.

Last night on his return home from work at the library a heavy cream-coloured envelope had been waiting for him behind his front door. He had opened it with curiosity rather than apprehension. His bills were paid, he did not even own a car and as far as he knew all of his few remaining relatives were in good health.

The letter was from one of Edinburgh's leading firms of solicitors. It begged to inform him that he was being given advance warning of the three months' notice required by law to terminate the lease on his flat. He must vacate the premises by 31 December 2005 or the owners would be forced to take all legal steps necessary to remove him. The gratuitous threat made him as angry as the prospect of losing his home made his heart sink.

Reading further he discovered that the building had been purchased by a management group and was to undergo extensive redevelopment. He was invited to apply for a new tenancy agreement in one of the refurbished apartments that would be available from January 2007.

Included were a glossy publicity blurb and an artist's impression of the new Holyrood Mansions. There was no mention of the rental for these palatial suites. The cost would be one of the attractions to the new tenants; it would keep out the undesirable. With another jolt Douglas realised that he was included in that list. The new owners were no doubt going to target members of the new Scottish Parliament and Edinburgh's up-and-coming glitteraty. The new elite who would consider an address just off the Royal Mile to be very cool indeed.

Douglas had read the letter three times, not wanting to believe what it said. Then he made a telephone call to an acquaintance in the law faculty of the university, a man whom he had helped out on several occasions with sources of obscure references. This individual confirmed Douglas's suspicions that the purchase of the building and his subsequent eviction were perfectly legal. Even if Douglas took the new owners to court, the procedure would be expensive and the result unlikely to be favourable.

That night Douglas had taken out the bottle of the Edradour single malt he kept for special occasions. The level in the bottle dropped considerably but no solution presented itself to his bewildered brain.

Next morning Douglas washed, dressed and went out to work at his usual time, taking some small comfort from the familiar routine. He walked up the High Street to the National Library of Scotland on George IV Bridge. His office was on the second floor of the large white building.

Two years ago he had been promoted to be head of the ancient history and archaeology section. Even so his salary was modest. Certainly it would not stretch to cover the rent of a luxury apartment. He started slightly at the touch on his arm.

"I said good morning, Douglas. Are you not speaking to me or has your mind not yet returned from ancient Greece?"

Douglas turned and looked down on his diminutive colleague. "Margot, I'm sorry, I've got something on my mind."

"I've sort of worked that out for myself."

Margot Lynagh worked in the decorative arts section. She

was just over 150 cm and had a head of long curly black hair into which she liked to wind coloured scarves. Today she was dressed in some sort of floaty dress and over-tunic with a swirly pattern in bright colours topped off with enormous earrings. The outfit said 'lady artist' rather too loudly for Douglas's taste. She was twenty-six years old but looked several years younger. On the other hand Margot certainly had the personality to carry off wearing the most outrageous clothes if she chose to do so.

Whilst they worked in different parts of the building, sometimes their paths crossed when Margot needed information on classical designs. Professionally, Douglas undoubtedly knew his stuff when it came to the antique world. Socially, she had always found him pleasant enough if just a little distant. Today he looked not just distant but distracted. Douglas was never what you might call a snappy dresser but his tweed jackets were always carefully cleaned, his brushed cotton shirts pressed and she knew nobody who had such a wide selection of tweed ties. On the other hand, she knew no one else who would want one.

Today he looked as if he had thrown on the first things to hand. The beard looked ruffled as if he had run his fingers through it many times, his cheeks, usually smooth, looked unshaven and his longish hair unbrushed.

She took hold of his jacket again. "Come to my office," she commanded. "I'll make you a cup of coffee and you can tell me all about it."

For a moment she thought he might pull away. He was a very private man. He never took part in the usual staff room gossip, and she realised she knew very little about him, despite the fact they had been colleagues for nearly five years. Instead he allowed himself to be led away almost like a child.

Margot's office was more like a short, narrow corridor than a conventional room. Margot had had shelves constructed on the two longer walls to give herself some storage space. It did, however, reduce the width even more. There was just one spindly chair apart from Margot's own posture-contoured chair behind the desk. Douglas sat quite still on the uncomfortable visitor's chair looking down at his large hands with their long sensitive fingers.

Margot fussed with the coffee maker and glanced at Douglas from time to time. Eventually the fragrant scent of coffee filled the book-lined room, and she placed a mug in his hands. She might not know anything about his private life but she knew that he took his coffee black and that he had a weakness for chocolate biscuits.

"Tell me the problem," she asked gently.

"The building where I live has been sold to developers. I'm going to lose my flat."

It took all her self-control not to laugh. Of all the disasters she had feared this was one of the least serious. Still, another person's burden is never heavy, she thought.

"How long have you lived there?" she asked

"Fifteen years, ever since I left university."

"Have you contacted a solicitor?"

"I phoned Harry McIntire last night. He did not hold out much hope."

Margot knew Harry by reputation at least. He was one of the keenest brains in the law faculty. If he said there was no chance, then there wasn't one, so move on.

"So where would you like to live?"

"Pardon?" Douglas looked at her as if she had suddenly started speaking in Chinese.

"If you can't continue in your little *pied á terre* in historic Scotland, where would you like to live? A small house with a garden somewhere like Linlithgow, so you could commute into Edinburgh by train? Would you rather have a more modern flat in the new town? Do you want to move out to the student district around the university or would that be too downmarket?

"I am going to voice some personal questions, so please don't tell me if you would rather not, but you do need to start to think about them. How much can you actually afford for rent? Do you have enough saved for a deposit to buy, rather than keep on renting a place? It would be more economic in the long run. You know anything you tell me will go no further than this office."

Douglas continued to stare at her.

"My friend Catherine is an assistant manager in her father's estate agency. She'll be able to give you some idea of what's available and what it will cost you."

As he continued to look bewildered she added, "Look, if you want, I can book a half day's leave and come with you. Catherine is very efficient, I'm sure she will have some ideas, but remember you've only got four months and that can flash past when you're house hunting. I found that out when I moved to Edinburgh from Glasgow. I thought I'd just walk into somewhere and I ended up doing six weeks in a grotty bed and breakfast place." This was not strictly true but Margot felt that Douglas needed a kick up the backside.

"Thank you, Margot," Douglas said at last. "I would appreciate your company. I find I have no idea where I should start. Shall we meet in the foyer at say one o'clock? I must be getting to my office now. Professor Solomós from Athens University said that he would call me this morning."

Douglas got up and wandered towards the door, still looking as if he were a man who could not feel his feet.

Margot looked after Douglas with regret. He must be nearly forty yet he seemed about as practical as a bunch of flowers. He lived on his own and as far as anyone knew, he had never had a serious girlfriend, not unless you counted a life-long love affair with Pallas Athene as a relationship. Julian Sneddon down in records swore Douglas was not gay and if anyone would know, Julian should.

Douglas was a good-looking man, very tall, 190cm, and he held himself well, not slouching as many tall men did. He was not overweight although there was the beginnings of a little paunch under the checked shirts. In the last year or so his dark wavy hair had become noticeably more flecked with grey and there was a little bald spot on the top of his head that the over-long locks did not quite hide. *Anno domini* was catching up with Douglas Grey. Yet many women, herself included, would still think him very tasty.

When she had first joined the library five years ago her boss had told her that there was no one to touch Douglas for depth of knowledge on the ancient world. The man spoke classical Greek quite fluently and was no slouch conversing in modern Greek; apparently he spent all his holidays over there and was always chatting to one museum principal or another.

On the other hand, her boyfriend at the time, what was his name? Gregory, no Gordon, that was it, had loathed Douglas on sight. Apparently the two of them had had a stand-up row right in the middle of the reference library. A few weeks before, Gordon had approached Douglas for help with an essay. Douglas being Douglas had found him an article in some obscure magazine, long since folded, which covered the topic. Gordon being Gordon had reprinted the article word for word presenting it as his own work.

Gordon's essays were not usually so well thought out or even so grammatically correct, and his tutor was suspicious. He approached Douglas as the best source of information on the classical world. The rest as they say is history. Douglas had told the youth he was an idle layabout and did not want to see him in the library again. Not that Douglas had that sort of authority, of course; still, he had been right, the tosser was an idle layabout. Margot had finished with the slippery Gordon when she had found him stealing a £20 note from her wallet. Gordon had dropped out of university not long after.

Even Isabelle, her colleague in the dramatic arts section, had warned her about consulting Douglas.

"The man's a monumental bore," was the acid comment. "Once he gets started you come away hours later with your head ringing and so much information you don't know what to do with it. I once casually asked him about dance in the classical plays and he was still bringing me cuttings three months later."

Isabelle was a lovely person but even her best friends had to admit she was an airhead.

When Margo was doing her own project incorporating a classical frieze, Douglas had indeed devoted hours to getting her just the right selection of pipers, dancers and the rest. She remembered fondly a series of figures of the god Pan that she had placed in the corners, the little figure alternatively mocking and encouraging the dancers. That particular piece had won her quite a prestigious prize.

Margot felt a moment's regret that she had become so immersed in library life that she had let her own creative work slide. The telephone rang and she had to abandon her musings and get on with the work she was paid to do.

Douglas let himself into his office and relocked the door behind him. It was something he had never done before, but he felt as if he could not cope with any more fatuous queries at the moment. The excuse about the call from Professor Solomós had been a lie. He had just wanted to get away and think things out at his own speed.

Margot had been both sympathetic and practical. He was grateful for her help. He had always thought of her as a sort of female Hermes Logius, fleet of thought and tongue. Queen of the staff coffee room, gossiping away with a mixture of fact and outrageous stories. Still, she had proved his friend today.

On the other hand, he had caught the flicker of amusement in her face when he had blurted out his problem. Perhaps having to find a new home was not a world-shattering catastrophe. So why did it feel as if it was? He liked his flat. It was large enough to take his collection of books, well almost. He liked the thought that his building had been standing when Mary was Queen of Scotland. It had seen the troubles and turmoils of four centuries. He would never live in such a place again. It was sad, but not a life-threatening disaster.

As a boy he had lived with his parents in a large Victorian manse house on the outskirts of Inverness. His father had been an Episcopal minister and had a small but dedicated congregation. What money they had came from his mother's side. Sometimes he wondered what had attracted the practical and business-like Agnes McClaren to the dreamy, scholarly Wallace Grey. Yet as far has he knew the marriage had been a happy one. They had not been exactly short of money during his childhood. His father's stipend had been tiny, but his mother was a director in her family's transport company and her fees had covered all the domestic comforts.

He had been educated privately thanks to a legacy from his

mother's brother. Looking back it might have been good for him to go through the rough and tumble of a comprehensive. Uncle Fraser had left money for Douglas's education, and rigidly correct, Douglas's father had decreed that on his education it would be spent and on nothing else.

Still he had gained sufficient 'highers' to take him to university in Edinburgh. The one thing his mother had stood out for was that her son should go away from home whilst he studied for his degree. Father had made no secret of the fact that he would have liked Douglas to enrol at the college at Inverness and remain at home.

Wallace Grey had suffered a massive stroke when Douglas was in his first year of university. When Douglas went home for the funeral he had offered to give up his place at Edinburgh and return to Inverness. After he had made his fine speech he realised with horror that for the first time in his life his mother was about to slap him.

Instead she controlled herself, thanked him for his offer and packed him off on the first train back to Edinburgh as soon as the funeral tea had been cleared away.

His mother had then removed herself from the manse into a comfortable bungalow near a golf course. She had taken a greater interest in the family business and joined a considerable number of local organisations that she ran with great efficiency. When Douglas had indicated he would like to remain in Edinburgh after getting a double first in ancient languages and history, she seemed relieved rather than unhappy.

Douglas had no debts to speak of, but he had never saved much either. Most of his money had gone on travel, mostly to Greece, but also Italy and Turkey. He hoarded every day of his annual leave from the library to spend in antique lands. The only luxury he permitted himself apart from books was top-of-the-range photographic equipment that he changed on a regular basis as technology developed.

Still, he was not without resources. Douglas felt a terrible stab of sadness. His mother had died the previous year. She had developed breast cancer. For reasons he would never understand, she had told no one. She had not even visited her GP until the pain became too much to bear. By that time secondaries had developed and there was nothing that could be done. Agnes had spent her last two weeks in a hospice and no one who loved her would have wished her to live longer.

His mother's investments, savings and sale of the bungalow had resulted in quite a substantial sum. He had, however, tied it up in an investment account to give himself some much-needed extra income. It would take some time to release the money even if he wished to do so. Perhaps this friend of Margot's could come up with a solution. On the other hand, he had ceased to believe in fairies with magic wands a very long time ago.

He got up and released his door; it was time to get on with some work. In fact, he might as well ring Dionysos Solomós. There was a reference he did need to check and the old boy always had something interesting to relate.

The morning dragged on. Douglas was not concentrating too well and material that yesterday had been fascinating could no longer hold his attention. At noon he rang Margot.

"Hello, it's me, Douglas. How do you fancy wrapping up early and going along to the Vine Leaf for lunch before we brave the rigors of the estate agents, my treat?"

Margot was surprised but happy to comply. She had never been to the Vine Leaf, but she was hungry and unfussy about what she ate. Douglas was coming out of his shell with a vengeance.

Edinburgh was crowded; it was Festival time. They walked across George IV Bridge then turned left down Chambers St. alongside the rather ungainly tower of the museum of Scotland. They passed several groups of obviously excited people chattering in half a dozen languages and any number of weirdly dressed folk handing out leaflets for Festival fringe events.

"Will we get a table?" Margot asked. "Everywhere is so crowded in August. Sometimes I think the ordinary citizens of Edinburgh should all just go away for the Festival and leave the place entirely to the foreigners."

They dodged three young men in silver boiler suits with sparkly antenna on their heads.

"I phoned Hala who's the chef at the Vine Leaf. He knows me and will certainly save us a place. As for the Festival, it's only for a month, and it shakes the old city up a bit. The worthies of Edinburgh can get a bit pleased with themselves."

"Have you been to see anything this year, either from the Festival proper, or on the fringe?" Margot was interested. Most of the Edinburgh people she knew distanced themselves from the annual bacchanalia as if it would contaminate them.

"I support the Edinburgh Renaissance band so I go to all their performances. I know most of the players from when I was at the university and I have a great fondness for St Cecilia's Hall."

"They are the group that play medieval music with original instruments, aren't they? Their director came to see me about costumes once."

"Reproduction instruments, but yes that's right."

"Where's St Cecilia's Hall?"

"Margot, how long have you lived in Edinburgh?"

"Don't get all superior, I'm not into the classical music scene."

"The hall is one of the oldest purpose-built concert halls in Europe. I've got to admit it looks like a concrete box from the outside, but it has the most beautiful set of rooms inside with lovely acoustics. You must let me take you one evening when this flat business is settled. To hear, say, the music of Hayden in that setting is like stepping back in time to when Marie Antoinette was queen of France."

"Okay then," said Margot. To her surprise it did sound rather attractive. "What else have you been to see?"

"I did not bother with the ballet this year, a bit too avant-garde for me. I will go to a couple of the orchestral concerts, although the seating in the Usher Hall is still penitential despite the millions the city council has spent on refurbishment."

Margo was amazed that in the course of a ten-minute walk she had learned more about Douglas than in the last five years working with him.

"Every year the critics say that the fringe is not what it was," Douglas continued. "Yet if it were the same as the year before it would not be the fringe. Can you imagine anything worse than the same tired old artists performing the same material year after year? Do you know that this year there is a group playing ancient Greek music on replica instruments? I had to go and see them of course."

"Were they authentic?" Margot was intrigued

"Who can tell?"

"Well you, if anyone can."

"Their scholarship was not contemptible but to be honest some of the pieces sounded more like a racket than something the men and women who enjoyed Homer and Aristophanes would appreciate. It was fun nevertheless."

Somehow Margot had not imagined Douglas and fun in the same context.

"Here we are." Douglas stopped in front of an iron railing. They were across the road from the Festival Theatre. A narrow iron staircase led downward. The restaurant was quite tiny. A room no bigger than the average living room was split in two by a dividing wall. The walls were whitewashed although there had been some attempt at decoration with stencilled vine leaves and some rather dull copperware. A set of shelves held bottles of preserved peppers, herbs and some brightly painted pottery. A small, brown, balding man in a white apron greeted Douglas warmly and led them to a table for two.

They sat in silence for a while studying the menu. Douglas ordered a bottle of white wine and one of water. Margot was not sure that wine at lunchtime was a good idea. Still, perhaps Douglas needed a bit of Dutch courage to face the estate agents. She would also have liked to be consulted as to her preferences. On the other hand, the wine when it came was cool and crisp with tangy, green fruit flavours.

"If the only Greek wine you have had is holiday retsina I thought you might like to see there are some acceptable alternatives. This is Kretikos."

"It's very good," she admitted.

There was a bit more silence. Then Douglas asked her, "How

well do you know this estate agent person?"

"Catherine McFarlane, we met at school. We were best friends. The sort of best friends that only schoolgirls away from home for the first time can become."

"Was this a school in Edinburgh?" he probed gently.

"It was a boarding school, one of the rather posh ones where you can take your own horse if you want to. I'd be grateful if you didn't spread that around at the library," she said quickly.

"Why would I want to?" Douglas was definitely puzzled. "Anyway, your secret's safe with me."

"My father died in a rather nasty accident at his work when I was five. There was rather a lot of compensation. Mother did not want to touch a penny of it for herself. She said it felt like blood money. So she splashed out on my education. I don't think she realised what a handicap it could become in later life. As soon as someone knows you've been to a school like Whitegrove, they automatically think you're stuck up and have more money than is good for you."

"What about Catherine?"

"Well, she certainly isn't stuck up, but daddy does have an awful lot of money. In her case I think sending her to boarding school was a mixture of wanting to getting rid of her for long periods of time and wishing for her to make the right sort of friends rather than getting a decent education. A success rate of one out of three was way below daddy's average."

"One out of three, explain."

"I doubt if they saw their daughter for more than a couple of weeks in the year. In term time when she was at school, the only time they visited was sports day because it was sort of compulsory for parents to attend unless they were actually out of the country.

"In the holidays she went on those outward-bound courses. You know the ones where they take you abseiling and running through the mud. Otherwise she stayed with friends whenever she could. In the last couple of years I know she spent more time with me at my mother's house than she did with her own."

"Why did her parents want to get rid of her?"

"Mummy had some problem with her nerves. It was never

actually spelled out what was wrong, but I suspect she was an alcoholic who had to go and dry out at regular intervals. Daddy has more enterprises than just the chain of estate agents. He went abroad a great deal on business."

"So what went wrong?"

"An engineer's daughter from Glasgow was not considered the right sort of friend for Princess Catherine. Unfortunately, by the time Catherine's parents found out it was too late, we were inseparable.

"On the academic side, Catherine was certainly bright enough, but she would not work. She did not do anywhere near well enough to be accepted into a university. I suspect that even if she had she would have refused to go. Daddy found her a job in one of his estate agent's offices, just for something to do until she got married."

"Are you sure this is the person I should be seeing?" Douglas sounded panicky.

"Absolutely certain. She worked her way up from general dogsbody to assistant manager and she has become very good at her job. She would do even better if she would leave daddy's company and join one where she did not have any relatives."

"I can see why that might be. If your father owns the business, there is always someone who will say that any success you have is due to family influence rather than your own hard work."

"You're so right. There is also the undoubted fact that if daddy owns the business you're unsackable. Catherine very rarely resists the temptation to take a long lunch hour to do some shopping or leave early to go to the gym if they are not busy."

"You said this job was to keep her occupied until she is married. Is there a prospective Prince Charming on the horizon?"

"There is, with a diamond the size of the koh-i-nur to prove it."

"You sound a bit cynical."

"Michael, that's the fiancé, is daddy writ small. He's about ten years older than Catherine and was, in fact, her father's friend before he was her's. As Catherine's brother turned out to be unsatisfactory, Michael is now crown prince of the empire."

"What does he do?"

"He describes himself as a business man. Which as you know can cover a multitude of sins. He spends even more time travelling than daddy."

"That must be a bit inconvenient for the loving pair."

"Surprisingly enough, Catherine does not seem to bother very much. I suppose that the man in her life doing a great deal of travelling has become the norm."

"So when's the happy day?"

"In two years' time. The great hall at Edinburgh castle has already been booked."

Douglas said something non-committal. He had been groomsman enough times to know about the planning and expense that went into a great Scottish wedding and how far in advance those plans had to be made. He had always thought that if, when, he wanted to marry he would willingly settle for a modest ceremony if it meant a more rapid launch into married life. Still, even he recognised that when the decision was to be made, it would not be his alone to take, when or if.

The main course had been cleared away. It had been a very enjoyable meal. Neither wanted pudding but they indulged themselves in second cups of dark bitter coffee. Finally, Margot realised Douglas was beginning to get cold feet about the project and was procrastinating.

"I'm going to the ladies' room," Margot announced, pushing her chair back. "Will you get the bill whilst I'm gone? If we don't go now, Catherine will think we're not coming at all." She did not wait for an answer but headed for the toilets in a swirl of pink and blue silk.

By the time she returned, Douglas was waiting by the door and the young woman who had waited on their table was looking particularly pleased. Not a mean man, then, Margot thought.

They walked down to the new town. Catherine's business was just off George Street and although Douglas had offered to call for a taxi, she thought the walk would do them both good.

They were indeed late for their appointment with Catherine but she did not seem to notice. She greeted Margot warmly. Margot hoped that the tooth scrub she had performed in the restaurant restroom and the mint she was sucking covered any remaining garlic fumes.

Under the cover of the embrace, Catherine whispered, "We need to talk. I've just heard from Robert. He's being chased by pirates in Greece."

Chapter Three

Robert kicked to thrust himself deeper into the water. He felt the sting of salt in his eyes and nose. Only when his lungs were bursting did he allow himself to surface. He concentrated on putting as much distance as possible between himself and the boat before he permitted himself to look round. Costas had cut the engine and the boat was rolling on the swell.

As far as Robert could see there was no one in the cabin. Costas was probably below using his limited medical skills on his captain. Costas fancied himself as a first-aider. He had trained in the army whilst doing his national service. However, Robert had found out firsthand just how inept the little mate could be, when he had accidentally cut his hand open on an old tin can that had been dredged up with a net full of fish. Robert could even find some sympathy for the injured Yánnis.

The young man took the opportunity to rid himself of trousers and trainers then began to swim towards the land with all the strength in his powerful shoulders. The water was neither cold nor particularly rough but the boat had been further out than Robert had realised and the harbour wall seemed to be getting no nearer. A crack split the evening air. Bloody Costas was shooting at him. The chances of the mate hitting his target from a tossing boat at dusk were minimal, but Robert dived again. When he resurfaced the fishing boat was much further away. Robert resumed swimming on the surface trying to splash as little as possible.

Eventually he heard the engine of the boat start up. Would they cut their losses and go, or would they continue to search for him? Robert floated for a moment. It was time to start praying, except he had not been a believer for a very long time. Eventually Robert realised that the engine noise was getting stronger. The boat had turned round but Costas did not seem to be searching for him but heading straight back into the harbour. Robert kept himself as low as possible in the water, willing his head to look no more menacing than a piece of flotsam. The boat passed apparently without seeing him. Certainly there were no more shots.

His plan to swim to the harbour wall and climb up one of the iron fisherman's ladders fixed at intervals along its length had to be abandoned. He struck out to the left. The peninsula might not offer safe haven for boats but there had to be some sort of landing place for a lone swimmer. It took nearly an hour to get near to the shoreline. By that time his arms were almost too tired to move and he was regularly taking in large gulps of acrid seawater. His leg caught a hidden rock with mind-numbing pain. He cautiously tested the depth of the water. He could feel a jumble of weed-covered boulders beneath his feet, nothing that would give firm footing.

A wave caught him and smashed his shoulder against another hidden obstacle. He gave thanks for the lazy Aegean tides. In the Atlantic he would have been smashed to pieces on the rocks long before this. In the uncertain light he thought he saw a square-cut rock. Robert headed for it with all his remaining strength. Nothing was square in nature. He remembered Margaret's talk of the old temple of Poseidon. If the ancients had gone to the trouble of smoothing stone down here then this might be the place to make landfall.

The water deepened and he had to swim once more. Suddenly a wave caught him and he was helpless in its hold as he was propelled towards the shore. Then, gently as a mother laying down her baby, he was on the shelf of rock. Though every muscle ached, he scrambled higher before the next wave could pull him back into the sea. He cut his hands, scratched his legs and bruised his naked toes but somehow he crawled up the bank until he was able to grasp handfuls of coarse grass. One last heave and he was lying uncomfortably on a rough pebble path. Spent, he remained stretched out panting. Sharp stones dug into him but he did not having the strength to do anything about it.

When he could think of anything at all beside the fact that he had escaped those ghastly rocks, he considered what to do next. Painfully he got to his knees, then hobbled to the side of the path where the grass was less hard on his bare feet. Moving more quickly he gained the shelter of a grove of pine trees. He knelt on a bank of pine needles and brought up the seawater that had been sloshing about in his stomach. He got up and stumbled on a bit farther. If there was a path it must lead somewhere. The locals were not likely to be friendly but right now he would have welcomed Yánnis and Costas if they had offered him a drink of clean water before they shot him.

Robert was conscious of the honey scent of the island vegetation overlaid by the clean smell of the pines. Then there was another scent, wood smoke; of course, the students. Margaret had said that the archaeology students had a camp near the temple of Poseidon. They might be willing to brave the professor's wrath and help him. If not, what other choice did he have? Robert stopped walking and listened carefully. There was the sound of the sea endlessly shushing against the rocks. Trees sighed and creaked; occasionally there was the scrabbling sound of some small animal deep in the undergrowth. Then he heard what he had been listening for, voices, some distance away but certainly voices. He shuffled onwards.

He must have looked like something from a horror film when he reached the camp. By this time he was crawling. He was bleeding from dozens of cuts and covered in dust and dead pine needles from his repeated falls in the dark.

There was a group of people round a small fire. He could just see others beyond the firelight near the tents where there were some oil lamps on tables. Robert made a sound something between a croak and a cough. He was incapable of speech.

"What the hell is that!" shouted a young man who had been

holding forth on the uselessness of Greek football teams.

The first surprise over, they were remarkably efficient. Two of the men lifted him to his feet and brought him into the circle of light. Someone passed him a bottle of water. It was the most delicious thing he had ever tasted. It was snatched away far too quickly.

"Hey, slow down," said a voice. "You'll be sick." Then after a moment added, "Again."

They provided him with some warm water to wash, stuck band-aids over the worst of his cuts and loaned him some clothes. The shirt buttons strained over his chest and the pants were baggy at the waist and short in the leg but were clean, dry and felt wonderful. They had even come up with a pair of trainers that were a reasonable fit.

Eventually he sat by the fire in a camp chair sipping a mug of coffee whilst they hurled questions at him.

"Who are you?"

"Where have you come from?"

"How did you get like this?"

Then a voice he recognised. "It's Robert from the fishing boat." Margaret.

"Hello," he said and tried to grin.

"What happened to you?"

"I had a falling out with Yánnis and Costas, they tried to shoot me."

"I don't believe it, they've always been perfect pets."

"I've never been as impressed with them as you. That Pedro the fisherman act was always a bit too good to be true for a pair of smugglers." This was the girl called Rena; she sounded a bit acid.

"A few cases of cigarettes isn't real smuggling," protested Margaret.

"If it was just tobacco in those cases."

"What else would it have been? The prof. wouldn't touch drugs."

"Once you get involved with characters like that it escalates. You can't help yourself."

"You're beginning to sound like the religious tract society."

Margaret turned to Robert. "What were you carrying?"

"As far as I know it was cigarettes. Then tonight the boxes came down from the villa and one broke open."

"Boxes came down from the villa?" Margaret did not sound quite so sure of herself.

"Yes, that nephew character brought them down. The box that broke open had about ten different pieces all encased in bubble wrap. I saw what looked like a perfect female head, about 18cm across." Robert was conscious that his audience had gone very quiet.

Eventually Rena said, "Nothing like that has been found on this site. I've catalogued everything that's been uncovered."

"The professor's scrupulous about sending everything to Athens. I boxed it all up myself." Margaret was sounding stunned. Almost as if she had heard about a death amongst her close family rather than an extension to the smuggling exercise she obviously thought quite fun.

"He's found it, hasn't he?" This was one of the boys.

"The bastard's found it and he's shipping the prime pieces to Turkey." Another angry male.

"He's had us grubbing about on this piss-poor bit of worked-out rock and all the time he's been keeping the prime site to himself."

"I'll see he goes to gaol and never comes out." Margaret was very angry.

"What are you talking about?" Robert cut into the rising fury.

Several of the students kept up a low muttered conversation in the background, but Margaret calmed down enough to explain.

"If you remember when we were talking down at the harbour. There has always been a legend on this island that there was a wealthy and very beautiful temple to Athena back in the hills. There have been several attempts to locate it since the French archaeologists were here in the nineteenth century. McKenzie, however, has always been adamant that the Poseidon site was the only one.

"If all the boxes that Phillip brought down to you contain

artefacts, then McKenzie has not only found the prime site, he is systematically robbing it and selling the treasures."

Robert noticed that Margaret was no longer giving her boss his academic title. In her mind he had already been stripped of all his honours.

"For a man who was once a leading light in his field there is no worse betrayal." Margaret sounded near to tears.

"What happened with the cigarette scam?" Robert asked.

"McKenzie bought the fags from a contact in Turkey. The fishing boat brought them in every other Tuesday. We took them up to the villa, put archaeological stickers on them and registered them as 'finds' on the site documentation. The ciggies all had an extra red label and there is a contact in the ancient history department at Athens who ensures the special boxes are extracted and sent on their way along the chain."

"Does no one in the university realise that half their so-called remains are disappearing through the back door?" Robert was interested.

"The university is understaffed and overwhelmed with finds. They are about three years behind in their recording and logging. By the time they get round to the Sigandros material, some clerk will assume that the lazy holiday students got it all wrong. Our internal contact ensures that the paperwork detailing what is received at the university corresponds with what is put into storage."

"What did you think of all this?" Robert probed gently.

"Running a dig is expensive, even one like this that's only open for a few months of the year. I know McKenzie has put a lot of his private wealth into it. I respected him for it." The tears were back again. "A little slight of hand with tobacco duty did not seem such a terrible crime."

Especially if it gave you a cheap holiday on a Greek island, surmised Robert, but he kept the thought to himself.

"Plundering what might be one of the great modern finds to keep this site going is criminal," Margaret finished with energy.

Not only is it criminal it's stupid, thought Robert. When Margaret has calmed down a bit she'll realise that too. If the prof. was after academic recognition then surely he would have declared the Athena site in order to publish scholarly works detailing how he became the modern Schliemann, the hero of the discovery of Troy. As it was, the man's reputation was zilch and he was smuggling out his finds with a trio of dishonest fishermen. This was fishier than the hold of the *Herakles*. Meanwhile, he had his own problems.

"Can you get me off the island?"

"The ferry doesn't come in again till next week. Even so I would imagine that Costas and company will keep a sharp eye on who goes on and off. It's not as if there will be a crowd you can get lost in."

They thought for a moment.

"Is there anyone you can ask for help?" Margaret asked.

Robert thought about his father. It was unlikely he would lift a finger to help. He knew his mother cared but he doubted she would have the resources, either mental or financial. There was Cat, of course, all grown up now and with a lot of intelligence beneath that 'don't care' façade she used as a shield between herself and a world she had found bewilderingly hostile. He knew her telephone number too. She had forced him to memorise it during one of their very rare phone calls. Fortunately, he had always had a good memory for numbers.

"My sister, Cat, Catherine. Do you have a mobile?"

"Yes but the battery's pretty low."

They devised the shortest possible text message that would make sense. It was a long shot, but what else could he do?

"You can stay here in the students' camp until we hear from your sister. You'll blend in just fine. I'm sure the locals think we all look alike. There isn't a spare sleeping bag but I think we could borrow some blankets for you. I can do that three-blanket sleeping bag trick I learned in the Girl Guides."

At that moment the light of several powerful torches shone into the camp, blinding eyes used to firelight.

"I see we have an unexpected guest." Phillip's voice was thick with sarcasm.

Several of the students jumped up to face the intruders. The group dropped the beams of their torches. Phillip was backed up by four of the burlier villagers. At his side, holding a gun, was the squat shape of Costas.

"I think you would be more comfortable at the villa, Robert McFarlane."

Chapter Four

Douglas watched the two women meet and greet one another. There did indeed seem to be real warmth between the two of them. They gave each other genuine hugs, not the air kisses he'd seen exchanged by other fashionable women colleagues. He studied Catherine. No one ever looks like the mental image you have of them. He had supposed that she would be a slightly more businesslike version of Margot.

In fact, he was very impressed with her appearance. Catherine was very tall for a woman, perhaps 180cm. She was also very thin, which made her seem even taller. The black suit she wore had wide shoulders and a rather short skirt. It was made of a heavy shiny-looking material that looked expensive. A red silk blouse complemented her dark hair and creamy skin. It also prevented the funereal look that black suits can often give.

Her calves had the hard muscular look of someone who exercises regularly. When she moved forward to greet Douglas in his turn she moved with ease and grace. Douglas felt hot and embarrassed. He did not know what to say to this elegant and sophisticated woman. He was very grateful to Margot for promptly coming to his rescue and explaining the problem. It did not help, however, that he still did not know what he wanted if he could not have his present home.

She led him through to her office. In one corner was a

conference area with comfortable leather sofas and a smoked glass table with an improbable-looking modern sculpture on it. She indicated they should sit.

"To start off with let's not bother with what you might want. After all, right now you don't know what there is to choose from," she said kindly. "Instead tell me about your present home. What you like about it, what you would change if you could."

Douglas thought for a moment. "It's on the top floor of a three-story building. On a clear day I can see the Pentland hills from my kitchen window. One room has an oak table that must have been installed as the house was being build. It's too large to get through doors or windows. It's part of the landlord's fixtures and fittings so I suppose they will smash it up when they do the refurbishment."

"Catherine doesn't want to know that kind of stuff," Margot interrupted.

"Shush, Margot, this is exactly what I do want to know." She turned back to Douglas. "Do you do a lot of cooking and entertaining?"

"I don't as it happens, but why the devil do you want to know that?" Douglas was embarrassed; it was if he was confessing to being at best inhospitable or at worst incompetent.

"If your major use for your kitchen is to prepare a bowl of cornflakes for your breakfast, then a big, well-equipped kitchen is less important to you than if you regularly give dinner parties for a dozen guests," explained Catherine gently. She could see Douglas shudder at the thought. "Similarly," she went on, "if you like to go out to eat in the evening then a little farmhouse tucked away in the hills would be less attractive than a flat in the centre of town no matter how interesting the history of the building."

Douglas said nothing, and she could not gauge his reaction. Probably he did not care to go to restaurants alone but did so anyway when he got fed up of ready meals.

"I understand you don't have a car at the moment, Mr. Grey, but can you drive? Would you like a car if you didn't live in a place where parking was a nightmare?"

"It's Dr. Grey actually, but please call me Douglas."

Catherine looked annoyed with herself for the slip. She also noted that whilst he did not answer her question it had made him look thoughtful. Turning, she began to look through the folders in a filing cabinet. "I might have to do a bit of digging to get somewhere you really like. I shall certainly consult with the other offices in our group. Here are a few possibilities. Don't hesitate to discard any you think you would hate. That's how I get to know what might suit you best."

She put a dozen folders on the table. "Start with these and I will see what else we have." She walked to an alcove at the rear of the room, indicating to Margot that she should come with her.

They looked back at Douglas, who seemed to be engrossed in the brochures.

"What's this about Robert?" Margot hissed. It was supposed to be a whisper but Douglas could hear her quite clearly.

"I had a text message from him on my mobile."

"He's in the navy, isn't he?"

"Merchant marine, not the same thing at all."

"So what did he say?"

Catherine got out her mobile and showed her friend the text.

CAT! HV HD 2 JMP SHP, TRBLE WIV SMUGLRS, NO MNY NO PPRS, AM WIV STDNTS N SIGANDROS, CYLADES, CM & G8 ME ROBERT.

"What does that mean when it's at home?"

"'Cat', that's me of course, 'have had to jump ship, trouble with smugglers, no money, no papers, am with students on Sigandros, Cyclades, come and get me, Robert'."

"I've never heard of Sigandros. Is it an island?"

"I don't know. I called in at the travel agent's this morning and asked if they had heard of it. They looked it up in their directory but they couldn't find anything. On the other hand I suspect if I had asked if they had ever heard of England I might have got the same blank look."

Douglas was not even pretending not to listen by this time.

"Sigandros is a small and rather barren island in the Cyclades, halfway between Milos and Ios," he said rather hesitantly.

"You've heard of it then?" Catherine strode back to the office area.

"I spent a week there about ten years ago. Who is Robert if I may ask?"

"Robert is my brother. He's four years older than me and rather a black sheep. Daddy wanted him to go into the business. When he left school Daddy forced him to go to university and to do business studies. He lasted about a year."

"Did he fall or was he pushed?"

"He didn't even take the exams. I think he had been planning his escape for some time. The first thing we knew about it was a postcard from Gibraltar saying everything was all right and he would write soon. We're still waiting for the letter. Daddy went storming down to his college and found out that Robert had formally given up his place at the university and joined a cargo freighter as a junior crewman."

"A bit of a shock for your parents. Could he not have discussed his plans with them?"

"Daddy is pretty determined when he has his mind set on something. I think Robert drifted along until he found he simply couldn't do what my father wanted. He then showed equal determination to get the life that suited him."

"What happened?"

"Daddy got very Victorian for a while. All the photographs that had Robert in them were destroyed, even the ones of us both as babies. Mummy and I were forbidden to speak of him. I think Daddy's reaction hurt my mother far more than Robert's running off to sea."

The bleak tone showed that it was more than Catherine's mother who had been hurt by the temper tantrums.

"We received postcards at infrequent intervals from all over the world. Usually saying 'Lots of love, Robert'. After a year or so Daddy let Mummy keep them."

"How close were you to your brother? How did you feel about his disappearing act?"

"We had been pretty close before I went to Whitegrove, the school Margot and I both attended. Well." She hesitated. "As close as you can get with a four-year age gap. He was never mean to me, never complained when I had to tag along. When he could, he took me along to school rugby matches and the like. Once I was at boarding school, we did drift apart a bit. He was never a letter writer and personal telephone calls had to be taken in the secretary's office."

"When was the last time you heard from him?"

"Must be three months ago. A postcard of some mountains in New Zealand and a line to say he was going to make his way home."

"Has he ever done this 'rescue me' bit before?"

"No, never." Catherine seemed a bit offended.

"Where did the text message come from?"

"Sigandros, I suppose."

"No, what number did the call come from?"

"It was a mobile number. I've tried both voice mail and text but the only response I've had is an official voice telling me that the unit has been switched off."

"What are you going to do?"

"Daddy is away at the moment. I've not wanted to worry Mummy, she's not too well at the moment."

Margot, who had till this point kept in the background, asked, "What do you know about Sigandros, Douglas?"

"Well, I'm not too surprised that the travel agent did not have anything on the island. It's certainly not on the usual tourist run."

"Why were you there?" Catherine sounded a bit suspicious.

"I was there because I had been reading one of the essays by Philistophanese. I was there for a week because I was stupid."

"This is intriguing, explain please," Catherine requested.

"The summer of '95 I planned to go island hopping in the western Cyclades. Before I went I looked up some of the ancient texts that refer to that part of the Aegean. Philistophanes was one of the minor philosophers, but a great traveller and an even greater gossip. He wandered about the islands sending scholarly and salacious reports back to his masters in Athens, some of which survived and were collected by the Vatican in mediaeval times.

"One of his gossipy newsletters concerned Sigandros, where there was, so he said, a cult dedicated to Athena who was worshiped in a magnificent temple. It was apparently very wealthy and young girls from many of the surrounding islands would come to make offerings and spend some time there before their wedding night."

"If it was for young girls how come they let the old lecher in?"

"They didn't of course. All Philistophanes is reporting are rumours picked up in the waterfront taverns. But anything to do with girls interested him. He also mentions a temple to Poseidon on the peninsula. That site was found way back in the eighteenth century by some French archaeologists. On the other hand, temples to Poseidon were as common in fishing communities as churches dedicated to St. Nicholas are today and for the same reason."

"What's that?" asked Catherine.

"They are both patrons of fishermen and the sea. In an uncertain world of winds, weather and tides, there comes a point where knowledge and skill just won't help you anymore. So that's when you put your trust in the supernatural."

"That's a bit cynical," commented Margot. Douglas did not reply.

"So why were you there for a week?" Catherine persisted.

"I was on Ios, paying tribute to the poet Homer who is supposed to be buried there. One day when I was taking a stroll along the harbour I learned that the ferry to Sigandros was coming in that afternoon. It seemed too good an opportunity to miss. I got my things from the taverna, paid my bill and was on the ferry within a couple of hours. It was not until I had disembarked and the ferry was steaming away from the island did I think to enquire when the next ferry was due. There was nothing for a week.

"Fortunately, I had enough Greek currency on me to pay for room and board for that length of time. I did not have enough to pay a fishing boat to take me to another island. So I made the best of it.

"It's a small island but very hilly. It has no beaches, just the one deep-water harbour. I spent some time at the temple of Poseidon excavation. After half a day's exploration I managed to find the Venetian fort, which is really no more than a pile of rubble. I walked for hours in the hills looking for the temple of Athena. I came across a couple of possible sites but nothing conclusive. I also did quite a lot of sleeping in the sun as there was very little else to do."

"If there were no beaches, where did you do your snoozing?" said Catherine.

"On my second day I met Professor McKenzie. He was professor emeritus at Franchester at the time, but was building a villa on the island. He planned to make the history and archaeology of Sigandros his life's work. He invited me up to his place just outside the town, which was just a couple of rooms then, although he had plans for a young palace eventually. He laughed a bit at my predicament, but he was very hospitable and let me have free run of his garden when exploration lost its appeal."

"So what happened?" Margot again.

"Another ferry eventually came in. I wished the professor goodbye and sailed into the blue Aegean night with a strange mixture of regret and relief. I sent the professor a nice present once I reached home and we corresponded for a while. It eventually became very infrequent as sometimes happens. He never seemed to get any further with his search for the temple of Athena. Then there was some trouble at Franchester, he lost his chair, at which point correspondence stopped altogether, embarrassment, I suppose."

"So do you think the students Robert mentions will be working for Professor Mackenzie?" said Catherine.

"Perhaps. I believe he's still there, although he may no longer be in charge."

"Why couldn't Robert just go to the police?" asked Margot.

"There is no police presence on the island, no officials of any sort unless you count the priest or the mayor," said Douglas. "If he has got into trouble with smugglers he is probably reluctant to approach the islanders because he will not know where their sympathies lie. I can well imagine that he thinks the best plan is to merge with the foreign students until someone can go and get him."

"What are you going to do, Cat?" Margot asked again.

"Fortunately, Daddy is coming home today, he's been on a trip to Athens. I'll talk to him as soon as he gets in. He's bound to know the best thing to do, he might even have some business partner out there who can help right away."

Catherine had begun to look rather upset and it seemed wise to go back to the far less interesting task of looking at flats. There were a couple available for immediate viewing near the National Portrait Gallery that seemed to have possibilities, although the costs seemed astronomical.

"What time do you finish at the library?" asked Catherine

"Tomorrow I am on early shift so I finish at four."

"If you come straight here I'll make appointments and we can go and see these places. I'll probably also have some more suggestions by then."

They shook hands and Douglas and Margot left.

Funny sort of character, Catherine thought. He seemed so focused when he was talking about Greece, yet as wet as a lettuce when it came to where he wanted to live. Still, he was a good source of information. She would show him round the properties herself for the time being. If Daddy could solve everything with a couple of phone calls then she would pass Dr. Grey on to the office junior. It was nearly four now. If she was going to have a late night tomorrow she felt she was entitled to pack up early and go to the gym.

Daddy was expected home at six. He had insisted that he did not want to be met, he would take a taxi from the airport. She knew the routine by this time. He would bang in, leaving a trail of suitcase, briefcase, and coat in the hall. Go straight to his room have a long bath, an even longer whisky and finally go through to his study to flop in the great leather chair that was his and his alone.

It was only then that she could be confident of approaching him. The timing was fairly critical, because if he started on his post and the messages that had accumulated in his absence he would not talk to her again until next day.

She popped her head round the study door. "Do you want anything to eat?"

"Not a thing. I ate on the plane. Don't know why I do it, it's always rubbish."

"I need to talk to you, Daddy," she said quickly, coming into the room and sitting cross-legged on the rug in front of him. "I've had a text message from Robert, he's in trouble."

"Robert?" Her father seemed momentarily unfocused as if he could not place whom she was talking about. Then his face hardened. "What does that rubbish want?"

Catherine quickly told him about the text message.

"Show me," he demanded.

Catherine produced her mobile but could not bring up the message. Her father snatched it off her but the message was gone.

"You empty-headed idiot, are you sure there really was a message or have you gone completely off you head like your fucking mother."

Catherine was shocked. Daddy was often abrupt, but she could not remember him swearing at her before.

"I showed the message to Margot Lynagh. I don't remember deleting the message, I never intended to, but it could have happened then."

"You showed a message concerning private family business to that arty-farty waste of space you used to cling to at school." Her father's face was flushing deep red. "How many other people have you told? Have you broadcast it on Radio Scotland by any chance?"

"Daddy, that's not fair."

Her father got up from his chair and stood over her. His eyes were hard and his expression unforgiving. "Who else have you told?" He enunciated very clearly as if she were deaf.

She scrambled up to face him. She was beginning to feel frightened. "The only other person who knows is Dr. Grey who works with Margot at the library." Catherine was recovering her courage. Daddy was being completely unreasonable. "He once visited Sigandros," she tried to explain. "It's not an island that anyone knows much about. I thought that some local knowledge would be useful."

"If you ever had anything that could be called a thought it would be your first. You fool, you utterly brainless cretin. Don't you realise this sort of thing has to be handled carefully? Do you want to kill your brother?"

"Daddy, Margot and Dr. Grey won't tell anyone, why should they?"

"Just the way you didn't tell anyone I presume."

"I just wanted someone to talk to, you're never here."

"Listen to yourself, Catherine. You sound as if you're six rather than twenty-six. Well, if you want to be treated like a child I am happy to oblige. Go to your room and stay there. I don't want to see your face again tonight."

"What are you going to do about Robert?"

"None of your business, now get out."

"It is my business, he's my brother."

Her father did not bother to reply but seized her shoulder roughly and ran her out of the room and threw her down the hall. He banged the door behind her and she heard the key turn in the lock. Catherine picked herself up and went to stand for a moment outside the door, trying to control her breathing. Almost immediately she heard the electronic tune of the computer being turned on. Slowly she turned away and went up to her room. Her father had never been an easy-tempered man, but he had always treated his daughter with a fair degree of indulgence. Suddenly, Catherine had a great deal more sympathy for her mother.

Catherine went to sleep early, something she had always done when hurt or upset. It was a good way to hide when things became too much. As a result she woke in the early hours feeling extremely thirsty. She had not brought any mineral water up to her room with her and she detested the taste of the bathroom tap water.

She slipped out of bed and made her way downstairs. As she passed her father's study she could see that the light was still on. He was speaking to someone, presumably on the telephone, but his voice was too low for her to make out what was being said. She moved quickly into the kitchen. With Daddy in his current mood she did not want to be found eavesdropping.

Chapter Five

The bellboy at the Hotel Grande Bretagne in Athens led Professor McKenzie to his usual room on the second floor. It had a balcony with a fine view of the Acropolis. The boy anticipated a good tip. The professor was a regular visitor and known to be generous. He was also interested in the other little services a discrete and knowledgeable hotel staff could provide, for a consideration.

The professor was a big man; everything about him seemed big. He was about 180cm, with a thick body and chunky arms and legs. Even on that bear-like body his head seemed over large, with a big square face and bushy hair that had once been black but was now well mixed with grey.

James McKenzie slipped the boy a 20 Euro note. If he was lucky at the casino he would double that later. The pigskin case with which the young man had been struggling contained what the professor thought of as his city clothes. Fine silk and worsted suits, expensive underwear, silk shirts and ties. A world away from the scruffy denim and Fruit of the Loom that was his island wear. Still, it was the island and its little industries provided the finance for these very pleasurable trips to Athens.

"Is Georges on duty?" the professor asked in excellent Greek.

"*Nai kírie*, yes sir."

"Send him up to me immediately, please."

APOLLO IN TWEEDS

The little services were being needed somewhat sooner than expected. It was the use of the word please as much as the Euros that made the boy go and look for Georges as soon as the bedroom door had closed. Georges was enjoying a surreptitious cigarette behind the dustbins. The management was very strict about enforcing a no-smoking policy amongst the staff.

The boy was surprised at the speed at which Georges put out the fag, unwrapped an extra-strong mint and smartened his uniform.

"Hey, where's the fire, Georges? The old guy isn't going anywhere."

"You don't know our good professor. When things are going his way he's every inch the benevolent gentleman, polite to the staff, generous with tips. If something happens not to please him he can be vindictive. His speciality is a letter to the management after he has left. It usually results in someone losing their job. He also has a vicious tongue and can speak Greek as well as we can so muttering at him does not work."

With a last swipe at his hair, Georges hurried to the second floor. This guest would bear watching, thought the boy. Within half an hour the call girl Kleopatra was being discretely escorted up the back stairs to floor two. Kleopatra was a regular visitor to the hotel. She was beautiful in a wild, gypsy sort of way and pleasant enough to the staff. She was, however, very discrete and never stopped for a drink and chat about the clients afterwards as some of the girls did. It was also rumoured she did not object to a few bruises if paid well enough.

Relaxed and bathed, James McKenzie felt good. He looked round the room. The Grande Bretagne was a cut above the average business hotel. It had been built as overflow accommodation for the Greek royal family in the nineteenth century and it had retained a certain grandeur and style. That little desk by the window was certainly valuable. The carpets and draperies were of a quality well above the usual hotel functional. It suited him very well. It came at a cost, of course, but for once in his life money was not a problem.

He would have dinner at the casino, but that would be much later in the evening. He fancied something light now; smoked salmon sandwiches and champagne might be the cliché for the snack food of the wealthy, but it was still delicious. The Grande Bretagne prided itself on importing salmon from one of the finest smokeries in Scotland. As he reached for the telephone, it rang under his hand. Expecting some query as to his comfort from reception, he answered brusquely. "McKenzie."

"Uncle James, is me Phillip, we've got a problem."

The professor's heart sank. He was not unaware of his nephew's tendency to bossiness or the resentment it caused in some of the brighter students. "What's happened now?" he said wearily, expecting to hear that some key member of the team had gone off in a huff.

"The new guy on the fishing boat broke open one of the special packing cases. He saw the head of Athena; you know, the little one you were so pleased with? Yánnis tried to kill him but he jumped overboard. I caught him in the students' camp and locked him in the cellar." The words had all come out in a rush. Phillip drew breath and then said in a hopeful sort of tone, "What do you want me to do now?"

"Tell me again what happened, this time slowly and fill in some details," the professor said patiently.

So the story was told again with Phillip putting the best possible gloss on the incident in the harbour. After Robert had jumped overboard and the shooting incident, Costas had returned to the galley, smeared the captain's face with oil, given him some brandy then headed for the harbour. The harbour master had phoned the villa and Phillip had taken the van down to the sea to pick up the injured man.

The island did not have a doctor but the professor's housekeeper had been a nurse on the mainland for a while. She set about cleaning the muck from Yánnis's face and applying some soothing salve of her own. The professor wondered if even the super tough Yánnis would survive these ministrations.

Once a straight story could be got from Costas, Phillip had gone back down to the harbour. The usual layabouts that haunted the waterfront were sure no one had swum in from the sea. There had been someone on the quayside ever since the *Herakles* had returned so dramatically. That meant the seaman must have headed for the far side of the promontory. It was the only logical choice.

If the man had got his brains dashed out on the rocks, problem over. Somehow he did not think it was going to be so easy. The other scenario was that the swimmer had made it to the old temple landing stage. If so, then there was a chance he would be able to pull himself up onto the path.

Phillip decided he would go down to the students' camp and ask if they had seen anything. Perhaps he could get the idle sods to search the woods. In the end it was not necessary as the missing man was sitting by their fire as if he had just dropped in for a chat. The tale Phillip told his uncle was slightly more dramatic.

"Do Yánnis or Costas know you have the rogue seaman?" the professor asked.

"Yes, Costas was with us at the pickup."

"Restrain them at all costs. There must be no revenge killing, for now at least." The professor thought for a moment. "Keep the guy secure but do nothing else." The professor's voice was stern. "I will ring you back with instructions later this evening. Give the villagers some money and send them back to their homes. Swear them to secrecy, but I don't suppose it will do any good.

"I need to talk to some people. So please, Phillip, do nothing else on your own initiative. Do you understand me?"

"Yes, sir." Phillip's voice was sullen.

"You've done well so far," the professor coaxed. "We can't afford to have either the students or the villagers talking about mysterious disappearances. I'll talk to some people and then let you know the plan."

"Okay, Uncle." Philip sounded more cheerful.

The professor put down the phone and walked out onto the balcony. He searched in his pockets for cigarettes and lighter. Great Goddess Athena, he thought, blowing smoke at the Acropolis. What a mess. One drunken seaman gobbing off about wonderful treasures from a site that every archaeologist worth his salt knew was played out could have been shrugged off as spite or dementia. Shooting, dramatic escapes, midnight chases in the woods and they might as well have put up a banner saying 'Nefarious doings going on here'. Still, that is the penalty for dealing with criminals. They lack the logical mind.

What was needed now was damage limitation. He considered briefly going back to the island and sorting things out himself and saying nothing. No, too many people were now involved with the schemes. His partners were going to be very much less than pleased when he told them. If, however, they found out from another source they could get positively dangerous.

The problem had started with that comic duo who called themselves smugglers. Well, the Shadowman could deal with them. He took a big enough cut; it was time he did some work for it. Good God, the Shadowman, it sounded like the villain from one of the comics he had enjoyed as a boy. On the other hand, the professor really did not want to know this character's real name. That would be very dangerous knowledge indeed. As many students as possible must see the resourceful Robert alive, well and leaving the island cheerfully and without restraint.

Thinking about the students, it was perhaps time to send them home, not immediately but in the next week or two. Perhaps they could be transferred to another dig for the remainder of the summer. He'd have to pay their ferry fares and for accommodation on the new site but it would not be that much. It would certainly give them something else to think about besides a wandering Robinson Crusoe.

One or two were beginning to question the amount of resource expended on a distinctly unimportant site. Perhaps the temple of Athena could be discovered during the winter and a completely new team recruited for the next season. It would be nice to do some real work for a change.

The professor crushed out the remains of his cigarette. He realised what he was doing. He did not want to make that first telephone call and he was daydreaming in order to put it off.

First, however, he needed a drink. To hell with champagne, he needed a brandy. He called room service and requested a bottle of Remy Martin; it was going to be a long night.

When room service had come and gone, he opened his case and took out his mobile phone. This was one call that must not go through the hotel switchboard.

The call was answered on the second ring.

"Michael?"

"Yes."

"It's James. I'm in Athens."

"What the devil are you doing here in the middle of the season?"

The professor had known this call was going to be difficult. "I had to see Solomós at the university. Listen, there has been a problem."

There was a long silence and James took a bracing sip of cognac.

"Go on."

"There has been trouble with the transport. There was a new crewmember. One man has been injured, one absconded but persuaded to return."

James had spent some time working out what he would say. Enough to convey what had happened, neutral enough not to alert any unfriendly, listening ears.

"Is the situation stable?"

"For the time being."

"Where are you?"

"The Hotel Grande Bretagne."

"You do yourself proud, don't you, on your little business trips? I hope you're not going to claim your stay on expenses. I'll meet you at the Santorini in the Plaka in thirty minutes. Walk; don't try to take a taxi."

"You're in Athens?"

"How the devil could I meet you if I wasn't? Get a grip, I thought you were supposed to be bright."

James found himself listening to the dialling tone. For a moment, James felt like a first-year student being dressed down by one of the more irascible masters. Of course he would walk to the Plaka, the old town at the foot of the Acropolis, most of it was off limits to cars anyway. Where the hell was the Santorini? He would ask some stranger when he got to Sintagma Square. He felt he'd been indiscreet enough at the hotel for one night.

The Santorini turned out to be a cheap and cheerful tourist restaurant halfway down a narrow back street. It had taken McKenzie longer than he had calculated to find it and he arrived late. He tagged on to the end of what was obviously a coach party of German tourists filing their way through the blue and white doorway. How was he going to find Michael in this crowd? Would they be able to hear one another over the amplified bazouki music?

Michael was sitting at the bar. McKenzie extricated himself from between two hausfraus and went to join him. Perhaps this was just a place to meet. They would find somewhere a bit more upmarket to eat. Michael slipped off his barstool as soon as he saw the professor, leaving half a glass of milky ouzo on the counter. Without even a greeting he led the way up an iron stair to a tiny table for two at the back of a balcony overlooking the area where the floorshow was performing.

An elderly man with dyed black hair and an over-ruffled red and white shirt was warbling a folk song. He might have been good twenty years ago but now he was having difficulty hitting the higher notes.

"God help us, who employs that ancient gigolo to ruin a perfectly good song," McKenzie said testily.

"Stamati is the owner of the place. Anyone who suggests he isn't up to singing anymore will be out of the place within five minutes, customer or employee, so keep your voice down."

A waiter threw two menus at them and asked if they wanted anything to drink. Without consulting his companion, Michael ordered a jug of the house white wine. McKenzie shuddered and put down the large and garishly illustrated card.

"I don't want anything."

"You will order, eat it and at least appear to like it. You will do nothing to attract attention to yourself, do you understand?" Michael's voice was easy and pleasant but the words etched like acid. "Take off that poncy jacket, roll up your sleeves and put your tie in your pocket. Tonight you are just another stupid tourist soaking up a little Greek culture. So lose that sour expression and smile."

What Michael was saying made sense. McKenzie realised but resentment roiled inside him. Who was this jumped-up accountant to talk to him like this?

"I'm the man who is going to pull your chestnuts out of the fire," said Michael as if he had read his companion's thoughts.

The wine came quickly. The food service would be slower. Profit in these places came mostly from the booze so they gave you plenty of drinking time. McKenzie ordered Greek salad and lamb kebabs. They were the plainest things on the menu and the least likely to be spoiled by over-enthusiasm in the kitchen. Over the edge of the thick glass tumbler McKenzie studied the younger man.

He was older than he appeared on first acquaintance, nearer forty than thirty. He was not much more than middle height, compactly built with very clean-looking iron-grey hair that flopped over his forehead. A pleasant face that smiled easily and dark, dark eyes that looked as if they never smiled at all. He was wearing a black t-shirt with a badly printed copy of the Hippocratic oath done in gold on the front and black jeans, a businessman on holiday to the life.

McKenzie watched Michael observe the surrounding tables. They were jammed in like sardines but the occupants were either watching the troupe of dancers who had followed the singer onto the stage or busy with their own meals. They were certainly paying the two men no attention at all. After listening to the various conversations for a moment—English, German and one of the Scandinavian languages—Michael switched to Greek.

"So tell me about your cock-up."

"Your people started it," McKenzie protested.

"Just tell me."

"One of the crew of the transport team became ill over on the other side." Even though they could not be understood, McKenzie was still careful. "Something quite serious, strangulated hernia, certainly a hospital job."

"Heaven help the poor bugger," commented Michael. Turkish hospitals did have a certain reputation.

"If they were to make the run on time they needed a replacement quickly. They took on this English guy who was apparently working his way back to Britain from New Zealand. He came recommended by someone known and had a master's mate certificate. He was told the cargo was tobacco and seemed to have no problem with that."

"Whose story is this?" Michael asked

"Costas, the captain, Yánnis was injured."

"Go on."

"He did several trips, apparently this was to be his last run. The guy wanted to sign on with a freighter going north. This was fine with the crew as Yánnis thought he was getting a bit too nosy."

"So what happened last night?"

"Phillip says that when they were loading last night, the guy deliberately dropped a box and saw enough for him to know what it was that was being shipped."

"That's what Phillip says. What does Costas say?"

McKenzie had forgotten that Michael had met Phillip. "The same I suppose, I have not spoken to him directly but he was there when Phillip told me the story."

"That nephew of yours is a liability. When he returns to his university don't invite him back."

That wasn't fair. McKenzie started to feel angry again then deliberately pushed the issue away. This was not the time to discuss it.

"The next bit is still confused. Apparently they cleaned up and the boat set off for…well, started to return. Yánnis had a temper tantrum and went to fillet the Brit before they even got out of the harbour. Unfortunately, the guy had started to brew some coffee or something. Anyway, he threw a pan of boiling water over Yánnis and went straight over the side. Costas tried to stop him with a gun, but with a screaming Yánnis and the boat to see to, he missed. Costas brought the boat back into harbour and my housekeeper is trying to care for the injured man."

"What about the missing crewman?"

"He got to shore and made it as far as the students' camp. Philip and some villagers picked him up from there."

Michael ran his hand through his hair. "Is the Brit still alive and in good shape?"

"Yes, I told Phillip he must stay that way, at least for the time being. There is one more thing you ought to know."

"What's that?"

"The Brit's name is Robert MacFarlane. It could be a coincidence but do you want to take a chance?"

Michael looked stunned. Unfortunately, the food came at that moment. Fussing with plates and bowls and ordering more wine gave Michael time to compose himself. It was not often that you saw the smooth Michael at a loss.

The second jug of wine arrived. Mackenzie wondered what had happened to the first one. Neither of them had seemed to consume that much. Still, it was not bad wine.

"Stamati imports this stuff by the barrel from his native Santorini," Michael commented. "It's decent plonk and the trade supports some of the relatives back home. Back to business. I want you to return to the island tomorrow."

"There isn't a ferry till next week," Mackenzie protested.

"Then hire a yacht. You need to be there. Charge the hire to the business if you must."

That was unusual, Michael must be seriously worried. The dark eyes were unfocused as he concentrated on what must be done.

"Tell Costas to hire a couple of the more reliable islanders to crew the boat. Get him off on the first tide. Fill Yánnis up with booze and painkillers and send him with them. The islanders are to come straight back, not wait for the next cargo. Make sure they have enough money for the ferry fares and accommodation."

"They can make do on the boat," protested Mackenzie.

"I want them off that boat as soon as it lands. If they have to wait for transport tell them to wait on another island. They are not to stay in Turkey. Impress it on them." Michael stared at the professor until he was sure the pompous oaf understood.

He would have to tell the Shadowman what had happened. Yánnis and Costas would not be returning to the island. Then with a complete switch of personalities he began to clap and cheer with the other men as the belly dancer made her entrance.

"A belly dancer." McKenzie was torn between disgust and amusement. The average Greek hated Turks with passion, yet everywhere you went there was evidence of a shared culture. Greek delight, Greek coffee are indistinguishable from their Turkish equivalents. Now rashaki dancing that might have come straight from an Istanbul nightclub. The professor let his eyes stray to the silk-clad female who was doing a spectacular shimmy. She was not bad, not bad at all.

When the crowd had settled down, Michael rapped the table to attract McKenzie's attention and continued with his instructions.

"Tell Phillip to keep this Robert character in the cellar till you arrive. When you do, make a great show of letting him out. Shout at everyone for locking him up. Apologise, feed him, let him have a bath and dress him in some decent clothes. Have a big party with all the students there to thank them for their help. But whatever you do, don't let this Robert character off the island. If the ferry comes in before we can get out to you, promise him anything, chance of a job, holiday in the sun, boat going to England or wherever he wants to go, anything to keep him there until my partner and I arrive."

"Does the Shadowman have to know?" Mackenzie asked. "About this Robert character that is."

"Yes." Michael's eyes were obsidian chips. "He has spies everywhere. We would not last long if he discovered we were keeping anything from him. I've seen it happen before and to people who were very high up in the organisation. He is a generous friend but a deadly enemy and he decides who falls into which category. I think, however, I can persuade him that if Robert is who we think he is he need not be eliminated."

"What if he isn't...isn't who we think he is?"

"The students still need to see that the adventure in the night was all a misunderstanding and this Robert character, whoever he is, remains safe and well. My partner and I will offer the man a lift on our yacht to wherever he wants to go. He will sail off into the sunset, never to be seen again, by anyone. Now do you have any other questions?"

The professor's head was spinning. The wine—somehow they were on their third jug—the smoke and noise of the nightclub were all making thinking difficult. He knew what he had to do and he could do it no question. There was nothing else. Then he remembered the temple.

"Michael, will you ask the Shadowman about opening up the Athena site? The brighter ones are questioning the validity of the Poseidon excavation. Someone is going to call the attention of the authorities to it soon. If the site could be 'discovered' this winter it would give a reason for continued excavation on Sigandros. Some material would have to be sent to the university, but the business could go on as it always has."

"And you would get some professional kudos out of it? Save your academic reputation?"

The professor tried for a smile and failed. "My dear Michael, there is nothing that can do that. I have, however, been a loyal and generous friend to the university. There is no reason to think that if the temple of Athena was located this winter that I would not be put in charge."

It did not take a genius to see that the old fool had a double agenda. That did not mean he was wrong about the Poseidon temple reaching its natural end. He would mention it when he talked to the boss. Meanwhile, the show had finished and customers were starting to move to the tiny dance floor. He paid the bill with a generous tip and the two men made their way out into the night.

Michael stood by the door and watched the professor stride away. Only when he was out of sight did Michael turn back into the restaurant and make his way to the manager's office to pay the extra required for absolute discretion and a table whenever he wanted it in a nightclub that was always fully booked.

McKenzie returned to the hotel. He did not acknowledge the friendly greetings of the doorman. Instead, he went straight to reception and announced his departure first thing next morning. On being informed, the night manager came scuttling out of his office to enquire if there was anything wrong or if there was anything they could do to help. For a moment McKenzie was tempted to ask about hire of a yacht, there was always a chain of relatives and connections who could get you just about anything you wanted. Then he thought better of it. It was as well to keep business and pleasure separate as much as possible.

Once back in his room, McKenzie phoned Philip. The boy sounded less than alert. His uncle wondered if he had been drinking, then realised that it was very late. Slowly he went through the instructions. They were simple enough but there must be no more mistakes.

"I will return tomorrow. Keep the Brit safe till then. Always have at least three men present when you take his food or remove his slops. Recruit a couple of the most reliable fishermen, get Yánnis and Costas off the island as soon as possible. The islanders must return immediately, impress it on them."

Reluctantly McKenzie told his nephew where he kept his cache of emergency funds, well, at least one of them. He was conscious that he would have to change the hiding place once he returned to the island. His nephew had a positive lust for money that certainly did not come from his side of the family. McKenzie finally terminated the call after forcing Phillip to repeat the plan one last time. As soon as the line cleared he redialled for one more call.

Professor McKenzie passed the rest of the night without much sleep. He worried that something else was going to go wrong. As soon as dawn broke, a taxi collected him to take him down to the harbour at Piraeus. He went immediately to the harbour master's office. Here his excellent Greek stood him in good stead.

"I'm Professor McKenzie," he announced.

This did not elicit much response.

"I am the archaeologist in-charge at the very important dig on the island of Sigandros."

A little more interest.

"I came to Athens to discuss the work in progress with Professor Solomós at the university."

They had certainly heard that name. In this ancient city, top archaeologists had the status of minor pop stars.

"I have just been told that one of my staff has had a terrible accident. I must return immediately."

More interest, accident watchers every one, the ghouls.

"There is no ferry till next week. Can you help me hire a reliable vessel to take me out there now, this morning?"

The bearded harbour master had come out of his office to investigate what was going on. One of his staff repeated the story, although it was clear he had already listened to every word.

"It will be very expensive," he rumbled.

"Cost is not a consideration," the professor said nobly. "I must get back to my people."

There might have been a twitch of a smile under the beard.

A vessel was found within a very short space of time and the documentation completed on the spot.

The professor insisted on making a donation to the fisherman's orphans fund, although he doubted if the children would see any of the money.

One of the secretaries escorted him through the maze of commercial and private vessels to the hire-craft. It was done within ten minutes. The cost was well over the going rate but the business could afford it. By the time the sun was well up they were skimming over the sparkling waves. McKenzie experienced none of the pleasure he usually felt on leaving the grey skies of smog-polluted Athens for the clearer skies of the islands. He had the uneasy feeling that the trouble would not be covered over as simply as Michael envisaged.

The Shadowman would not be pleased at the sudden visibility of the operation or the costs incurred. Despite the huge profits gained from the double operation of artefacts from Sigandros to Turkey and goods from Turkey via Sigandros to Athens, the Shadowman and his agents watched expenses as if they were the Inland Revenue rather than a bunch of crooks. Perhaps that's why they watched each other so carefully, they knew someone would start to skim off given the slightest opportunity.

At least part of costs of this incident would undoubtedly be taken from his share of the profits. If the Shadowman thought the operation was fatally compromised then the professor was under no illusions that not only Yánnis and Costas would die. He, too, would soon suffer a fatal accident. James McKenzie shivered despite the heat of the sun.

Chapter Six

Next day Douglas rose feeling a bit more cheerful. The previous evening he had looked through his notes and got out those that related to Sigandros and Professor McKenzie. It had been better than thinking about new houses. He would photocopy the documents at the library and give them to Catherine when he met her that afternoon. He put them in his briefcase. Walking slowly from room to room he felt something like pain at the thought that his time in the old building was limited. He was, however, slowly coming to terms with the fact that he must move.

Perhaps it was time to get out of the city altogether. He thought briefly of a cottage deep in the Trossachs, Rob Roy country. He smiled as the impracticality of such a dwelling came to mind. You might cut yourself off from irritating neighbours but you would also distance yourself from libraries, live music and the unacknowledged blessings of a corner shop. What he would really like would be a villa on one of the more culturally orientated Greek islands.

"Commuting to the library in Edinburgh would be a problem," he said aloud as he locked the front door behind him and hurried down the stairs.

High Street was almost empty at eight in the morning. There were some people like himself plodding to work, a few backpackers either searching for breakfast or looking as if they were returning from some all-night rave. Then there was a sprinkling of super keen tourists wanting to photograph the ancient streets without a mob of people in the way. They did not realise that mobs of people were natural for this place. It was the old town, it was meant to have crowds of people, that was what it was for.

Douglas noticed a couple of the scruffier characters were coming up fast behind him. He moved to the edge of the pavement to let them pass. It was not wise to get between an addict and his fix. Then he felt a tremendous thump in the middle of his back that propelled him forward. Unable to save himself he went down hard, full length on the pavement. One of the louts stood on his wrist and wrenched the briefcase from his hand. The other closed from the left-hand side and put a couple of kicks into his ribs. Then they were gone, racing down one of the narrow closes and out of sight.

Too winded even to cry out, Douglas lay on the pavement. His wrist felt as if it was on fire. The pain in his side was knives. He could not breathe, it hurt too much. Within seconds a crowd had formed from the previously empty air. A woman screamed, someone asked him if he was all right, bloody stupid question, a man tried to get him to sit up. It was his turn to scream. Another person commanded that he be left alone. It did not stop the prodding or fussing. Some kind Samaritan put a coat under his head. He could hear mobile phones being used to summon the authorities. Inevitably some latecomer to the spectacle asked, "Is he drunk? At this time in the morning, too, it's disgusting." It must be nice to be so self-righteous.

Just about the time Douglas was beginning to think he might be able to move, the emergency services arrived with flashing lights and braying sirens. The crowd began to melt away, not wanting to get involved. As the paramedics helped him into the ambulance he could see a couple of police officers in yellow vests trying to round up some reluctant witnesses.

Slow hours passed whilst Douglas waited for nurses, doctors, x-ray technicians, more doctors, more nurses. Each and every one intent on knowing his name, address, date of birth and National Insurance number. He asked for an aspirin. His head had started to pound along with his arm and chest.

The request was denied with a certain amount of shock, they didn't have anything like that, this was a hospital.

It turned out that no bones had been broken. The wrist was severely bruised. It should be strapped and kept immobile for a few days. There might be a hairline crack on a couple of the ribs. Strapping was not recommended as it restricted breathing and could lead to chest infections.

"The last thing you need with a cracked rib is a cough," the young houseman said with cheery good humour. Douglas could not see the funny side. Which was perhaps as well because laughter was not recommended either.

The police appeared at one point. The young officers seemed vaguely disappointed that his injuries were not worse and very disappointed he could not describe his attackers. They also seemed determined to find some reason why the attack had been his own fault.

"Was it a very expensive briefcase?"

"It was leather, but ten years old, and not that expensive, even when new."

"Where you drawing attention to it?"

"I was not to my knowledge swinging it or doing anything else out of the ordinary."

"Do you walk along the High Street at that time every day?"

"When I am on the early turn, it is the only logical route from my home to the library where I work."

They had him on that one. "It's always as well to vary your habits, sir."

Did they expect him to make a half-mile detour via Princes Street to foil potential muggers?

"Do you regularly transport valuable articles?"

"No, I am a research librarian."

"What about valuable books?"

"Valuable books stay in the library."

The officers both looked sceptical. "What was in the briefcase?"

"Photocopied documents."

"What else?" More cynicism.

"A mobile phone, address book, paperback novel, packet of tissues, tube of mints."

The officers had lost interest. They gave him a crime number and asked him to come to the station within the next forty-eight hours to sign a statement.

Douglas went back to waiting and contemplating his headache. Right now the only thing he missed from his case was the latest blood and thunder by that woman pathologist. It would have helped to pass the time. Then to his utter surprise Margot ran into the waiting room, scarves flying, and flung her arms round him. She calmed down when she felt him wince. Behind her hovered the elegant figure of Catherine from the estate agency.

"Douglas, I have only just heard, I am so very sorry. How badly have you been hurt?"

"No broken bones but I feel like death warmed over. How did you find out where I was?"

"The police rang the library, trying to find out if you really did work there and were you in the habit of taking valuable books home."

"The bastards," Douglas moaned. "What did the boss say?"

"Old Carberry said that none of his staff was in the habit of removing books from the reference section to take home."

Loyal, if not strictly true.

"How long have you been here?" Catherine asked suddenly.

"Since about half eight this morning."

"What are you waiting for now?"

"Staff nurse said that they will strap my wrist as soon as they get the notes from x-ray. After that I don't know; I've sort of lost track. Please, whilst you are here, can you get me a cup of tea from the machine? If I go, that's sure to be the time when they call my name and if I miss it. That will be another hour on the waiting time."

To Douglas's surprise, Catherine did not go in search of the drinks machine but instead marched up to the harassed nurse on the reception desk. There followed a furious row that Catherine seemed to be winning. The x-ray notes were extracted from under a pile, bandage and sling produced.

Whilst the nurse did a bit of medicine rather than administration, Catherine had completed the formalities and called a taxi on Margot's mobile phone to the great displeasure of the orderlies. In a shorter time than Douglas could ever have imagined, he was sipping Earl Grey in his favourite squashy armchair in his own lounge. Margot and Catherine sat together on the settee.

"Thank you both," Douglas said with deep sincerity.

"When I found out what had happened to you I telephoned Catherine to cancel your appointment for this afternoon. Catherine asked if I had a car to get me to the hospital. When I said no, she said that she would get a taxi and would pick me up outside the library in five minutes. She was waiting for me as I came out."

"That was more than kind, but is this not above and beyond the call of duty for someone who only wants to buy or rent a very modest property?"

Catherine had the grace to look uncomfortable. "I really wanted that information on Sigandros."

"There has been no further word from your brother?" Douglas was surprised.

"I told Daddy when he got home last night. He's still angry with Robert even after all this time. I'm not sure if he will do anything to help. I tried to show him the message on the mobile but somehow I had deleted it. He forgot to give it back to me. So I don't know if Robert managed to text me again."

"If the mobile he was using was running out of juice, then there might not be another." Douglas was trying to be sensitive but he could see Catherine was getting more and more upset. Right now he just did not have the energy to cope with her.

Margot could see Douglas was drooping. He looked deathly pale and ten years older. "What have you had to eat today?" she asked.

"Eat?" Douglas looked as if the concept was alien.

She realised that her friend had probably not had anything since breakfast, whatever that consisted of in this bachelor household.

"I'm going to go for a carry out," she announced. "Anyone got any preferences?"

No response. Douglas looked as if he was beyond caring and

Catherine had retreated into a tight little world of her own. Margot grabbed her bag and said she would not be long. Douglas roused himself long enough to say, "Marco at La Rusticana is usually good about doing something decent to take away."

"Nothing greasy and no meat for me," Catherine stated flatly.

You'll eat what you're given, or not as the case may be. Right now it's not you I'm worried about, thought Margot. It was a bit of a trek to La Rusticana. Margot's heart sank when she asked for Marco. A thin man, with long black hairs plastered over his bald head and a defeated expression, responded to her enquiry.

"I'm a friend of Douglas Grey," she said.

"Dear Dr. Grey, how is he?" The voice was beautiful, a musical tenor, soft as silk velvet. The little man smiled and suddenly Margot could see the heartbreaker he must have been in his youth.

"Douglas is far from well, Signor Marco. He was mugged this morning and he has only just got out of hospital. He has had nothing to eat all day and is feeling rotten." Margot had not intended to give the *War and Peace* version of the day's events.

"He is alone?" Marco was concerned.

"No, I and another friend are looking after him. I just came out for some hot food. Could you possibly help?"

"For three of you?"

"Yes, please."

Without asking any further questions Marco turned on his heel and marched into the kitchen shouting something in Italian to the young girl behind the bar. She approached Margot and said, "Please, if you would like to sit here at the bar the food will be ready in about fifteen minutes. Can I get you a drink? It will be on the house."

"A glass of dry white wine would be nice, but I'll pay for it myself."

Margot noticed the girl did not reach for the open bottle of house white on the bar but reached for an unopened bottle of Lacrima Christi from a chiller cabinet.

As she opened the bottle, the girl said, "I hear what you say to Marco. Dr. Grey very good customer here. Always very polite, very generous, a gentleman. We are happy to help. Please, how is El Greco?"

Margot was quick enough to realise that Douglas's love of ancient Greece must show even when having a spaghetti supper. She described the injuries and stressed they were not serious. She did not add that her friend was probably suffering from shock and hospital fatigue as much as the blows of his assailants.

Just about the time Margot was finishing the pale amber wine, Marco reappeared with a large box. He called to one of the younger waiters. "Pietro, go with this lady and be sure to carry this box carefully." Marco brushed away both her protests and offers to pay, and she was escorted back out onto the street. It was only as she and her companion were climbing back up to High Street that she began to wonder what dishes were actually in the mysterious package.

Back in the flat, Douglas cradled his third mug of Earl Grey in both his hands. Under the combined influences of the fragrant tea and three aspirins, the turmoil in his body was beginning to subside. He still hurt, but the pain no longer filled his whole mind. He could hear Catherine moving about the flat. He supposed it was a mixture of restlessness and professional curiosity. Let her wander, there was nothing even a maiden aunt, supposing he had one, could not see, more's the pity.

Catherine at first could see no further than her own misery. She was worried about her brother, still shocked by her father's reaction and uncomfortable that this attack on Douglas had come so quickly after her bringing his name to Daddy's attention. After a while, however, she began to appreciate the beauty of the old place. The walls were natural stone or white plaster. The wide floor beams must be original. They were uneven and full of knotholes, but polished, not to a shine, but to a warm glow.

Apart from the enfolding armchair and settee, the rest of the cupboards and bookcases were of dark wood, reproduction, but good quality. There was an enormous coffee table of glass and stone that must be modern but had a timeless quality. The dining table Douglas had mentioned when they first met was in a side room. She could see what he had meant when he had described it as part of the building. On it stood piles of books and papers. It was slightly dusty. Catherine thought it probably had not been used for its original function since Douglas had moved in.

There were no curtains on the small windows. She hoped Douglas had hung some in his bedroom but she was not going in to find out. There were some handmade rugs on the floor and throws over the worn fabric of the lounge furniture. These were in bright colours and it would not have surprised her to learn they had been purchased direct from the weavers in Greece. She had never seen anything quite as beautiful in all the years she had spent viewing houses for prospective clients.

She picked up a jug from the top of one of the bookcases. The man must have as many books at home as he had in his library. Well, perhaps not quite as many. The handsome blue and cream wine krater had a small lead tag proclaiming it an authentic copy from some museum.

Elsewhere there were black and terracotta jugs with the outlines of gods and warriors. In pride of place, a sculpture of a rather superior-looking owl looked at her with wide round eyes.

It was a good room, full of interest, easy to relax in. She thought of the thousands of pounds her parents had spent on the house in Morningside, which had all the comfort and homeliness of a show house. Catherine turned to the man in the big chair. He seemed to be a little better than he had when she had first seen him in the hospital. He still looked shocked and ill. She realised he was hardly in any position to help her even if he wanted to.

Still, Michael was coming home tonight. He would know what to do and there was no one better at coping with Daddy in one of his moods. She had first met Michael when she had gone back to live full time at her parents' house after finishing school. He was the director of an import and export business. Daddy and Michael had some deals going together and the younger man was frequently invited over to the house to talk business.

Daddy obviously liked him and after a while Michael would be asked to stay and have a meal with the family. It soon became the norm for him to come by taxi and for Catherine to take him home after so he could have a drink. Catherine had never cared much for either wine or spirits. They were empty calories and impaired her performance at the gym. It was no real imposition to stick to mineral water and drive the guest home at the end of the evening.

After a couple of months of leaving him at the entrance to his apartment, one night he invited her in for coffee. There had been no coffee. He had taken her into the bedroom and raped her. Well, that was what it felt like at the time. He told her she was very unsophisticated and when she was more experienced she would enjoy it more.

After that she became his escort whenever there was a party or function to which the businessmen were expected to bring wives or girlfriends. Each time she took him home he expected her to go to bed with him. Or rather have sex on the bed. For when he was satisfied, she then had to dress and take the car back to her parents' home. As he predicted, it did get easier with time and habit.

Michael seemed satisfied and eventually he and Daddy had had a long talk, the engagement ring had been produced and plans had been made for the wedding and where they would eventually live. Catherine had gone along with the plans more because she could not think of any alternative than because she was desperately in love. She did, however, admire Michael for his business acumen. He had a fine athletic body and he was one of the few people who was powerful enough in their own right to gain the respect of her father.

She was to meet Michael at the airport tonight. He was flying in from Athens. She would tell him what had happened and get him to use his influence with her father. They usually went straight to Michael's apartment when he came home. Travelling seemed to create a need in him. Afterwards would be a good time to approach him.

"You're looking sad, what's the matter?" Douglas voice cut into her thoughts.

"Just thinking about Robert," she said quickly. "Did you find anything else about Sigandros?"

"I had a few things, nothing dramatic I can assure you. Some photographs from my stay, a bit more about the island and its history."

"What did you find out?" Catherine asked more to keep the topic of conversation away from herself than any real interest in the barren lump of rock on which her brother had apparently been washed up.

"As I told you yesterday, Sigandros has nothing to recommend it unless you're a history nut. There are about two hundred Sigandrites as the islanders call themselves. Most live in the village surrounding the harbour, but there is another little hamlet, Hora, up in the hills. Hora was the main town in the days when pirates plagued the Aegean. It was hidden well away from any casual search and was very difficult to raid if the pirates did come ashore. These days the people make a living from fishing, plus export of their olive oil and honey."

"So where do the archaeologists come in?" Catherine was curious.

"The professor and his students are a major addition to what would otherwise be a very scanty income. The teachers and sometimes students stay in the domathios, the bed and breakfast accommodation. They eat and drink in the tavernas and buy from the supermarket. The dig employs some of the locals for the heavier work."

"I can see why the professor might be popular with the locals. Did you find anything more about the island?"

"Yes, surprisingly enough. The Germans used the island as a prisoner of war camp during the Second World War. The remains of the block houses are still there, although I did not see anything of them whilst I was visitor."

"Do you think Robert could be hiding there?"

"It's certainly a possibility." Douglas did not add the thought that Robert could also be imprisoned there if he was not already dead.

Catherine seemed to be having similar thoughts as she asked quickly, "You said you had something more on the professor?"

"Yes, I went onto the University of Athens' website. It cost me an arm and a leg to get a system that will show both Greek characters and our own alphabet."

"You can read Greek?" Catherine sounded surprised.

"It's necessary if you want to be a Greek scholar," Douglas said gently. "In fact, I'm not as fluent in modern Greek as I am in the classical variety. Still, I can get along in most situations."

"So what did this website have to say?"

"McKenzie is in charge of the excavation on Sigandros. That's unusual because the Greeks are very sensitive about the fact that there is more of their heritage in both museums and private hands abroad than there is in Greece."

"You mean the row about the Elgin Marbles?"

"The sculptures from The Parthenon in Athens purchased by Lord Elgin in 1812 and now residing in the British Museum are just the tip of the iceberg. Take the example of Sigandros. The best material is in either the Louvre in Paris or in Istanbul. That's because the original excavators were French and because Turkey ruled the island for many years. There are some artefacts in Athens and a tiny museum on the island itself. When I was there it was kept locked and to the best of my knowledge no one except McKenzie and some of his personal students have visited it for years."

"So the people of Sigandros are still being robbed of their heritage." Catherine was indignant.

"You could say that." Douglas looked uncomfortable. "On the other hand, you could consider it the heritage of all the Greek peoples. As such it is more accessible in Athens than on an island no one visits."

Catherine had lost interest in the rights of the islanders. "Does the professor have an e-mail address? Could you send him a message, ask him if he has seen Robert, talk to his students?" Suddenly, the aloof and slightly unhappy young woman was transformed into an eager girl. Douglas was suddenly conscious of how very pretty she was.

"There was no contact data on the website, but I suppose I could ask Professor Solomós. It's too late now to catch him in his office but I'll message him. Give me your e-mail and telephone numbers and I'll contact you straight away."

Catherine thought about her missing mobile again. She did not want her father to know she had confided again in someone outside the family. She gave Douglas her e-mail address and her home and office numbers. "If I'm not there, would you leave a message to ring Diana? I don't have a friend called Diana so I'll know it's you."

Douglas thought it was a bit cloak and dagger but did not have the energy to argue. Instead, he rang the familiar Athens number and left a message in Greek for Dionysos on his answering machine. Then booting up the computer he did the same with the message system. Catherine was deeply impressed. She could tell from the fluency of his speech and typing that the tall scholar had been over modest about his language skills.

Just as Douglas was finishing, Margot returned. She directed a hard look at Catherine. "Douglas should be resting," she said shortly. Then she turned, thanked the waiter Pietro for his help, and tried to give him a tip. The young man would have none of it. Instead, he addressed a few words in Italian to Douglas of which *buona appetito* was recognisable, then he ran lightly back down the stairs.

"You have hidden depths," commented Margot dryly.

Then they turned their attention to the box, which was giving out a tantalising smell. There was a clear soup with tortellini, a creamy-looking risotto with mushrooms, chicken pieces with artichokes in a cream sauce, garlic bread, a dish of mixed olives, and a huge portion of tiramisu, the traditional Italian pick-me-up. There were also a couple of bottles of Barolo, the deep red wine from Piedmont.

"What did you order?" asked Catherine suspiciously.

"I didn't. Marco chose this all by himself. I suppose he knows Douglas taste by now." There was a slight warning note in her voice.

While Margot and Douglas shared the soup and risotto,

Catherine nibbled on some of the olives and accepted a piece of garlic bread. She refused the wine and got herself a glass of mineral water from Douglas's fridge. The food was delicious. Margot wondered briefly if the paying customers in La Rusticana were eating anything half so good, then decided she didn't care. By the time they had finished, Douglas was looking much better and slightly sleepy. Margot promised to look in on him the next day and the two women left him to get himself to bed.

Margot said she would walk home so Catherine was left to her own thoughts in the taxi back to Morningside. She decided to pick up her car and go straight to the airport to wait for Michael. She did not want to spend more time at home than she had to until Michael could get her father to see sense. The long wait in the airport lounge gave her time to think. What if Michael took her father's side? What if they both refused to either go to the island themselves or commission one of their Greek agents to do so? Could she go by herself?

For a woman of her wealth and background she had travelled very little. There had been a couple of school trips, one to Paris and one to Rome when she was in the sixth form. She did not think those would count, as the teachers organised and supervised everything. She could speak French reasonably well and had some Latin, but Greek was all Greek to her. She laughed out loud at the foolish joke then clamped her lips shut. Stop it, she warned herself, don't get hysterical.

She had rarely been on holiday with her parents. Daddy always had business commitments and her mother was rarely well in those days, especially after Robert had disappeared. During school breaks she had been sent on adventure holidays. Most of them had been quite fun too. Daddy had not been mean with money and she had gone to organisations that had had good equipment and skilled instructors.

Running over miles of boggy heather had not been her idea of a good holiday. She had, however, enjoyed climbing and potholing, in fact become quite good at it. The best holidays, however, were the sailing schools. She had gained certificates in craft handling and navigation. For once Daddy had been very pleased. He thought her skills might be useful at some point and encouraged her to return to the school at every opportunity. There had even been talk of buying her a boat of her own, but that had fallen through. She had, however, been permitted to hire a craft for several weeks each summer to maintain and polish up her skills.

When she had become engaged to Michael she thought that she might travel more widely. Michael was as old fashioned as Daddy when it came to taking a woman on a business trip. When he did permit himself a holiday, he said that he travelled abroad enough on business. He wanted to stay in Scotland. So that's what they did, touring from grey, rainy golf course to grey, rainy golf course.

Business was never far from Michael's mind. If he met any prospective clients he would invite them to go out for a round next day. In those circumstances, she was left to get a lady's game if she could or explore the area by herself. Fortunately, most of the hotels they stayed at had a decent gym and she spent a lot of time working out. Enjoyable as that might be, it had not equipped her to take off for foreign parts alone and unprepared.

Douglas was used to travelling on the continent by himself. He knew the island and he even knew this old bird McKenzie. Would he go with her? Money was not a problem; she could afford to pay for them both. She had her regular salary from the estate agents. The generous allowance Daddy had provided when she did not have a job had never been cancelled. Living at home with her parents kept her expenses down. Even her health club fees were paid by the business. Her only real indulgence was clothes. She bought the best and bought regularly. Even so there was a tidy sum saved up for her marriage and new home. She would spend it all and more if it would bring Robert home safely.

Eventually she saw the familiar figure pushing a luggage trolley out of the customs hall. The iron grey looked slightly greasy. Michael had it cut and shaped regularly to keep it in the best possible condition but the journey had taken its toll. Everything about Michael was quality, expensively tailored suits, handmade shirts, fashionable ties. The ones with Disney characters he wore last year were horrible, but fashionably horrible. Thank goodness that the current mode was more restrained.

In repose, Michael's face was serious, perhaps formidable would be a better description. He was undoubtedly handsome but there was strength behind the looks. The heavy brows almost touched over his dark eyes. His features were regular and smooth, the mouth wide but a little thin lipped. His personal grooming was immaculate, he always looked closely shaved and there was always just a hint of expensive cologne.

Catherine ran up to him. He did not smile or greet her but pushed the trolley into her hands. "I want to go straight to your father's place," he said shortly.

"Don't you want to go back to the flat first, have something to eat, freshen up?"

"No, something's come up."

"Is it this business about Robert? I know something about it. I'd like to talk to you before you see Daddy."

"Not here, in the car." That was the last Catherine got out of him until she was well away from the airport buildings.

"Tell me what happened, start at the beginning and leave nothing out. Do you understand me?" Michael had never been overly romantic. But he had never been as harsh and demanding as this with her. For a moment Catherine thought about the gentle scholar, Douglas Grey, his courtesy and charm.

Catherine obediently told the story from receiving the original text message to Douglas being mugged for the contents of his briefcase. The only thing she kept back was the trip to the hospital and subsequent visit to Douglas's flat.

"Are you sure you have told no one else?"

Michael was beginning to sound like her father.

"Perfectly sure, but if I had I don't see why it would matter. Please tell me what is happening. I know Daddy always overreacts when Robert is mentioned. I was shocked and upset when he shouted and screamed at me last night. I could at least comprehend why he was acting so irrationally. Now you're angry and worried too. If you would only tell me I think I could help."

"Leave the thinking to the grown-ups, darling."

Catherine could not have been more shocked if Michael had slapped her. She drove on into the night with tears streaming silently from her eyes.

Chapter Seven

Philip placed the receiver very slowly back into its cradle. It was quite fun giving orders to the losers who came on his uncle's dig. They were so frightened of offending the great professor that they would take any amount of shit from his favourite nephew. Manipulating characters like these fishermen was not going to be so easy. Another thought occurred, he could just about manage enough Greek to give basic orders like 'come with me'. How was he to give the detailed instructions demanded by his uncle?

He thought briefly of taking the next ferry off the island and leaving the old man to sort out his own mess. No, attractive as that was, he did not want to risk terminating the regular stream of presents that made his life so comfortable. He thought of his fellow students. The little dark-haired girl, Rena, she was practically bilingual. He had not bothered with her much because she had a figure like a boy and a moustache like Kaiser Bill. She could be very useful now. He would go and see her in the morning. He could be persuasive when he wanted and this definitely called for the old charm.

It was time to go to bed, but first he had better check on their guest in the cellar. If he could be kept quiescent then life might be a bit easier until Uncle James could return and take over. He walked down the lime-washed steps to the lower storage rooms. One had been hastily emptied of its usual contents of Calor gas cylinders to accommodate the prisoner.

"Hey, Robert," Philip called.

"Who's that?"

"It's Philip. I'm Professor McKenzie's nephew. Look, I'm sorry about this. I've been talking to my uncle."

"I can't hear you, open the door," Robert interrupted.

"I can't do that, my uncle...."

"To hell with your uncle! Are you a man or a lap dog?"

"The professor thinks there has been some kind of mistake," Philip started again.

"Open the door!"

"I can't. Tell me what happened."

"That idiot Yánnis tried to kill me. He went for me with a knife, I bopped him with a pan the size of a coffee cup then legged it. I nearly drowned just trying to get away. Let me out, please, I need to go to the heads."

"Use the chamber pot."

"I'm not a cat to crap on a litter tray, let me out. Christ, man, where can I fucking go? You have all the islanders in your pocket, the students think I'm a homicidal maniac and the ferry apparently visits every other millennium if you're lucky. Come on, mate, let me out, I really need to go."

This made sense to Philip and it seemed needlessly cruel to lock the man up overnight with his own stink when they intended to let him go in the morning anyway. He turned the key in the lock. As soon as the bolt clicked, the door burst open and a hairy fist the size of a small planet caught him on the side of the head. Then another buried itself in his gut. As Philip rolled away, retching and whooping for breath, he thought he heard the clatter of feet on the stairway and the bang of a distant door.

After what seemed a very long time Philip was able to sit up. His first thought was to raise the household and search again for their prisoner. What was the point? Nothing could be done till morning. He limped towards his bedroom. He decided to delay searching his uncle's office until morning when he hoped he would feel better. Philip thought ruefully that it might be the last time that he saw any of the good professor's money for some time.

APOLLO IN TWEEDS

Robert had not expected to be able to talk his way out of the storeroom. That Philip really was a fool. As soon as the effete young man was down, Robert barrelled his way to the cellar steps and out through the front door. If he met Costas with his gun then he would deal with the situation when it happened. The house seemed deserted. As he ran into the night, Robert briefly wondered if he had done the right thing. To hell with it, anything was better than sitting in that stuffy hole waiting for others to decide his fate.

He ran headlong into the darkness of the trees. There he slowed down; a twisted ankle would be of no help whatsoever. He decided to wait for his much-needed pee. They would not get dogs out. The Greeks were not great dog lovers. If there were any mutts on the island they would not be trained trackers, or so he hoped, but it was best to be careful.

The plan, so far as he had thought it through, was to hide up in the forest till morning then somehow work his way back to the students' camp and see if he could get either Margaret or her Greek friend Rena on their own. If they would help him hide then he had no doubt that Catherine would turn up and whisk him away. If challenged he would not have been able to say why he believed so strongly that Catherine had even got his message, let alone travel thousands of miles to come and get him. Yet there was no doubt in his mind that his little sister was already on her way.

There was some moonlight filtering down through the branches of the olives. As his night vision improved, he made his way cautiously through the leaf litter, heading away from the villa and up into the timber. The gradient suddenly became much steeper and he was practically climbing a vertical bank when his arm met no resistance and he fell forward to land face down on a flat path. His fingers scrabbled for purchase. This was not a dirt track but a metalled road. It was clear of debris so someone must use this track fairly regularly. He decided to follow it, continuing in the direction of rising ground.

The road that wound its way up the hill was very steep in places. Robert thought he would not like to drive up in anything smaller than a four-track. On foot, however, he was able to put some serious distance between himself and the villa. Time passed and he reckoned that he must have travelled several miles. Just when he decided he might be climbing the Himalayas, the road levelled off and at the end of a circular clearing were a number of long low buildings.

Robert approached cautiously but there were no signs of life. The structure had all the hallmarks of military architecture, but it was well maintained and the doors securely padlocked. A wave of extreme weariness overtook him. This might make a good place to hang out till Catherine came but he could not explore properly until daylight. He did not think he could go much farther tonight. He withdrew a short way into the surrounding trees and chose one whose thick roots and slightly off centre trunk made a reasonably comfortable resting place. Then he put his head on his arms and allowed himself to drift into sleep.

Margaret McDonald woke up with the sun in her eyes. For a moment she took pleasure in the light and heat. There were many fair days in Scotland, but the constant presence of hot sunlight in the Greek islands was a joy to her. She turned in her sleeping bag to see if Rena was awake. Her friend was sitting cross-legged on her bed, staring at nothing.

"Rena, what's the matter?"

The girl visibly started. "Nothing, I was just thinking."

"Serious thoughts."

"Not really. I have decided to go home when the next ferry comes in. I have not been happy for some time. The events of last night, Costas with a gun, the smuggling, they are all just too much for me. I want nothing more to do with the professor or the island right now. I don't even know if I want to continue with the archaeology course. I will talk to Professor Solómos when I get back, perhaps I will transfer to the History of Greece course in the autumn."

"I don't blame you. I've been thinking on similar lines. When you go I'll come with you. My return ticket to Edinburgh is not valid till next month, but I will try to sweet talk the ticket desk at the airport into changing it."

Rena looked shy for a moment then blurted out, "You would be very welcome to stay at my home. I know my mother would love to meet you. Athens is a wonderful city. I could show you some of the things the tourists always miss. The university is open. If you wish, I could get you permission to work in the library."

Margaret held up her hand. "Enough, enough, you've convinced me. If you're sure your mother wouldn't mind I would love to spend the rest of my time with you in Athens."

"Mitera loves company. Unfortunately, she does not get out much these days as her knees give her trouble."

"Then it's settled, we'll just keep a low profile until Friday when the ferry comes in, then we'll disappear without a fuss."

At the villa, Philip too was waking up. His stomach felt sore and he had a blinding headache. The thought that his uncle would arrive that evening gave him a sinking feeling in the gut. He washed down four aspirins with water from the bottle on his bedside, then stuck himself under the shower for five minutes. Once dressed, he began to feel better. The smell of coffee and fresh bread was drifting up from the kitchen. He would think of something, he always did.

After breakfast, Philip went to his uncle's study. He had not explored in here before even when his uncle had been off on one of his business trips to Athens. Mainly because he never expected the old man to be so stupid as to leave money just lying about. In fact, the cache Uncle James had told him about was not all that well hidden. The money was in an old metal box screwed to the underside of the desk. The key was taped behind a photo of the professor at some academic bash. To Phillip's disappointment there was barely enough to cover the necessary expenses, let alone provide some much-needed pocket money. Still, if there was one secret hiding place there might very well be more. There would be time enough to do some serious exploration later; meanwhile, he had better get on with the tasks his uncle had set him.

Philip walked down to the dig where the students were drinking coffee and looking miserable. There was not much sign of any work being done. He plastered a smile on his face and called out, "Dreadful business last night. It all seems a bit James Bond in the light of day." There was not much response. He tried again. "My uncle is charting a boat from Piraeus, he should be here by this evening. Meanwhile, I think we should get Yánnis to some qualified medical assistance."

"What's all this about your uncle finding the temple of Athena!" shouted one of the boys.

That flap-mouthed sod, thought Philip. Aloud he said, "It's a damned lie. That Robert character made it all up to get your sympathy."

"If he made it up then he's damned good, because he was half dead of exhaustion when he got to our camp."

"Good God, man, this island's not that big, you've all been hiking in the hills. Where do you think the prof.'s keeping it, behind the dustbins at the villa?"

The truth was that none of them had explored very far, the lazy buggers, but it's surprising what people will believe if you tell lies forcibly enough.

"Look all of you, come up to the villa. I'll get Yánnis and Costas to tell you the real story. I'll also ask Mayor Nikos Ritsos to come up. His family has farmed on the island for five generations. Rena will you help translate. Costas's English isn't that brilliant and Mr. Ritsos has difficulty saying good morning. I don't want there to be any misunderstandings."

"No, I want nothing to do with it." Rena was distressed. However, she relented as the other students pressed her to use her skills.

"Come up at twelve and we'll have lunch." Philip favoured them all with a big smile, then scarpered before they could realise that they were not going to have their explanation straight away. Still, the promise of food should hold them.

Philip practically ran back to the villa. He yelled to Ékaterina to prepare food for the students. He thrust some money at her and told her to get help and provisions from the village if she needed them. Costas was with Yánnis, trying to calm him down. Philip spoke slowly to the two men, regretting for the first time his lack of modern Greek. He told them that he would get them off the island as soon as he could. First they must talk to the students. Yánnis was beyond all caring but Costas was surprised.

"Why we need tell them anything?" he protested. "They just fools."

"That damned Robert has told them about the finds. They are angry and ready to complain to the university. We've got to keep them quiet. Admit to smuggling cigarettes, they know all about it anyway. Say you took nothing back but some black market booze for the Greeks in Marmaris."

"*Endaksi*, okay, but get us off this damned island quick." Costas was grudging.

"I've spoken to my uncle and he's authorised me to pay a couple of the local fishermen to help you get the boat back to Marmaris. Chose a couple of men you can trust. You can leave straight after you've spoken to the students. There's also money for a doctor back in Turkey. Just be discrete, *malista*, yes? I need you to do something else," Philip added urgently.

Costas rolled his eyes up to heaven.

"When you are down in the village, speak to Mayor Ritsos and tell him he's to tell the kids 'no temple of Athena'. Got that? 'No temple'."

"*Fisika*, of course, I'm not stupid," Costas returned.

Philip bit back the obvious remark and encouraged the fisherman to hurry. He then raided his uncle's stores of wine and found ouzo and bottles of the fiery white raki the islanders distilled themselves and which Philip thought privately might be better used to fuel trucks rather than to drink. Distraction, distraction, distraction, he thought to himself. Feed them enough alcohol and grub and nothing will seem quite as bad.

Obediently the students filed up to the villa at noon. Philip played the genial host to within an inch of his life, pressing drinks and mezzos on his guests. As soon as he could, he tried to get Rena away from the others but she seemed reluctant to leave the shelter of Margaret's shadow. So eventually he invited the two women into the study. He went again over the story of getting Yánnis to the hospital or at least a competent doctor. He then went on to explain that two of the island fishermen were going to help Costas with the boat.

"I need to be sure that the two men know exactly what I want them to do."

"What is that?" Rena sounded suspicious.

Blast the woman! "They are to take the *Herakles* directly to Marmaris. As soon as they have docked they are to leave the boat and come straight back. If they can't get back directly they are to wait on another Greek island."

"Why can't they wait and come back with the *Herakles*?"

This one was easy. "They are fishermen with families. They won't want to be away from home longer than they can help."

"Why can't they wait for a lift in Marmaris?"

"Who comes to Sigandros? They are better off island hopping. Anyway, as you know very well, Greeks are not that welcome in Turkey. Yánnis will be okay, he has contacts there."

It made sense and Rena indicated that she was willing to do as she was asked.

"Please," Philip pleaded at the last minute, "do ensure that these characters really understand what they are supposed to do. Tell them I will give them the money for the return journey and my uncle will pay them for their work when they return." That would save at least some of the cash. He would explain the 'mix up' if it ever became an issue.

The two fishermen received their orders stolidly enough. Best now to get Costas and Yánnis to do their piece and get them beyond questioning. Ékaterina was barbecuing steaks of young goat by the time they got back to the terrace, and the meeting was already turning into a party.

Yánnis truly looked dreadful. He had a bandage over his eyes and did not seem to be able to walk unaided. When invited to give his side of the story, he mumbled something about Costas and seemed ready to cry. No one wanted to press him for more. Robert reflected that with something like a bottle of his uncle's finest brandy inside him it was a wonder the old reprobate could stand at all.

Costas on the other hand was in fine form. Speaking slowly so that Rena could translate each sentence, he described how he had always mistrusted the young seaman. They were fishermen, but fishing in the Aegean was poor. They supplemented their income with transporting a few cigarettes. It was no secret. The new man had tried to get them interested in drugs. That was something they would never touch. He swore it on his mother's life. Roberto had threatened to tell the authorities about the cigarettes if they did not do as he said.

Then he said he would make up a story that would finish the excavations on the island. The clever students would have to excuse him there. He did not understand exactly what had been the nature of the threat. He and Yánnis had barely been to school before starting work, let alone attended a university. Yánnis, however, had been enraged to think that this criminal might blacken the good professor's name. A fight started, that was when the scoundrel had thrown boiling water in the captain's face and swum for the shore. By the time Costas had sobbed his contrition for dealing in duty-free cigarettes, most of the students were as angry with Robert as they had been at the professor.

Mayor Ritsos spoke next. He assured the students that he and his family had explored every inch of the island. They would like nothing better than to find a new archaeological discovery. It would bring more visitors to their poor island. Unfortunately, there was nothing. The legend of the temple to Athena was regretfully no more than that, a legend. The mayor was applauded and his health toasted. Ékaterina's nephew turned up with his bazoukie and pretty soon there was dancing and singing.

Costas and the fishermen helped Yánnis down to the *Herakles* and they set off. Philip pressed on them bottles of brandy and food wrapped in layers of foil like children taking goodie bags away from a birthday party. Anything to get them on their way. When Professor McKenzie arrived at six that evening, most of the students could not have cared if he had been personally responsible for the removal of the Elgin Marbles.

Robert woke gradually from a dream of mountainous seas. He had slumped uncomfortably sideways during the night. As he stretched his cramped limbs, his much-abused muscles protested vigorously, sending cramps along his nerve endings. He was horribly thirsty and his head pounded. He scrabbled to his knees then, after what seemed to be a long time, made it to his feet. He realised he could not go on for much longer without proper rest and shelter.

Half-staggering, half-shuffling, he returned to the buildings. They looked impregnable. The doors were secured with chains and padlocks and the windows fitted with heavy metal shutters. Whatever was in here was well-guarded. Robert prowled round the buildings once more. What was needed was a housebreaker or lacking that a Sherman tank. Then he remembered one of the crewmen on a dirty little freighter in the South China Seas, Frank Wu. The man had obviously had a colourful past. He used to say 'padlock friend of thief, one good blow on base and open sesame'.

It was worth a try. Robert scoured the area. He soon found what he was looking for, a large round lump of heavy marble. Then he returned to the doors and examined each one. He was searching for one where the door did not fit too well. The baking heat of a Greek summer was no friend to wood; it shrunk and warped. He found one door where he could jam the hasp of the padlock into a deep crack. Held in this makeshift vice, Robert brought the marble down onto the base of the lock with all the strength left in his powerful arms. The padlock sprung open just as Frank Wu said it would. Robert removed the chain and lock and pocketed them. There was also a Yale lock on the door. Another blow from his rock burst the door inwards.

The interior of the building was dark compared to the

brilliant morning sunshine outside. Robert slipped inside and closed the door after him then allowed a few minutes for his eyes to get used to the gloom. There were boxes stacked against one wall, but no other furniture. He moved cautiously from room to room. All were empty and dusty. At the far end, though, there was something more interesting. Someone obviously stayed here on a regular basis. There was a camp bed with blankets and pillows neatly stacked. Nearby sheets and pillowcases were folded separately and looked freshly laundered. Beyond lay a crude bathroom. It contained a foot-bath loo, a stained tiled area with a hook from which hung a shower head and length of rubber hose connected to a tap, beneath which was a drain hole. The last room of all was a kitchen. A sink, two-ring gas burner with bottled gas underneath and some cupboards.

Robert threw open the cupboard doors. The first one contained cups, plates and a couple of pans. The drawer above was home to cutlery and a can opener. The next cupboard was the real find: two plastic-wrapped four-packs of mineral water, a dozen assorted tins of meat, vegetables and fruit plus a jar of coffee. Robert scrabbled a bottle of mineral water from its shrink-wrap, unscrewed the cap and sucked at it greedily. It was with difficulty that he restrained himself.

Too much all at once and you'll throw up, an inner voice warned him. It's all yours, just take it easy. He took another brief swig then opened a packet of biscuits. They were a bit stale but not bad. Taking a handful to nibble on, Robert walked back to the first room with the boxes.

They looked like the cartons of cigarettes he had brought in from Turkey. Something nagged at a corner of his mind. They were too heavy and there was double packaging tape round the edges, neatly done but still detectable. They had been opened and resealed. Robert walked back to the kitchen and selected a long thin knife that looked reasonably sharp. He sliced open one of the boxes. Under the innocent buff cardboard lay long fat packets of honey-coloured granules. A second nick and the taste and aroma told the experienced Robert that here was first-processed opium resin. Even in this crude state he must be looking at a million Euros worth of drugs. If they found him now he was not just in trouble, he was dead.

The two villagers half carried Yánnis down to the boat. Grumbling about having to start a voyage mid-afternoon, they would have to do most of the journey in the dark. In the shallow waters there was the danger of rocks and in the deeper channels there was always the chance of meeting one of the commercial ferries. They never posted proper lookouts. Still, the promise of a generous payment from the professor did a lot to dispel the *kakos tiheros*, bad luck. They bedded the captain down in the cabin and headed out of the harbour. The two villagers had been helping to sail fishing boats since they were able to toddle. Costas had no problems letting them handle the *Herakles*.

He was worried about Yánnis. The man had a short fuse sure, but they had sailed together for a long time. They were as close as brothers. If that bastard Brit had ruined Yánnis's sight he was going to die, however long it took and whoever was looking after him. All that business of locking the young idiot in the cellar had not fooled him for a minute.

Okay, he was willing to play along for the time being whilst the professor and that stupid nephew of his were handing out Drachmas, curse it, Euros, would he ever get used to the new money? He would return to the island and then he would finish what the captain had started. Only this time there would be no fancy fighting or giving any warnings. It would be a knife in the dark and no mistakes made.

Costas watched over Yánnis for a while but the man was asleep. Best to leave him to his rest. Time enough for trouble when he woke up. They sailed at maximum knots for several hours. The Aegean was full of islands, some were big enough to be inhabitable, if someone was mad enough to want to try, others were little more than nameless rocks. He had been sailing through them all his life and knew enough to respect them. A sudden storm could drive a boat onto their teeth and those hungry rocks could tear the bottom out of a boat and crush the crew against the needle-like projections.

"Where will you be staying in Marmaris, Alexis?" Costas asked the older of the two fishermen.

"We're not staying in Marmaris. The young *daskalos*, teacher, was very insistent we return straight away. We have money enough for ferry fares and up to a week in hotels although we would not want to be away that long. If we stay in Turkey then the deal is off and we don't get paid for our time. Who would want to stay in that pig-loving country anyway?"

"I did not think young Phillip's Greek was that good. Did you understand him okay?" Costas said cautiously.

"Philip can barely ask his way to the bog. No, the *fititria*, the student, Rena, told us what he wanted to say. She's a sweet piece that little girl. Modest, polite, she's been well brought up. I'm a modern man, I don't mind an educated woman, provided she knows her place," Alexis said expansively.

Costas lit another cigarette and watched the phosphorescence on the waves. He did not like what he was hearing. They worked for dangerous people. There had been a cock-up. It wasn't their fault but when had that ever been a consideration? If the boss was going to get rid of all witnesses and start again, then perhaps it was time to think about Yánnis and himself disappearing before someone else could do it for them more permanently.

Just then Costas heard Yánnis shouting from the cabin. He threw his cigarette over the side and hurried down the companion ladder. The captain had pulled the bandages away from his eyes. He looked a mess. His face was scarlet with large white blisters. The flesh was swollen and the eyes gummed shut with what looked like puss leaking from beneath the lids.

"I can't open my eyes, I can't see. The bastard has blinded me, I wish he'd killed me." Yánnis's voice was breaking.

"Calm yourself, my captain, or you'll be dead before you can wish for it, me too." Costas took out two of the sterile pads provided by Ekaterina and rebandaged Yánnis's eyes. As he worked, he explained what the fisherman had told him. "I think they are planning to get rid of us permanently," Costas finished.

"You are right, my friend." There was no trace in Yánnis now of either the bad-tempered bully or the whining invalid. He was calm and serious. "Alexis is related to my wife, he and his cousin will help us to a certain extent, particularly if it does not put them in danger. We have to leave this boat before we reach Turkish waters. This is my plan." Yánnis reached out a hand and groped for Costas's shirt. Pulling him closer, Yánnis whispered in his mate's ear.

Chapter Eight

Catherine pulled up outside her father's house. Michael jumped out almost before she had engaged the hand brake and strode through the front door. She pulled herself out of the car feeling old and stiff. She had been so sure Michael would be able to put everything right. Maybe he could, but she had now seen a side of him she hated. It was too much like the way Daddy treated Mummy. She knew only too well how unhappy her mother was and the excesses to which it sometimes drove her still-loved parent.

Slowly she went round to the boot and removed Michael's topcoat and case. He had taken his briefcase with him. Catherine sometimes thought that he was more attached to his documents than he was to her. She took Michael's things inside and put them in the spare room. It was more than likely he would stay the night; he often did when business meetings went on into the early hours. Then she went back outside to put the car away and lock the garage. Like a good little girl, she thought bitterly.

Suddenly Catherine wanted to talk to a friendly voice very much indeed. She had not wanted a telephone in her room, preferring to use her mobile. Now Daddy had confiscated that for some mysterious reason. Then she had an idea. She went back to the spare room and searched the pockets of Michael's expensive vicuna overcoat. He had had it ready to use if he did not immediately spot her at the airport and had not had the opportunity to return it to his briefcase.

She carried it into her room intending to call Margot. On impulse she used the facility to recall the last ten numbers dialled. To her horror she saw that amongst the numbers with the Greek dialling code and her father's numbers, there was also the number for the mobile Robert had used on Sigandros.

With trembling fingers she brought up the last text message; it was in Greek. She put the mobile down on her bedside table as carefully as if it were a bomb. Think, she ordered herself. Michael spends a great deal of time in Athens, it would be very useful for him to know Greek, but why had he not told her? Daddy had obviously contacted Michael about Robert, why were they being so secretive about it? Was there something about their business dealings in Athens that they did not want to come to public notice? If so, would they risk their own security to rescue Robert? Daddy had seemed to hate her brother since the young man had run away, although surely he must still love his son deep down.

She got out notepad and pen. First she copied down all the numbers. Then, as carefully as she could, she copied the Greek text. Finally she repeated the saved messages. As she expected, there were several in Greek but one was in English.

"Michael, it's now nine o'clock, I've managed to hire a boat and am just leaving Piraeus. The crew tells me that we should arrive about six tonight. Phillip's taking care of things on the island. I'll contact you again when I know the real situation."

Catherine turned the mobile over and over in her hands. Then she remembered the Dictaphone she used when assessing properties. She located her briefcase then, juggling recorder and phone, taped the rest of the saved messages. It suddenly occurred to her that Michael, in his present mood, would not appreciate her borrowing his mobile, even for the original innocent purpose of phoning Margot. It suddenly seemed a very good idea to get the sophisticated little gadget back into hiding in his coat pocket. She was halfway to Michael's room when she heard his footsteps on the stairs.

"Hello, darling," she called. "I thought I heard your mobile ringing but it had stopped by the time I got to your room.

Anyway, I thought I'd bring it down to you."

Catherine held the gadget out to him. Michael eyed her thoughtfully for a moment then pressed the code for ring back. He looked at the display then slapped her one hard blow that knocked her on her back.

"Don't lie to me, *darling*." He drawled the last word making it sound like an insult. "You're really not clever enough. Now what were you really doing?" he snapped.

"I wanted to ring Margot," she whispered. "Daddy's got my phone."

Michael drew his wallet from his jacket pocket and threw some notes at her. "Buy yourself a new toy. You don't touch anything of mine unless you are told to do so. Do you understand?"

"Michael, what's going on?" she pleaded. "Why are you and Daddy so cruel? It must be something to do with Robert on Sigandros. It you would only tell me what's going on I wouldn't blunder about."

He looked at her for a moment, considering, then said lightly, "Leave it to me and your father, sweetheart, it's best that way. You be a good girl and I'll come and kiss you goodnight." Without waiting for a reply Michael turned on his heel and went back down the stairs.

Catherine went into the bathroom and bathed her stinging face with cold water. There would be a bruise there in the morning. She looked at her reflection in the glass and smiled. Maybe for what she wanted to do, it would even be of assistance.

Despite his promise or threat, Michael did not come to her room that night. Catherine had waited up till the early hours dreading seeing him again but knowing if he came she would comply with his desires. Finally she had fallen asleep only to be wakened what seemed like minutes later by the bedside alarm clock.

She secured her door with a chair then proceeded to pack a rucksack. The adventure holidays had ensured she had all the clothes and equipment she would need. In the hours before she fell asleep she had given careful thought to what she would need. Then she dressed in jeans and trainers. She did not expect to be seen, but if she were, she would claim she could not go into the office looking like an escapee from a women's refuge. She would tell anyone who asked that she was going to stay at their holiday home on Mull until she was fit to be seen. She had written a note to this effect to leave for her father.

Her father and Michael, they thought she was so frightened of them that they would not look beyond her explanation. She was not going to Mull, she was going to Sigandros. Alone if necessary but preferably with someone who knew the place and who could speak Greek. She was going to recruit Douglas Grey.

Douglas woke slowly, his first conscious thoughts being of the persistent ache in wrist and side. The mugging itself seemed a long time ago. It was almost as if it had happened to someone else. Douglas supposed that it was his mind's way of protecting itself. Even so, he felt much easier than he had the night before. Levering himself out of bed, he pottered into his kitchen to prepare tea and toast. Then he turned on his computer to check if there were any e-mail messages.

There was a moment of excitement when his system signalled 'receiving mail' but it turned out to be nothing more than a couple of circulars and a note from Professor Solomós. Suddenly his concentration was disturbed by a furious knocking on his front door. Tightening the belt on his sensible woollen robe, he moved towards the entrance to his flat and called out, "Who's there?" The events of the previous day had made him cautious.

"It's Catherine, come on, open up."

Douglas fiddled with locks and door chain. His first impression was of a far more lively and dynamic woman than the slightly bored executive he had met in the George St. office. Then he saw the bruise on her face. The purple mark on that lovely skin made him feel sick. He opened the door wide and gestured for her to enter. Then, conscious of his state of undress, he said, "I'll just get some clothes on. Wait for me in the lounge."

When he emerged ten minutes later he found Catherine reading his e-mail messages.

"Hey, what are you doing?" Douglas was really angry. He was very protective of his privacy even with his few friends. The thought of this young girl he had met only a couple of times going through his correspondence was totally unacceptable and he was going to let her know in no uncertain terms.

Catherine smiled up at him. Her face without makeup looked even more lovely and vulnerable. The bruise once more tore at his heart. "I saw the name Solomós on the screen. I thought it might have something to do with Robert. I'm sorry if I've upset you. I really am not the sort of person who reads other people's letters."

Douglas said nothing but pointedly turned off the computer. Then he turned to her and asked, "Why are you here? What has happened to you?"

"My fiancé Michael came home last night. I found out by accident that they know more about Robert on Sigandros than they are letting on. I also fear that my father will let his resentment of Robert overcome his feelings as a father. I regret he has always been a hard man."

Douglas noticed that she now spoke of her parent as 'father' rather than the childish 'daddy'. It seemed the young woman had done some rather rapid growing up.

Catherine smiled at him again. "I have come to you because I have some spoken and written Greek that I hope you'll help me translate." She dug in her bag for the note pad and Dictaphone.

Ignoring these, Douglas asked, "What are you planning to do? Are you going to go to the police?"

"I don't think the police would be very interested, do you? All I can report is an odd text message I no longer have, from a brother who's a known wanderer, on a Greek island supervised by a respectable archaeologist."

"Then what are you going to do?" Douglas persisted.

"I'm going to see for myself."

Douglas was stunned. Eventually he said, "How?"

"Money isn't a problem. I've been saving up for some time for my wedding." She touched her cheek. "I don't think that is going to happen anytime soon. Even if it were, I would still spend all my savings and more if it brought Robert home safely."

"Very commendable," muttered Douglas.

"I will get a scheduled flight to Athens then hire a yacht to take me to Sigandros. I have been sailing since I was fourteen and all my documents and certificates are up to date and valid."

"You can't go alone." Douglas was outraged.

Catherine continued to look serious but inside laughter bubbled. This was going to be easier than she had thought. "Never mind that for the moment. Will you help me with these notes?"

"Let me see," Douglas said wearily. Then remembering his abandoned breakfast he asked if she would like a cup of tea. In the end Catherine made fresh tea and toast for the pair of them whilst Douglas obviously struggled with Catherine's transcriptions. Eventually Douglas laid his pen aside and ran his fingers through his hair. "This is about as much as I an get. The text message is in very bad Greek."

"I'm sorry." Catherine was offended. She had taken great care with her copy.

"No, you misunderstand me. As far as I can tell you have made an excellent copy, it's the original that's downright atrocious. It is as if it's from someone who speaks another language and had picked up Greek as he went along rather than being formally taught."

"Okay." Catherine was pleased. "So what does it say?"

"Message understood, surplus packages will be disposed of as soon as crew have left."

"What does that mean?" Catherine was indignant.

"There is a limit even to my talents," Douglas replied straight-faced.

"Sorry," Catherine said again. "I've just got so wrapped up in this. What about the voice messages?"

Douglas paused a moment before answering. "As you know there were six voice messages, five in Greek, one in English. You did very well to record them at all." Douglas was learning tact. "But some of the words were obscured and the speaker had rather a thick accent. Here is my best reconstruction. They are in the order they were received."

Where's the stuff? It should be here by now.

Get the prof. back to the island pronto and make him sort things out.

I'll get rid of the crew, they know too much; you tidy up your end.

I don't care if it is Alistair's kid. If he's not safe, kill him.

You make one more cock-up and we've all dead men. The Shadowman does not accept excuses.

Douglas blushed. The word had not been cock-up.

"It may not be as bad as it looks," Douglas soothed, but Catherine had gone pale.

"My father's called Alistair. We have to go, now, right away. There's a plane that goes from Heathrow at two p.m. There's a connecting flight from Edinburgh. If we go now we'll catch it. Fling what you need in a bag, anything you forget we'll buy in Athens."

"Hold on a minute, young lady. I am not going anywhere with you and certainly not to Greece." Douglas was more amused than angry. "I have work, commitments and I certainly can't afford to fly off into the blue whenever I want to."

"Decide how you please, but never again call me 'young lady' in that patronising tone." Catherine was furious. "You have sick leave from your work for two weeks since that stupid accident yesterday. I organised it myself when you were discharged from hospital. According to Margot you don't go anywhere nor do you do anything except go to work so I don't know what these other commitments are.

"Finally, you don't have to afford anything, I will pay for your travel and any other expenses, fuck it all, I will pay you a thousand pounds for your time but you must come with me now. You're the only Greek speaker I know, you've been to the wretched island, you've met this mad professor and are respectable enough to be an independent witness if we need one. Sod it, you're bloody right I am too big a wimp to go alone." Catherine burst into tears.

Douglas produced a handkerchief, patted her shoulder and made vague soothing noises. The tears were real enough and Catherine eventually emerged from her cotton shield with red-rimmed eyes and a pink nose.

"I'm sorry, Douglas. That was inexcusable, but if an excuse can be made, I've had the worst couple of days in my whole life. Everyone I thought I could trust has let me down. I seem to have brought my troubles onto you, a complete stranger, and I have this overwhelming feeling that if I don't make some sort of effort to go and find my brother, today, right now, then I will never see him again."

"What do you think I can do?" The question was calm and serious. Douglas had spent the whole of his adult life helping others with their work. It was what he did, what he was. It was also true to say that the thought of an all-expenses-paid, if unscheduled, trip to the part of the world he loved the best was not all that unattractive.

Catherine made another swipe at her face then tried to marshal her arguments in a logical manner. "The first thing is the language problem. Whilst I know that many Greek people have a facility with other languages that puts the British to shame, there is no substitute for speaking to people in their own tongue. I have been thought of as an airhead all my life. Let's face it, I have acted like an airhead. If I need to convince this professor chap or if I need to go to the authorities it would do no harm at all having someone with me who could provide some gravitas. Finally, of all the people I could have met with, you know this obscure little island that no one else has even heard of."

"It's a wild impractical scheme," Douglas complained. Whilst the arguments swayed to and fro for a while longer it was at this point that both of them knew he would go.

Once the decision had been made, Douglas packed and made ready for travel in a very short space of time. A body belt with documents and a stash of Euros leftover from his last trip abroad, plus a soft hold-all held his clothing and toiletries. Finally he filled a haversack with books, papers and writing kit. Catherine, who had been admiring the economy of his preparations, exclaimed at this bulky object.

"My dear," Douglas closed his mouth sharply on the rest of the phrase, "whatever we do or do not do on this trip one thing is certain, there will be hours of waiting around doing nothing. If you don't want me to go completely mad or have for your companion a bear with a very sore head then I must have some reading matter and a little work to do."

Catherine tested the weight of the reading matter and wondered how much she was going to have to pay in excess baggage. Most people she knew contented themselves with a couple of paperbacks when they went on holiday and usually brought one of them back unread.

Catherine had left her car in the New Street car park. She walked down to get it whilst Douglas closed up his apartment. She marvelled at how easy it had been to get the scholar to do what she asked. Perhaps it was an omen that for once in her life things would work out the way she wanted them to.

At Edinburgh airport, booking a flight to Athens was no problem. Especially as she was prepared to pay for club class. Douglas removed a rather large and battered volume from his haversack for light reading on the plane. It almost seemed as if he resented being parted from his treasures as the grey-green package went bumping along the luggage bands. Catherine reminded herself that he was a seasoned traveller. It was she who was a relative novice at these things.

When they reached Heathrow, Douglas surprised her by using the time between flights to visit the duty-free shops to buy a multiple pack of high-quality cigarettes and two bottles of single malt. She had not realised he was a smoker and had not taken him for much of a drinker. He looked with amusement at her horrified face. "These are not for me," he assured her. "Sometimes a small gift can ease the way when even hard cash cannot get you what you want. The Greeks, like most of the people of continental Europe, have a passion for Scotch Whisky. Once you have been in the vicinity of a Greek cigarette then you will realise why the American brands are much appreciated."

They settled down in the bar and Douglas bought a glass of white wine for himself and a mineral water for Catherine.

"What do you have in the way of money?" he asked her

"I have about £300 in sterling and my credit cards."

"Then you need to visit the Bureau de Change in the airport and get yourself as many Euros as your credit cards will allow."

"They take plastic everywhere these days," Catherine protested.

"Even these days there is no substitute for hard currency, especially if speed and secrecy are on your agenda. What are your plans?"

"As soon as we have collected our baggage and cleared customs I want to get a taxi to take us down to Piraeus. There I want to hire a small yacht and buy the charts necessary for Sigandros and the surrounding waters." Catherine had given a lot of thought to this but Douglas shook his head.

"It's August, yachts for hire will be at a premium. I'm sure you have all the right qualification but chauvinistic Greek boat owners will be reluctant to entrust their valuable craft to a woman, especially an attractive young woman. No!" He held up his hand. "Don't bristle up at me. These are facts; you have to accept them before we can work round them. If you have hard cash, it will make things a lot easier. Similarly, as speed is of the essence, we would be better advised to use the ferries."

"You said the ferry only went to Sigandros once a week. What chance do we have of one waiting to waft us directly to the island?" Catherine protested indignantly. "Even if we do, then it might be pleasant for you to spend another week in that benighted place but it won't do for me. If we do find Robert and he is in trouble I want to get him home as quickly as I can."

"Calm down, Catherine, I didn't mean to give you the impression I wanted to take the Sigandros ferry. Let's start again and let me explain properly before you jump down my throat."

"Sorry, Douglas." Catherine realised she had been apologising quite a lot to the tall scholar. He had no obligation to help her. If she exasperated him thoroughly enough she might find herself completely on her own.

He seemed to read her thoughts. "Look, I might have been, indeed I was, reluctant to get myself involved with what still seems like a wild goose chase. However, I gave my word, I said I would go with you and use what skills I have in finding your brother and pulling whatever chestnuts he has burning out of the fire. I'm not going to go back on that, ever."

Catherine looked at him in amazement. He had certainly not said that directly to her. She suddenly realised this strange character with more than half his mind permanently back in the time of Socrates was completely honourable. He was not halfhearted nor did he deal in half promises. Getting used to him would definitely take some time.

"Let's deal with the finances then firm up on our plans. It won't be long before they start to call our flight," Douglas's voice broke into her thoughts.

The Bureau de Change was rather taken aback with Catherine's request. They were rather more used to changing £10 worth of currency than the sum Catherine mentioned. The duty staff ushered her into the manager's office and it took several telephone calls to head office and to Catherine's service provider before they would part with that volume of cash. It was only the thought of what that level of transaction would do to his dwindling monthly figures that persuaded the manager to co-operate at all.

Meanwhile, Douglas visited the gift shop and bought a body money belt, then he looked for and purchased the sort of cloth purse that fits beneath the waist band of dress or trousers and finally he chose a leather bum bag. He was waiting for Catherine as she emerged from the bureau.

"Go back in," he whispered urgently. "Ask to use their

private facilities or at least a private office. Put about 1000 Euros in the bum bag with your passport and tickets. That's to go on show. Divide the rest between the body belt and the waist belt so that no bulges show. Put no more than 100 Euros in you handbag. Quick now, they're calling our flight."

Catherine's first reaction was to ask why and protest against the uncomfortable strapping. Then she remembered that this was the one person who was helping her. She turned immediately back into the office. The staff used the airport facilities so she used the manager's office to undress. One of the female clerks helped her distribute the money and strap it on to her person whilst the manager huffed and puffed in public section.

"Your friend's no fool," the clerk commented as she helped arranged the money. "Something to show on the surface so any random mugger won't look any further and the bulk of your cash well concealed. Just remember, never try to pluck at it in public. You'll simply advertise you have hidden cash. If you need money you can usually gain some privacy by insisting you have to go to the bathroom. Even today most men are still baffled by the mysteries of women's plumbing."

Catherine and Douglas ran along the miles of airport corridor as the tannoy boomed out last calls for passengers Grey and McFarlane. The aircrew received them with frosty glares but then forgot about the two late arrivals as they busied themselves with the pre-departure checks.

There was not much chance for conversation during the safety video, take-off and the first rush of information and instruction from the crew. Eventually they were settled with more drinks, wine and Malvern water for Douglas, double Malvern water for Catherine.

"Let's go back to the conversation we were having in the airport," Catherine began. "What alternative is there to either hiring a yacht or catching the Sigandros ferry at Piraeus?"

"There are a couple of possibilities. One is to catch a ferry to one of the larger neighbouring islands, say Milos, then hire a yacht for the last jump to Sigandros. Or if we're really lucky we could get a domestic flight out of Athens for Milos. That would save us several hours but would be a lot more expensive."

Catherine thought about it for a while then attracted the attention of one of the cabin staff. Apparently a query about connecting flights to obscure Greek islands made a pleasant change from the routine requests for extra booze and mix-ups over vegetarian meals. The young woman disappeared into the flight deck and emerged sometime later with the information that there was an evening flight to Milos which was due to depart about an hour after the Athens flight landed. The timing was tight but not impossible.

Douglas extracted his large leather-bound volume from the plastic bag of duty-frees and remained incommunicado for the rest of the flight. Once Catherine glanced over to look at his page; she might have known, the text was in Greek.

Chapter Nine

Robert resealed the packages and disguised the signs of tampering as well as he could. His watch, which had survived his many adventures, showed him the time; it was nearly noon. He had a wash in the simple bathroom then made himself some coffee and raided the food stocks. By this time he was feeling quite a bit better physically even if he was still worried.

It was time to go and find Margaret. He followed the road back down the hill, keeping to the side of the track ready to head into the trees at the first sound of a vehicle.

He must have walked a couple of miles before he saw the smoke. It was just a thin trickle of blue haze against the cloudless sky. Proceeding cautiously to the next bend in the road, he saw a ramshackle stone structure with a rusty tin roof. The door was open and a fine cockerel emerged, placing its feet with delicate precision. Somewhere ahead he heard a dog barking. This must be the village in the hills, Chora or Hora, well, something like that. Phillip might not have put out a general alert to the islanders but it was not worth taking the risk of walking right through the centre of the place. The hill on the right side of the road rose steeply so he made his way behind the hen house, continuing more or less in the direction he had been going.

The ground was rocky and the ancient gnarled olive trees widely spaced, not a lot of cover but easy walking. Robert hoped that the villagers would all be sleeping off their lunch. Suddenly he saw another clear path through the trees, crossing at right angles to the way he was walking. It was stony and very steep. To the right it clearly headed to the road he had abandoned but where did it come from? On a whim he decided to follow it.

It curved down the hillside, twisting and turning. In some places he slipped and slid down the scree. Soon he began to catch glimpses of blue-green sea between the trees. Eventually he emerged at the head of a tiny cove. The rocks rose steeply on either side. There was no beach but a set of worn marble steps led down the last section of sheer cliff to the clear water. They reminded Robert of the steps that had saved his life outside the temple of Poseidon. Was this another legacy from ancient times?

Out to sea and half hidden by heat haze was another island. He squinted against the glare. It looked bare and desolate. Perhaps it had been more inviting when Pericles had been a boy. Slowly Robert turned and made his way back up the roadway. It seemed a lot farther going up. Plodding mechanically he was at the village road before he realised he should have turned again into the trees. There was no one about, he decided to risk the road. He was starting to get thirsty again and wanted to get to the students' camp as soon as possible.

At the villa, Rena was bored. She had never been much of a drinker. A glass of wine with a meal was very pleasant; guzzling it just to get drunk was disgusting. She did not like Philip; the few times he had spoken to her in the past he had been rude and arrogant. She mistrusted his recent attempts to be friendly. She had avoided him as much as possible after translating the speeches for the fishermen and the mayor. The island was not lucky for her and she longed for Friday to arrive and the ferry that would take her away from this place for good.

She had liked Robert, she remembered with pleasure the lunch they had had together in the taverna by the harbour. She could not believe that he had been so wicked.

On the terrace Ékaterina was now trying to teach some of the students a folk song. It was about an old woman who had lost her pig. Rena remembered her grandmother singing it to her when she was a little girl. Filled with homesickness, Rena wandered into the kitchen. One of Ékaterina's nieces, Anna, was trying to wash dishes whilst watching the pots bubbling on the stove.

"Can I help?" Rena asked, quickly turning the flame down on a pot of pasta sauce that was about to boil over.

"Our lady, bless you," was the reply. "Thia Ékaterina asked me to help with the clearing up. Now she is trying to understudy Nana Moskouri and I'm left to do everything."

They worked together in companionable silence for a few minutes. Then the girl said, "Did you know that dreadful Robert character?"

"I only met him the once, he didn't seem all that bad to me. Still, you can never tell with men," Rena replied carefully. "Where did Philip put him? I've not seen him since Phillip and the men took him away from the student camp."

"Didn't you hear? It was dreadful." Anna was delighted to gossip. "They locked him in one of the storage rooms in the cellar. Then late last night Phillip went down to see if he was all right and the devil burst through the door, knocked Phillip flat and escaped."

"Where is he now?" Rena asked, concerned. This island was not friendly to someone without water or shelter.

"Nobody knows. He just ran off into the night and no one has seen him since. I'll be sure to keep my door locked tonight. Who knows what a villain like that might get up to."

In truth, Anna seemed more excited than scared at the thought of a dangerous criminal on the loose. She had probably watched too many reruns of *The Fugitive*. Then Ékaterina started shouting for some service and they were too busy ladling pasta and sauce into huge bowls, chopping salad and cutting bread for much more conversation. Eventually

Ékaterina came back into the kitchen to supervise and Rena made her escape. In the garden she looked over to the dark green forest and wondered about the young Brit. Her feelings were still mixed, yet running away like that must surely prove a guilty conscience. On the other hand, what would she herself do if she was falsely accused and locked up in a cellar?

"What's the matter, Rena?" It was Margaret. "I've been looking for you everywhere. I began to wonder if Phillip had finally had his wicked way with you."

"That would be a fate worse than death indeed." Rena smiled, then serious again, "Have you heard about Robert?" Quickly she repeated the story of the escape.

Margaret looked concerned. "He could be in real trouble out there. I don't trust Phillip or Costas, come to that, farther than I could throw them. Let's leave this lot to their bacchanalia and see if we can find where he's gone." Rena nodded her agreement. "We can't go like this," she indicated her dress and sandals. "Let's go back to the camp and pick up our boots and a daysack."

"We could do with a few provisions, too. He's likely to be dehydrated and starving." Rena slipped back into the kitchen. She returned a few minutes later with a bulging plastic grocery bag. "The professor caused all this trouble in the first place, he can help put it right." Giggling, they scampered down the path to their tents. It did not take very long to change.

"I need to pee," commented Margaret. "Pity I didn't think of it at the villa, the prof.'s facilities are a great deal better than our smelly latrine." She walked over to the bog tents that were discretely situated behind some thick bushes and nearly lost control of her bladder as Robert suddenly appeared in front of her.

Some things are more important than others. Mumbling, "Got to go, Rena's back there," Margaret disappeared into a cubical.

Robert walked in the indicated direction. He was concerned to see the scared look on Rena's face and the way she stepped back from him. Clearly something had occurred during his capture and escape. He sat on one of the campstools and tried to look as unthreatening as possible.

"Where is everyone?" Robert asked.

"Not far away," was the nervous reply. There was some more silence and Rena continued to stare at him, her enormous dark eyes still wide with surprise. Robert was glad when Margaret returned looking more embarrassed than frightened.

"The rest of the students are up at the villa having a party organised by a suddenly affable Phillip," Margaret stated. "We have heard another version of your escapade on the *Herakles*. According to Costas it's you who's into drugs up to your neck and the tale about the artefacts was just made up to get back at the crew when they would not fall in with your plans. What do you have to say about that?"

"Only one thing," said Robert calmly. "Why didn't Phillip and company call the police?"

"There are no police on this island, you know that," Margaret replied.

"Think, woman," he said impatiently. "The shower at the villa have e-mail and telephones. The nearest island with a cop shop is less than an hour away by fast launch. If all these characters are so innocent, how come there aren't officers of the law doing their duty all over the place?"

The two women were silent.

"Why are you here," Robert continued, "and not at the knees up at the villa?"

There was some more silence. Then Margaret asked, "Where have you been?"

Robert told of his night's adventures, leaving out the drugs and the visit to the tiny harbour. As he told the tale he realised that the two women had not been convinced of his guilt and had probably decided to come and look for him. The abandoned supermarket bag spilling its contents into the dust confirmed his theory. These were nice women and he felt a momentary pang at involving them in his troubles. It was, however, only for a moment because he needed their help. Fortunately, Margaret asked the right question. "What are you going to do?"

"My sister is coming. I know that as sure as I know the sun will rise tomorrow," Robert told them eagerly. "I'll continue to hide out up at the army huts. Please, will you look out for her? When she arrives, try to get her on her own and tell her where I am."

"We can do that till Friday, but we are leaving for Athens on the next ferry. I, for one, don't want to spend another week on this island." Rena was adamant.

"That should be long enough." Robert sounded perfectly confident.

"There's another problem," Margaret continued. "Professor McKenzie is due to arrive this evening. Whether he is or is not a criminal mastermind is immaterial for the moment, what he certainly is, is clever. If he knows about the army huts he'll guess that's where you are and he'll come for you with reinforcements."

Robert acknowledged the truth of her words. He had been congratulating himself that two or three nights in the hut would be no problem. Now he would have to find a far less comfortable alternative. "Any suggestions?" he asked tentatively.

"How much mess have you made at the huts?" Rena asked sharply. "Will they know you have been there?"

"I haven't made any mess," Robert responded indignantly. Then he thought about the broken lock, the food and water he had taken. It would be obvious to anyone familiar with the place that there had been a visitor. "But yes, I reckon they would know I had been there," he admitted.

"What about the old Venetian fort?" Rena asked.

"What fort?" Margaret asked.

"There are remains of an old fortress on the west side of the island. It's not easy to get to and it's just a ruin. I read about it before I came and have been to visit it on a couple of Sundays when there was nothing doing at the dig. The villagers don't go there because there's a legend that it's haunted."

"It sounds delightful," Robert commented sarcastically.

"You could go back to enjoying Phillip's hospitality. I'm sure I don't care either way." Rena was angry.

"Don't be a prick, Robert." Margaret was on Rena's side. "You can hardly book into the Sigandros Hilton. There are snakes on the island so camping out in the open isn't a good idea. Most of the students have been convinced by Costas's little performance so you can't hide here in the camp. What do you propose?"

"Sorry, Rena, I guess I left my brains in my other suit." He had not realised about the snakes; the thought of his hours under the olive tree made him shiver. "Tell me more about this fort."

Rena was quiet for a moment, then said, "As I was saying, most of the place is a ruin but there are a couple of rooms in the tower that are still intact. We have some food here for you and you could borrow some more from the huts if they will know you have been there anyway. The haunting legend can work to your advantage. The villagers aren't going to go running to the prof. if they happen to see a light or some movement in the old tower. Apparently pirates occupied the tower for a while back in the eighteenth century. They tortured to death some of the islanders and then buried their bodies in unconsecrated ground. The ghosts are supposed to be the spirits of the victims looking for Christian burial."

"So what do I do if a skeleton clanks at me in the middle of the night?"

"Point the way to the cemetery I suppose." Rena smiled at him.

They decided that going through Hora twice in one day was not a good idea so going back to the huts straight away was not an option. From the students' camp they took some bedding, the food they had brought from the villa and some more bottles of water. Then Rena led them along the goat track that led to the old fort. Robert did not think he would have been able to find the place if he had not had a guide. The brush was so thick and the path so stony that no one would be able to sneak up on him without making enough noise to wake the dead. Cancel that thought, it was not something to dwell on.

The girls did not linger after they had dumped the supplies they were carrying. They stated their intention of going back to the party and being conspicuous when the professor docked. The tower was made of massive grey stones now thoroughly twisted with vines and creepers. The floors in the surviving rooms were dusty but not too rough. Robert thought longingly for a moment of the army huts on the hill, especially the crude shower and toilet. Still, Margaret was probably right, once the prof. was home it would be one of the first places he would set the villagers to look.

Breaking out a bottle of the island's dry white wine, he went to sit on the remains of the old rampart with a book the girls had loaned him—a murder mystery set in ancient Greece where the detective was helped by the philosopher Aristotle; he might have guessed.

Professor McKenzie could not settle to anything. Half a dozen times he had opened a book, stared sightlessly at a page for a few moments then put it away again. He had tried to telephone the villa a dozen times but the line rang out without anyone answering. What could have happened? Even if that Robert character had turned nasty, there were more than enough people to cope. McKenzie thought briefly about contacting Michael, then discarded the idea. If there were some simple explanation, if all was well, he did not want to draw any more attention to his problems than he had already.

In a flood of self-pity he wished he had never got involved with the Shadowman. In his imagination he saw himself once more with a chair at a prestigious university, a string of best-selling publications bearing his name, a greenfield site to excavate, an untarnished reputation.

At the last thought he gave a twisted smile. He had burned his boats. The dream could never have been a possibility even before he came to Sigandros. There were, of course, compensations. This small difficulty would be straightened out and forgotten. It was hardly his fault after all. He would show that he had acted promptly and efficiently. The Shadowman might even change his mind about the Athena site.

The daydreams burst as the yacht entered the closed

harbour. He could hear the sounds of music drifting over the still water. The garden of his lovely villa seemed black with people and there was faint blue smoke rising that indicated a barbecue in progress. Had Phillip taken leave of his senses? As the elegant craft slid into a mooring, the professor instructed the crew to wait until he found out what was happening at the villa. The three seamen grumbled and swore it would spoil their schedule even though they had no intention of sailing any farther that night. As they hoped, the old fool promised them a bonus if they would stay.

McKenzie almost ran up the hill; fortunately for his labouring lungs the yacht had been spotted and a reception committee was on its way down the hill to greet him. The garbled explanations, however, left him more confused than ever. Forcing himself to smile and play the affable academic, he finally managed to reach his study and shoo out all the students except his nephew. McKenzie saw with concern that the lad looked glassy-eyed. It was not yet five in the afternoon. Calling on all his remaining patience, the professor sat Phillip in one of the leather armchairs and poured the young man a large glass of mineral water and himself a small brandy.

"What has been going on, Phillip? Explain yourself."

Even through the wine fumes, Phillip knew it was not the time to mess his uncle about. Phillip caressed his thumb to show that this was the first point. "Yánnis and Costas went off in the *Herakles* this morning with a couple of the local fishermen. The islanders have strict instructions to return straight away, just as you said. I got the student Rena to translate so I know they understand what they have to do. Costas is okay, of course, but Yánnis looked to be in a very bad way."

"Why are all the students having a party here in the villa?" The professor's voice was still level but he was beginning to sound dangerous.

"Robert escaped. This is damage limitation to get the kids on our side and discredit Robert's stories. Let me tell you everything that has happened."

"Very well explain and your story had better be a good one or

I swear I'll wash my hands of you, and my sister can cope with you by herself."

This was the hard part. Phillip had rehearsed half a dozen stories but none of them made him sound anything but a prat. He could, however, try to put the blame on the absent Costas. The odds were that his uncle would not check up on this story with the rest of the staff.

"After I had locked Robert in the store room, apparently Costas went down to the cellar to taunt the guy and threaten what he was going to do to him. Robert, having more than two brains to rub together, challenged the mate mano á mano. Costas opened the door and Robert came out fighting. He got in a couple of fast low blows and scarpered up the stairs before Costas could get his breath back. There was nothing we could do at that time and in the dark."

"So why the party?" McKenzie was almost screaming.

"Robert had been telling all sorts of tales to the students. They believed him. They were getting really stroppy. I had to put in some damage limitation." Phillip realised he was starting to sound panicky and tried to slow down. "I got Costas to confess to cigarette smuggling, which they all knew about anyway. He then told the kids that it was Robert who was into drugs and he who made up the false stories about the temple of Athena when they wouldn't play ball.

"Yánnis was there, looking as if he were at death's door, nodding in the right places and going for the sympathy vote. Then the mayor swore there was no temple on the island. Rena did the translation again, so they thought they were getting a straight story. Fortunately, none of the foreigners knows what a corkscrew the man really is.

"I've filled the mob with food and wine to take their tiny minds off escaping muggers. I'm afraid it has got rather out of hand, the Greeks love a party too. Once they started the bazouki music and everyone got to singing and dancing it was a bit hard to stop."

The professor looked grave but at least he seemed to have calmed down a bit. "Where is Robert now?" he asked at length.

"I don't know. The natives have been looking out for him, but apart from one old granny up in Hora who regularly sees Turks under her bed anyway, there has been no sign of him."

"What about Robert's friend amongst the students, the girl from Scotland." The professor was considering possibilities.

"She's been here all day. You can see her down on the terrace trying to do Zorba's dance with Ékaterina's nephew and a few of the others."

Sure enough, Margaret's distinctive copper top was bobbing about with a dozen others.

"This is a dry island. Unless he has got help from somewhere, thirst would have driven him into the open before now." McKenzie finished his brandy and poured himself another. He thought hard for a moment then said, "Have you sent anyone up to the old German prisoner of war camp?"

"No, it's all locked up. Even if by some unlucky chance he found it, he would not be able to get in." Phillip had completely forgotten about the old army huts. He could have kicked himself but he was not going confess this to his uncle.

"I'll take the van and look for any signs of a forced entrance. That old woman in Hora might not be as crazy as everyone thinks." McKenzie looked at his nephew. "You most certainly can't drive. In your present state you would crash straight into the nearest olive tree."

"Look, Uncle, I had to play the genial host." Phillip stopped; he realised how pathetic that sounded. "What shall I say if someone wants to know where you are?"

"Phillip, I used to think you were very bright, I'm beginning to change my mind. Please go down to the harbour, tell the crew of the yacht that they can go whenever they wish." The professor walked out of the room, leaving his nephew to curse himself, his uncle, but most of all that damned interfering Robert.

On the drive up to the army camp, McKenzie was not worrying about his nephew, he was wondering how he was going to explain these latest developments to the supercilious Michael. Unwelcome as the thought was, it would have to be done. The village looked deserted, it always did, but that did not mean that no one was watching. As the road rose to the top of the hill, the professor changed down a gear and drove even more carefully. He knew from experience the track could be treacherous. The villagers were paid well to keep it in good order but a sudden storm or one of the drivers showing off could ruin the surface overnight.

The huts had been a legacy from the Second World War when the Germans had used the island as a prisoner of war camp. Built with typical Aryan efficiency, the buildings had still been in reasonable condition when he had first come to live on the island. They had been a godsend for putting up visitors who were not wise to advertise to all and sundry. There had been some local opposition to restoring the relics; the islanders had not had a good war. Money, however, salves a lot of consciences and he had gained goodwill by restoring the village church at the same time.

By the time he pulled up in front of the huts, McKenzie had still not decided what he would tell Michael. A brief examination, however, told him Robert had visited the old camp but was there no longer. So where was the bastard?

McKenzie lit a cigar and walked to the cliff edge. It was nearly sunset and the sea looked like molten gold. The ground dropped gently away at first then there was a sheer drop into deep water. The islanders said that the bones of many of the prisoners of war lay at the foot of the cliff. Those men and women the soldiers had disposed of and those for whom death had become a welcome alternative. The old folk swore that the cries of the doomed souls could still be heard on moonless nights. Still, what could you expect from a bunch of ignorant peasants?

Where was Robert? How many places were there to hide on this island? Then it came to him, the old fort. The crafty blighter must have realised that sooner or later someone would come and search the huts. He was probably trying to camp out in the old citadel. Well, let him try a night or two in there. He might be a bit less cocky when they did come for him. The professor threw the remains of his cigar away, being sure that it was completely extinguished. He did not want a forest fire to complicate his life any more than it already was.

He drove at reckless speed back down to the villa, composing his message to Michael in his head. The first thing he did on his return was to indicate to Ékaterina that the party was over and he would appreciate the students leaving as soon as possible. The housekeeper would do this with greater ease and certainly with more tact than Phillip would. Even as he walked into the villa he could see her dousing the barbecue and calling to her relatives to start clearing up.

Locking the study door, he dialled Michael's number. Michael answered as usual with the one word "Yes."

"The packages have been dispatched with instructions for onward delivery." McKenzie thought this was rather good. There was, however, no response. He continued, "The visitor has declined our hospitality but is in a secure location." This was a bit obscure but he hoped Michael would not ask for clarification on an open line.

"Can you maintain the situation there without prejudice?"

"Yes." The professor was not at all sure he could, but now was not the time to show weakness.

"I have returned to Scotland. I need to consult. If there are any further developments let me know immediately."

"Certainly," the professor started to reply but realised he was speaking to the dialling tone. There was nothing more he could do tonight. He was weary and suddenly quite hungry, he wondered if those gannet students had left anything worth eating. A tentative knock sounded on the study door. He got up and opened it. Ékaterina was standing in the corridor balancing an enormous tray. Opening the door wide, he helped her place it on the desk.

"It will take some time to get everything straight again. I have to say, though, it was a very good party. I thought you might like something to eat here in your study."

There was bread, a Greek salad, grilled fish and a plate of golden chips. Condensation was running from a dark green bottle of chilled white wine. It looked marvellous. There was even a slice of baklava running with honey, a sweet to which he had always been very partial.

"*Efharisto para poli*," he said with enthusiasm.

Ékaterina blushed with pleasure at his thanks. "When will the students be leaving?" she asked. McKenzie was stunned for the moment. Then he realised, in previous years, he had always had a party to mark the end of the year's excavation, although perhaps not as generous as this one had been. Ékaterina was obviously assuming that this had been it.

The housekeeper needed to know just when they would be leaving so she could manage her kitchen stocks. The logical departure date would indeed be Friday's ferry, three days hence. Tidying up the site and preparing to leave would give the blighters something other to think about than disappearing Robert, and if anyone complained about the early finish he could pass them onto another dig.

"I'm going to try to get them on Friday's ferry. I'll confirm with you in the morning."

Ékaterina inclined her head and left him to his supper. When the food was finished, he returned to the telephone. This time he called Professor Solomós in Athens.

After a few polite enquiries McKenzie mentioned his problem.

"The dig's not going well this year. We're not getting anywhere and there has been a bit of trouble. I'm going to close early."

Solomós quiet, educated voice indicated sympathy.

"The trouble is that some of the students have fixed flight tickets. Can you find them something to do for the next month or so?"

"My dear man, we can always find work for warm bodies to do, especially if they are not a burden on our budget."

The crafty old sod. Still, he had expected nothing less. "Of course, I'll cover their transfer and the pocket money for the rest of the season."

"How many will there be?"

"Not more than twenty. I can give you exact numbers tomorrow."

"Shall we say fifty Euros a day per student to cover food and accommodation?"

McKenzie had not expected that. "Where are you planning to lodge them, the Ritz?"

"It's the middle of the tourist season, everything is more expensive at this time of year."

McKenzie suspected he was paying for Solomós winter holiday but finally agreed to forty Euros.

"I'll have one of my staff meet your people at Piraeus. Depending on numbers I'll have either one or two mini buses to take them up to the excavations at Delphi. They should find that interesting."

There was another round of courtesies and they said goodbye. It was full dark now and the professor walked onto the terrace. It was still warm, that fool Robert might have an uncomfortable night but he would not come to any harm. Still, tomorrow he would have to go up to the fort and try to explain that if he was the son of Alistair McFarlane of Edinburgh they did not want to kill him but bring him into the family business.

Chapter Ten

The *Herakles* bucked in heavy seas. Costas made his way to the wheelhouse, thinking that the islanders had a heavy hand with a tiller. The boat might be old but she could move a great deal more sweetly than this if handled correctly. The sun had already disappeared behind clouds; soon it would be dark. If they were going to do it, then it must be in the next hour or so.

"Where are we now?" he asked casually.

The two islanders looked at each other. Was this Costas asking for a location? This was the man who claimed to have knowledge of every rock in the Cyclades.

"We have just left Astipalea behind on our port bow," came the equitable reply.

"If you steer south and west there's a fast current that takes you between Tilos and Chalki."

This was the first they had heard of it, but said simply, "South and west it is."

Costas stood at the back of the wheelhouse smoking cigarette after cigarette, his hard eyes scouring the horizon. From time to time he went down to the cabin to check on Yánnis. Eventually he brought the captain up the companionway and they both stood on the deck leaning against the rail.

"You're steering too far south," Costas called up. "You need to be much closer to Agía Triáda."

What was the fool up to? It was not safe to get too close to the barren rock named after the Holy Trinity.

"Starboard! Starboard! Now!" screamed Costas. "There's the Dragon's Teeth port and for'ard." The wheel spun just in time and an ominous grating against the hull spoke of a near miss. The almost completely submerged fang-shaped rocks hissed by. They were within a couple of cable lengths of the island.

"Follow the dark water and you'll be safe enough," Costas called.

Then suddenly the two men were over the side and swimming for the island. They could see that Costas had a length of line attached to the blind man's belt to keep him swimming in the right direction.

"What in the name of the Panagia are the two of them playing at?" the younger fisherman wondered.

"Watch your steering," his cousin said sharply. Until they were clear of these rocks it was not the time for idle speculation. Then he relented. "They knew or thought they knew something unpleasant was waiting for them in Marmaris. Costas was jumpy from the moment I told him we had strict orders to leave immediately. Play with the devil, you sometimes get burned. Between the devil and the deep blue sea they opted for the sea." The fisherman laughed at his own wit.

"What will they do now?"

"Drown"

"Alexis no, they were swimming well and heading towards the land when we last saw them."

"They drowned," said the older man again, and he casually threw a life belt into the sea. "We did what we could but we were almost on the rocks ourselves. We even have a fresh scratch on the keel to prove it."

"So what are we going to do?"

"We won't go to bloody Marmaris that's for certain sure. We'll go to Rhodes, that's the nearest island with proper facilities. The time it takes us to get there will allow Costas and Yánnis time to sort themselves out." The fisherman kicked the radio with his heavy boot. "Pity the radio isn't working, must have got damaged when that bastard Robert attacked the captain. We could have called the coast guard straight away."

"How can they sort themselves out? Agía Triáda is nothing but a barren rock."

"I'm sure Costas has thought of something. Anyway, remember, they drowned. We saw poor Yánnis clutch at Costas in panic and they both disappeared under the waves." The fisherman gave a sentimental sigh and crossed himself.

The younger man shrugged. If that's how his cousin wanted to play it, he'd go along.

Costas and Yánnis had both earned a living swimming for crabs and mussels as boys. They might have grown bellies since those days, and thank God for it, but they still had the shoulders and the skills. Yánnis responded to the gentle tugging of the line at his waist. The seawater soaked the bandages round his eyes and they began to chafe his skin. On the crest of an uprolling wave he tore the wretched thing off. Seawater stung his face and seeped under his burned lids, filling his face with fire. He had known worse pain. He struck out doggedly after Costas, thinking of nothing but the next stroke and the one after that.

Just as there seemed to be nothing in the world but the battering of the sea and the endless tugging of the cord, his feet touched bottom. Costas pulled Yánnis's arm over his shoulder and then they were staggering together out of the surf. Finally they stumbled towards a flattish rock and sat down. Yánnis wiped the water from his face with his hands and stared at Costas through a pair of bloodshot but bright brown eyes.

They yelped and whooped like madmen. "It was Ékaterini's foul gunk that blinded me. The sea washed it away." Yánnis was nearly in tears. Privately he promised a medallion to St. Raphael, patron of the blind, for saving him from a worthless and horrible life.

All too soon their elation wore off. "Well, we're off the boat what do we do now?" Yánnis asked. "Where are we? Does anyone live on this rock?"

"We're on Agía Triáda," Costas replied.

"The place where that mad old monk used to live?"

"Still does as far as I know, let's find out."

They trudged up the tiny beach. It was full dark now and they could hardly see where they were going. More than once they dashed their bare feet against stones or slipped on weed-covered rocks. After about ten minutes of struggling, they saw a yellow light flickering up ahead of them.

"It looks like the holy father is in," said Costas with a touch of relief in his voice.

As they approached the light they could see a tiny whitewashed chapel with a small stone house next to it. The light was coming from the chapel. They slipped through the open door and sat down on the single wooden bench at the back.

The priest with a pristine white gown over rather salt-stained black robes was chanting with hands raised in front of the sanctuary. Costas thought this quite remarkable. If he had been isolated on a barren island he was not sure he would have bothered to keep up with the services; after all, who was to know? The rather uncomfortable thought came back, God would.

The tiny chapel was lit by a couple of oil lamps. In a sand tray half a dozen beeswax candles were burning. They gave out a distinctive perfume which mixed with the smell of incense from the silver censer by the side of the altar. The walls of the chapel were covered with murals.

The priest must have heard them come in but he continued with his prayers. As Costas stared around, waiting for the old man to finish, he began to pick out the things he knew from the mass of painted figures. There were scenes from the life of Christ, the life of the virgin, images of dozens of saints, only a few of whom he could name with any degree of confidence.

In the scented gloom the low musical voice of the priest lulled his senses. He was halfway to being asleep when he became aware of black figure standing over him. The white robe must have been removed as he dozed.

"It is rare I have a congregation for the evening prayers," the old man said mildly, "but I think you should get out of those wet clothes and then you can tell me how I can help you over supper."

The priest extinguished the crystal oil lamps and led the way out of the church and into his house. He fumbled with matches for a moment and then a far more workaday lamp illuminated the interior of the cottage. A huge black kettle of hot water stood on the crude kitchen range. The priest poured a generous amount into the kitchen sink.

"There is cold water in the jug and here are soap and towels. Wash all over or you will chafe. Don't be shy, I have seen naked men before."

"Father!" Costas began.

"No, tell me nothing now, especially do not tell me anything that in the future you might wish I didn't know. I am Father Athanasius, you are Matthew and Mark, let that do for the time being."

Lulled into acquiescence by the almost fantastical world they seemed to have entered, they did as they were bidden. They took off their wet and sandy clothes, washed with the course household soap and put on clean but crumpled shirts and trousers that the priest took from a large cardboard box of similar clothing.

By the time they were dressed, the wooden table had been laid for supper. There was bread, butter, cheese, steaming bowls of vegetable soup and a jug of red wine that Father Athanasius poured into thick green glasses. The priest insisted on a long grace before they could touch the food. What else could you expect in a priest's house?

"Eat slowly," the old man warned, "or your stomachs will rebel."

They ate in silence for a while then the priest said quite calmly, "You are dead men."

The newly christened Matthew and Mark choked on their bread.

"The bodies of the men you were have been carried away on the current, they may never be seen again. Dead men can't be prosecuted by the police, neither do their enemies seek them anymore."

Costas realised his mouth was hanging open and shut it with a snap. "My wife, my children!" he exclaimed.

"It is not unknown for widows to remarry or for distant relatives to help raise the children of someone who has perished. These things can always be arranged."

"What other little arrangements do you have. How much will this cost us?" Yánnis was always suspicious.

"There is no charge," Father Athanasius said equitably. "If you are successful in your new life then you might feel you wish to make a donation to the church. Even if I have been taken into Abraham's bosom there will always be someone on this island. Most people find that they do want to make a contribution," he paused, "eventually. Sleep now, then in the morning go for a walk together, discuss your future then let me know what you want to do."

The priest busied himself washing the supper things, then produced a couple of folding camp beds and covered them with grey army blankets.

"Make yourselves as comfortable as you can, I have to go and say the night office. I will speak to you both in the morning."

Overcome with weariness and shock, they lay down. It was, however, some time before sleep came. The next morning they found fresh goat's milk, cheese and bread on the table. The two men ate in silence then walked out onto the headland. The tiny island could not have been more than a mile in length. Sagebrush and oregano barely covered the rocky landscape. There was a flock of thin-looking goats and some violently coloured blue beehives. So the good father did not spend all his time praying. In the small natural harbour a substantial-looking motor boat was tied up.

"We could steal the boat and get away from this dreadful place," Yánnis suggested.

"We could, but then what?"

"I'm not frightened of that poncy professor or his stupid nephew." Yánnis was belligerent.

"What about the professor's partners? They're pretty scary. If we suddenly pop up again we could be dead men in reality."

"Do you trust this priest?" Yánnis was scornful.

"No, but that's no reason for not accepting his help."

"If we do turn into Matthew and Mark, how do we get started

in our new life? The sea is all we know. Do you want to become a waiter or a taxi driver?"

"That's where we have a little advantage our holy friend doesn't know about."

"If you mean your money belt, he spotted that straight away."

"No, when we went over the side I had a little string bag attached to my belt. In it I put the best of those little toys the professor was shipping back to Turkey. In the right hands they should bring enough to start us up in business again."

"Who do you know who won't rob us blind? Have you any idea what those things are really worth? I know I don't. We can't sell them on the open market, and any crook is going to want his cut. Where did you hide them by the way?"

"Amongst the rocks where we came ashore."

They turned back towards the cove. Approaching then was the priest. Swinging from his hand was a string bag filled with large parcels covered in bubble wrap.

"These are yours I believe," Father Athanasius said pleasantly. "It's time for our little talk. Have you decided what you want to do?"

The two fishermen followed the priest back down to his house. They sat round the table and the priest poured coffee, which they drank, black and unsweetened.

"We would be very grateful for your help, Father Athanasius," Costas mumbled.

"Then it would be as well if you disappeared for a while," the priest said.

"What do you mean by that?" Costas started to worry that their disappearance might be permanent now the priest had found their cache.

The old man looked at him sadly. "When will you learn to trust me? If I wanted you dead I have had more than enough opportunities to kill you. You obviously need help and I am happy to give it, free and without obligation."

Neither of the fishermen believed this for a moment, but decided to play along. It wasn't as if they had many options.

"You cannot vanish in the islands, too many people know

you. It would be better if you went to Athens at least for a while."

"I hate Athens," protested Yánnis "I can't breathe the foul air and the dirt makes my skin crawl." Costas nodded, he felt exactly the same.

"It would only be for a few weeks. My brothers in God would be able to realise the best price on these little souvenirs." The old man indicated the string bag. "Then perhaps a boat, something a bit more upmarket than the old *Herakles*."

How did this hermit know the name of their boat? This old guy was spooky.

"There is a growing market for holiday cruises amongst the islands. It might make a better living for you than whatever caused you to end up on Agía Triáda."

Yánnis preened his moustache. He had seen those cruise captains sailing by in their white uniforms, a pretty girl on each arm. It might not be a bad life. Costas still had reservations. Somewhere along the line all this Christian help was going to have to be paid for. He could see it being very expensive indeed, but what could they do?

Father Athanasius pulled a very modern-looking mobile phone from the pocket of his robe. The push of a button dialled a stored number. He spoke rapidly in a language neither Yánnis nor Costas could understand.

"I shall take you in the motor boat to my mother house. They will find you a suitable disguise and transfer you to a monastery outside Athens. The abbot there, Father Ilías, will help you through the various business transactions. Now perhaps a short prayer to help you on your journey." The old man led the way back to the church then stood pointedly by the offertory box until Costas parted with most of the contents of his money belt. It's started, he thought.

Michael walked up and down the well-appointed study. Alistair McFarlane had never before seen this usually calm young man so agitated.

"McKenzie's a slippery bastard and I don't trust him." He paced a bit more. "He let what should be a little local difficulty blow up out of all proportion. The people with whom we are working are not a bunch of airy-fairy academics, they don't forgive mistakes easily."

"It's hardly his fault, he wasn't even on Sigandros at the time." Catherine's father nursed a small whisky and water. He, too, was worried but he doubted it was for the same reason.

"No, it was that bloody nephew. You've never met him, have you?"

"No, never had the pleasure."

"He's no pleasure I assure you. He's an arrogant know-it-all without a scrap of common sense."

"Will McKenzie be able to sort things out? He's back on the island now, isn't he?"

"He's taken care of the fishermen. I'm expecting confirmation from Marmais any time now to say that they're no longer a problem. The last message I got from the prof. indicated that something else has gone wrong. It wasn't wise to go into details over an open line."

"Is this Robert character my son or not?" Alistair finally put his concerns into words.

"Given the call to Catherine and the name he's using I'd say he is." Michael did not add the fiery temper, a tendency to violence and a large degree of resourcefulness also made it likely this was a chip off the old block. "But I thought you hated him?"

"No, I don't hate him. I was bloody annoyed because he would not do what I wanted and turned himself into a useless drifter. He's grown up a bit now, got himself some useful skills. I certainly don't want my son killed on the whim of a greasy wop like the Shadowman."

"Don't underestimate the Shadowman, he's not a man to cross," Michael warned

"What are we going to do?"

"There's only one thing to do. We'll have to go to Sigandros ourselves and make sure things are sorted out properly."

"How will we get there? I thought the island was at the back of beyond."

"We can fly to the neighbouring island of Milos. Luck is with us for once, there's a weekly flight out of Glasgow and that's tomorrow, Thursday. In Milos we can hire a boat to take us to Sigandros; it will be expensive but not difficult. We certainly don't want to be waiting around for ferries."

"Then let's do it. Anything is better than hanging about here waiting for news."

Michael put a call through to the travel service used by his office. It had twenty-four-hour staffing for the use of executives who regularly wanted to make last minute and complicated changes to their travel plans. He explained his needs to the operator. She promised to ring him back with reservation numbers within the hour. One reason for the agency's very high fees was that they boasted they could always get seats, even on fully booked flights.

"What shall we tell Catherine?"

"Don't tell her anything. She and I had a bit of a falling out," Michael drawled carefully. It might not have been wise to hit her in her father's house, especially if the old man was getting all paternal. "She'll probably go away and sulk for a bit."

Uninterested, Alistair let it go. He'd seen to that overeducated librarian. Catherine would probably cry a bit, then go shopping. It would be good to have Robert home.

"Don't pack more than a tote bag," Michael warned.

"Save your bullying for Catherine," Alistair remarked shortly. "I travel just as much as you do."

Temper, temper, thought Michael but this time he wisely said nothing.

Next morning Alistair found the note from Catherine. He puzzled a bit over the phrase 'fit to be seen' then dismissed it from his mind. Catherine was getting to be more like her mother every day.

Waiting at the airport was no pain as they had use of the executive lounge. Both men had work to do. It was not easy for men as involved in business as they were to drop everything at a moment's notice. There were meetings to cancel and deputies to be instructed.

It was not until they had to board the Milos flight that the real pains of travelling tourist class became apparent. Screaming babies and restless children were the least of the problems. The adults were even louder and more fidgety than their brats. Alistair thought that if the stewardess banged into him with the drink's trolley just one more time he would thrust both it and her out of one of the emergency exits.

Michael was also in a foul mood. He had had a text message before departure from his contact in Marmaris to say the *Herakles* had not arrived. The hours passed eventually and the plane made a bumpy landing at the tiny airport. Alistair found it remarkable how all Greek airports managed to look exactly alike. Hot, dusty concrete boxes built on the edge of a dozen scrap yards. There was the usual interminable wait for luggage. The officious bastards at Glasgow had not let him take his overnighter on the plane as cabin baggage even though it was well within the regulation size. No amount of shouting had been able to shift them.

He glanced over to the carousel carrying the detritus from the internal flight from Athens. Great lumpy brown paper parcels, cardboard boxes with more tape than cardboard and battered suitcases secured with string. How could the airport authorities allow such rubbish on their planes? It couldn't be safe.

Then his heart jumped. He saw a girl with long dark hair who reminded him strongly of Catherine. Then she picked up a child, a man presumably her husband put an arm around her and they became lost in the crowd. Funny how the mind plays tricks. The blare of the warning klaxon distracted him. The carousel stated to move, and Alistair became involved in trying to spot his bag and get out of the airport before all the taxis were taken.

Michael meanwhile was frowning at his mobile.

"Bad news?" Alistair asked.

"Don't know," Michael said shortly. "Let's get out of here and down to the harbour. I'll fill you in when we can get some privacy." If not bad news, it certainly wasn't good.

Douglas did not speak to Catherine again until the stewardess announced that the flight crew was beginning preparations for landing. Reluctantly he put his book away.

"There is not going to be much time between collecting our bags and catching our connecting flight."

He was looking uncomfortable; Catherine wondered what was coming next.

"It would be sensible to divide our efforts and one of us collect the luggage whilst the other goes to buy the tickets."

Suddenly Catherine saw the problem. Common sense dictated that she pick up the bags and he as the Greek speaker did the negotiation with the ticket desk. Romantic good manners, however, had the man lifting the heavy weights. On top of that he would have to ask her for money. Another no-no in whatever fantasyland he inhabited, where women played the gracious Guinevere and men jousted with dragons.

She touched her money belt then remembered the advice about not fiddling with it in public. She made a dash for the loo, earning herself another black look from the stewardess. On returning to her seat, Catherine passed to Douglas a wad of notes.

"You buy the tickets, use that for now, tell me when you need some more. Please don't worry about me lifting your two-ton book bag. If I can't manage to get a couple of suitcases on a trolley then I have been wasting my time at the gym all these years."

Douglas managed to look uncomfortable and grateful at the same time. Catherine was amused to see that when the plane landed Douglas left knight errantry behind. By some very ungentlemanly pushing and elbowing, he was one of the first to leave the aircraft. The wait for baggage seemed interminable, with all the usual worries that one or more pieces had gone to the other side of the world. Eventually the last piece emerged and Catherine set off at a run past the bored customs officials to where Douglas was waiting for her, waving a brightly coloured folder.

They had to leave the airport building and re-enter by another door. It took a great deal of rapid Greek to get themselves accepted on the flight. They ended up pushing their trolley out onto the tarmac and handing over their cases to be thrown directly into the hold. Catherine suspected they would not have been successful if the young woman with the clipboard had not been so obviously taken with the ever-courteous Douglas.

As they fastened their seatbelts and listened to the pre-flight checks once again, Catherine took another discrete look at her companion. All she had seen when Margot had first brought him into her office was an elderly academic with too much hair and the need for some accommodation. Even when she had decided to recruit him as an ally in the search for her brother she had seen the facility in Greek rather than the man.

Now she saw what the young woman at the airport had presumably seen, kind eyes and pleasant regular features, of course, but more than that, the indefinable goodness of the man that was core to his being. Douglas had got his book out again. He must have felt her gaze because he looked up and smiled.

"Don't worry, luck is obviously with us, we'll sacrifice to Melos Aphrodite when we land."

Catherine was not at all sure he was joking.

The journey was over before the stewardess could get to every passenger with refreshments. This time they left the plane with a little more decorum. Because their luggage was last in, it was first out. Douglas, to salve his manly pride, put himself in charge of loading it onto a trolley. Suddenly, Catherine caught at his arm.

"Douglas! My father and Michael are standing at the next carousel, what shall we do?"

Chapter Eleven

Robert twisted, turned and finally admitted to himself that sleep had deserted him for good. He picked up a bottle of water and some biscuits and went onto the ramparts to watch the sun rise over the Aegean. It was a beautiful sight but it did not distract him from the fact that he was cold, stiff and dirty. Life in the professor's storage locker might be preferable to an existence as the prisoner of Zenda.

He tried to calculate when he had sent the message to Catherine. It must have been Monday evening. This was what, Wednesday morning? It couldn't be, so much seemed to have happened, and yet repeated calculations on his fingers told him that less than three days had passed since that carefree lunch with Margaret and Rena.

If his sister had acted immediately she might arrive today, but he knew he was kidding himself. Catherine was good hearted and loyal but she did not have the strength of character to take off for an unknown destination with no more than a moment's notice. So when could he expect her in reality? Friday would be about the earliest. Would she use the ferry or travel independently? He knew that she could handle a boat. Could he last out in this ruin even with Margaret and Rena helping him? It would be hellishly uncomfortable and bloody boring but he supposed he could do it, he would have to.

Then he heard the sound of someone moving through the olive trees. They were taking no care to muffle their footsteps.

Could it be one of the islanders? No, Rena had said that they avoided this place because of the ghosts. Robert carefully moved round until he could see the path. A few minutes later a figure walked into view. A big man in his late sixties, perhaps early seventies, with a head of bushy white hair. He wore a well-pressed khaki shirt and pants and carried a brass-headed stick. The stranger stopped at the bushes guarding the entrance to the fort.

"Robert, Robert McFarlane," he called. "I'm James McKenzie, I need to talk to you."

Robert said nothing but continued to watch.

"Blast, you boy, I know you're in there. There is nowhere else you could be. You've caused more than enough trouble, now come out and talk to me like a sensible fellow because I'm blowed if I'm going to bellow out my business at the top of my voice like a market woman selling fish."

There were a few minutes of silence. Even the birds were quiet, as if the shouting had scared them into hiding.

The professor looked round and seated himself on an outcrop of rock. He shrugged off his haversack and extracted a flask. As the older man poured, Robert could see steam rising from the liquid in the early morning chill and the smell of coffee made his stomach clench.

In a far more ordinary tone the professor said, "Your father's name is Alistair, your mother's Diana and you have a younger sister called Catherine. You have seen by now that I am quite alone, and a young man like yourself could probably tie me in knots if he wanted to. Now please come out and listen to what I have to say."

Robert moved cautiously until he was within three metres of the seated man. "Throw your walking stick out of reach," he called. "I've seen sticks like that before in the Turkish bazaars. It's a sword stick."

"You have a good eye, young man. It is indeed of Turkish manufacture. However, this one is not a sword stick. One of the troubles with weapons is the fact that they can so easily be taken off you by a stronger opponent. Whereupon you have doubly armed your attacker. This stick has a more peaceful purpose."

The professor unscrewed the handle and poured a splash of amber liquid into his cup. Robert emerged from his hiding place and said, "If you have another cup in that bag I would be grateful for some coffee but I don't think I will take any spirits right now."

"Very wise. I don't usually take whisky before breakfast myself, but this morning I needed a little Dutch courage. You have the reputation of being an extremely violent young man."

"Yánnis was about to fillet me with a knife," Robert protested. "He had completely lost it and was going to kill me for sure. A pan of boiling water may not be a gentleman's weapon but Yánnis wasn't fighting by the Queensberry Rules either. As for your nephew, I didn't give him more than a push, whatever the little bastard might have told you."

"You pushed Phillip, did you? That's interesting." Robert waited but McKenzie said no more. The older man indicated the haversack. "I think it would be better if you searched in here yourself until we have come to an understanding. You will find another cup and some sandwiches wrapped in greaseproof paper, take whatever you want."

Robert thought he had never tasted anything quite as good as that hot coffee and soft fresh bread wrapped round thick slices of ham.

McKenzie waited until the first hunger was appeased then said, "You have probably been able to work out what's going on by now for yourself."

"Drugs in, antiquities out," Robert replied through a mouthful of bread.

"Very succinct and essentially true, yet I think you would understand better if you allowed me to tell you the full story."

Robert said nothing and after a moment McKenzie resumed in his best classroom manner.

"It must be twenty years since I first came to this island. I had just been appointed to the chair of ancient history at Franchester. As a small celebration I hired a yacht and a local guide then set off to explore the Cyclades with a group of friends. Men and girls who were as obsessed by the ancient world as I was and who also liked to have some fun.

"I don't know who suggested Sigandros first, but most of us knew the story of the lost temple of Athena. Pretty soon we were all convinced that we would find the legendary site and become rich and famous. Well, we found the temple of Poseidon; you couldn't really miss it. The French have never been particularly neat excavators. But no sign of the mysterious and secret site dedicated to Athena. Eventually we became bored and sailed off in search of new sites and a bit more entertainment than this bit of rock could afford.

"Yet somehow the old story had caught my imagination. I came back the following year on my own and spent a month here. Then I did some research in the Louvre, looking up the records of those two old frauds, Annonay and Guimet. I went to Athens and scoured their records. I met Dionysios Solomós who had just been appointed director and was as keen as I was to locate a new and important find that would make his name. We became friends and he managed to get me permission to run an excavation here. An honour rarely granted to someone not Greek by birth. I spent all the time I was not positively compelled to be in Franchester here on Sigandros.

"Ten years ago I came out to live on this island permanently after parting company with my university under something of a cloud. The only problem was money. I had a pension, some investments but nothing like enough to continue with what I now thought of as my life's work.

"Then I met your father; or rather he was washed up on my shore. He had been cruising in these waters when a sudden violent storm forced him to head for the nearest island. If I were superstitious I would believe the great god Poseidon had brought him to me. He appreciated my difficulties and was able to suggest a solution. It started with cigarettes coming in from Turkey and the odd case of brandy going back. Illegal certainly, but not enough to twinge the conscience too severely.

"A contact had been set up at the University of Athens. The artefacts from the temple of Poseidon, a perfectly legal and certified dig, were sent to the archaeology department on the mainland. The extras were sent along with them and spirited away by someone on the staff. An anonymous benefactor, supposedly an islander who has made a fortune in business, supports the dig. After every successful run a little more money is donated into the funds. It's then up to me to do some creative accountancy on my side to produce a clean set of books if they are ever required.

"Once used to bending the law a little and, of course, accustomed to the extra income, other things were introduced. It was then that I became aware that your father was not the mastermind behind this little enterprise. He was running it for another who is referred to a little dramatically as the Shadowman. Most people are happy to know this character by, I presume, his nom de guerre. Those who are more curious tend to die quite painfully.

"Then I made my breakthrough. I found the temple of Athena. For fifteen years it had been almost under my nose but I had not seen it. I could say with Howard Carter 'Wonderful Things'. Unfortunately I had made my discovery too late. The publicity attending a find like this was not acceptable to those who preferred to do their business under cover of darkness. It was put to me, however, that I could excavate, make notes, do all the scholarly work and at some time unspecified when the island was not needed for other matters I could then publish.

"I agreed and fell right into the trap that had been laid for me. A report of the sort of finds I was making got back to the Shadowman. I was persuaded to let some of them go to collectors, for a consideration, of course. In effect I have been stripping my wonderful site in the very worst tradition of the nineteenth-century plunderers who called themselves archaeologists. The site cannot now be another Troy, but it could still be a footnote in the published literature.

"Then you came along and all that careful planning has gone rather pear shaped. You may be a black sheep but no one wanted to make you a sacrificial lamb without your father's specific agreement. He has decided that you might be worth taking back into the fold if I am not stretching a metaphor too far."

The professor stopped and looked at Robert, who gave every impression of a man who had been hit with a baseball bat.

"Your father and that rather unpleasant young man Michael, who is, I believe, your sister's fiancé, are travelling out to talk to you. We expect him to arrive on Friday. They are also going to have some rather strong words with me. Although what I could have done to prevent the problems you have caused I rather fail to see. Unfortunately, when you work with a character like the Shadowman, shifting blame becomes part of the job description, if you wish to live to enjoy your ill-gotten gains that is."

"Please, this is not making sense," Robert pleaded

The professor looked as if one of his students had claimed not to understand the causes of the battle of Thermopile.

"Oh, I get how you sank down the slippery slope into a life of crime," Robert assured him.

McKenzie looked pained. Robert was not impressed. He believed the former academic had not taken too much persuading to leave the straight and narrow.

"I even appreciate the sweet little deal that is going on here. What I cannot understand is why you think you will be able to continue to use the temple of Poseidon as your cover. All this year's students know the site's played out and are beginning to wonder why you were bothering, and more to the point, why Athens lets you. That sort of speculation is not good for secrecy. You're either going to have to rediscover the temple of Athena soon and that will stop your games with the antiquities, or you will have to stop using this island as a staging post. Whatever, this Shadowman character is not going to be pleased either way. Perhaps you should be grateful to me for causing a diversion."

Suddenly, McKenzie could see that this was indeed Alistair's son.

"Tell me more about my father's involvement and about this Michael character. This is the first I've heard about him."

"Your father works under the title of businessman, which can and does cover a multitude of sins. Amongst his many enterprises he has a controlling interest in a soap and disinfectants factory just outside Athens. This plant provides an ideal cover for the export of less legitimate finished products all over the world. Michael Buchanan is that very rare bird, a Brit who has a facility for languages. He speaks Greek without any trace of an accent. He has a working knowledge of other unusual languages too, including Turkish and Arabic.

"Michael and your father met at some conference or other, years ago, probably just after you had flown the nest. They got on well despite the difference in ages. Alistair wanted a partner who could speak to the natives. Michael needed the older man's business contacts. It worked very well for both of them. Somewhere along the line he became heir apparent to your father's business interests and settled the deal by becoming engaged to your sister."

"I take it Catherine was happy about this?"

"I have no idea, my dear boy, I never saw any symptoms of grand passion in Michael but then he is a very cold fish."

"Why are my father and this Michael character coming to Sigandros?"

"I suspect the first reason is to ascertain that you are who you say you are. The second is to do some damage limitation on what has become a very noisy episode."

"Why should they care, about me I mean? My father washed his hands of me years ago, and Michael is not going to want a rival in my father's regard."

"I can only suppose the business has expanded to the point where they need another director. A family member would be best but your sister is not, I think, management material. You have grown up a bit since you ran away to sea. Perhaps your father wishes to kiss and make up." The professor waggled his scholarly eyebrows; it was a good trick. "You might have to watch your step with Michael though. He could be persuaded to accept a junior partner but he won't tolerate a rival for crown prince."

Robert nodded, he had been thinking the same thing. Then he remembered. "I sent a text message to Catherine. She's coming out here to help me."

"I don't think you need to worry about that. She did get your message and got rather overexcited. She tried to persuade your father and Michael to do something to help you. They told her to forget about it and she seems to have gone off the idea. Apparently she has gone off to Mull to sulk, according to the latest e-mail from Alistair."

Robert said nothing. Yet the information did not sit well with his conviction that Catherine was coming for him. Claims to extrasensory perception did not go down well if you were trying to convince someone you were really quite a sensible chap.

Instead he asked, "What do you want me to do?"

McKenzie returned the question. "Who knows you are here?"

"You."

"Please don't play games. You must have had some help."

Robert thought about it for a moment but could not see the harm in answering. "Rena and the redheaded Scot, Margaret."

"Is that all?"

"Yes."

"Then wait till they come up to see you," the professor instructed. "Tell them that I found you and you have explained what happened. Tell them I believe you, but I am concerned that the islanders who took Yánnis and Costas back to Marmaris have reported your fight aboard the *Herakles* to the authorities. I am keeping you out of sight until I can get you off the island quietly. Say I have a friend on another island who will help.

"Once you have convinced the girls, go back up to the old German prisoner of war camp on the hill. Tell them you will be perfectly all right on your own. They are not to come near you again. Thank them, kiss them goodbye, exchange keepsakes if you must, but convince them that for your safety and their own this is the end of the line. In truth you can wait there in relative comfort until rescue arrives in the shape of your father on Friday. Is that clear?"

"Why am I not leaving on the ferry with the others?"

The professor thought for a moment. "Because that is how the gendarmes will arrive. A tuppence ha'penny dispute like this does not warrant getting out the royal launch. You will simply sail to another island and take up your wandering career again. They are good girls and don't deserve any trouble."

Robert took the older man's point immediately. He did not want this mysterious Shadowman to touch the lives of the two young women who had been his friends.

Robert watched the professor walk back down the hill then got his stuff together. The old man had done him the favour of leaving the haversack of goodies. So he filled in the time by finishing off the coffee and sandwiches and reading about dark doing in ancient Greece.

Occasionally he looked up from his reading to watch the fishing boats leave the harbour and wonder where the mysterious temple of Athena was located. It existed, McKenzie had admitted it. Moreover, he had seen the little head of the goddess when the packing case had broken open. Yet Sigandros was too small to conceal a find of those proportions for long.

It would all be explained eventually. As the sun warmed the stones, he began to feel his lack of sleep and gradually he dozed thinking of Athena Areia with helmet, spear and shield, her cloak edged with serpents, ready for war.

"A fine guard you keep!"

Robert jerked awake. Margaret was standing over him, another bag of groceries in her hand. Rena was hovering nervously behind her.

"Crisis over, at least for the time being," he told them. "Come and sit down. I have things to tell you. Starting with a visit from the professor this morning."

They looked almost disappointed that his troubles had been resolved. They said he could keep the fresh supplies and books they had brought. Robert and Margaret went through the motions of exchanging contact addresses then they did kiss and part.

Rena, who had held back from the pretend farewells, said, "There is much you are not telling us, Robert from the sea. So far I have believed that you were an honest man. Now I am not so sure and I am glad that our ways are parting." Rena turned on her heel and walked away from the fort.

Margaret seemed very struck with Rena's words. She paused for a moment, made a half-hearted wave then followed her friend without any further protestations of good will.

Robert pondered for some time if he had made the right decision then stopped trying to puzzle out the incomprehensible. He got together the gear he had collected on the short time on the island. Ensured that the evidence of his short stay at the fort was removed, he made his way back up the hill to the army camp.

Over the next two days Robert sent thankful thoughts to Margaret and Rena for the books they had enclosed with his provisions. The supplies at the army hut were more than adequate, but it would have been a tedious existence without the reading material provided by the girls. During the day he felt confident enough to go for walks and pick up the sounds of the students breaking camp and having a farewell party.

Professor McKenzie was worldly enough to send up a case of wines and spirits. Robert found it abandoned on his doorstep one morning, although he would have sworn that he had heard no sounds of movement in the night. On the other hand, as he lay on his cot wishing for sleep to come and eat up the hours, he had thought he'd heard the faint moans and prayers of the former prisoners of war. It was just the play of wind and waves amongst the coves and gullies of the rocks, but he would not be sorry to leave this place once the last student had finally gone.

At about 10 a.m. on Friday morning the Piraeus ferry arrived. Robert returned to the old fort to watch the students depart and observe who might arrive. There were a couple of broken-down old vans that chugged off the cargo deck deposited their loads and drove straight back on board. There were no official-looking characters who might be police officers. On the other hand, what did Greek detectives look like?

Robert thought he could see the black and red heads of Rena and Margaret. He wished them well, but he could not help feeling a little apprehensive on their behalf. He heartily wished he had not involved them in his adventures.

CHAPTER TWELVE

Douglas turned round and saw the two men Catherine had indicated. The younger one was staring at them. Briefly Douglas thought the sensible thing would be to go over and say hello, then Catherine's sense of panic seemed to infect him too. Quickly looking round, he saw a family struggling with bags of luggage and several small children.

"Pick up that little girl in the red tee shirt," he said urgently. To Catherine's eternal credit she did as she was asked immediately and without questioning the strange request. Douglas said something to the parents in Greek, bowing graciously, then draped an arm about Catherine's shoulder. Skilfully steering their trolley with one hand, he followed the harassed family to the exit.

"People mostly see what they want to see. Your father is not expecting to meet you here. He does expect to see Athenian families getting off the Athens flight. So we borrowed this delightful tot from parents who have too many to cope with and viola! We become just another group going on holiday."

Catherine was not sure about the delightful. The child was looking very doubtful about being separated from her mother and was beginning to wriggle. Douglas stopped and produced one of the boiled sweets distributed by the flight operators that are almost obligatory to ease the trauma of descent from the clouds. This was enough for the little one, who settled back crunching noisily.

Once past the barrier, the child was returned to her father, a lot of rapid Greek and handshakes were exchanged and Douglas issued boiled sweets to all the children. Catherine was astounded. She had not noticed Douglas take one, let alone a handful of the disgusting confections. The man definitely had hidden talents.

He steered Catherine to the coffee shop. "Men like your father and Michael will not want to linger around the airport. If you're sure you don't want to make yourself known to them, then let's have a decent cup of coffee whilst they presumably belt down to the harbour to hire a boat."

Catherine followed Douglas into the coffee shop. She found an empty table whilst he bought coffee and a couple of flaky pastry pies.

"I noticed you did not touch the ready meals on the plane, so you have had nothing since early this morning. It's time to do some more thinking and you might as well eat whilst we do so."

"I'm not really hungry," said Catherine, breaking her pastry in two.

"Spinach and cheese," Douglas told her, "perfectly safe."

She nibbled a corner. It was a bit greasy but tasted wonderful. They ate in silence for a few moments, then Douglas brushed the crumbs from his beard with a napkin and said, "Your father, for all his bluster, has obviously gone to a great deal of trouble and expense to look for your brother. I need you to tell me why you did not go rushing into his arms over in baggage collection."

It was a good question and Catherine suspected that if she did not have a good answer the adventure would end here.

She took her time arranging her thoughts. "All my life, right up to this week, I have thought of my father as the rock in our household. Mother has always suffered from various nervous complaints. When I was little she would suddenly vanish and reappear weeks later very quiet and looking thin and ill. I thought my brother Robert was wonderful, then he went off without a word."

"As I understand it, your father was also frequently away." Douglas was gentle, genuinely wanting to know.

"Yes he was, but he always went away for a comprehensible reason. He said when he was going, why, what his destination would be and when he would be back. He always returned when he said he would and called home when he arrived at his hotel. He never, ever disappeared."

Douglas nodded to show that he understood.

"Then this business with Robert blew up and it was if I was suddenly living with a stranger. All his reactions were wrong; there were mysteries and secrets when there should have been nothing of the sort. Even now, when my father looks like he is doing the right thing at last, I find I don't trust him anymore. I feel it's up to me get Robert home. If I don't do it myself, then no matter what my father may tell me, I'll never really know for sure that my brother is safe."

"What about Michael? This is the man you are, were, engaged to marry."

"I don't think I ever really knew Michael. He was there, he seemed to want me, my father obviously approved of him, and there was no one else in my life. It was a bit like an arranged marriage," Catherine said thoughtfully

"No one was forcing you into anything," Douglas protested.

Catherine thought briefly of the first night that Michael had taken her. She should have stopped the affair immediately. She despised the girl she was then, the one who had allowed that humiliation to happen without protest, the one who somehow thought she deserved that sort of treatment.

"Oh, nobody forced me, I went into it willingly enough," Catherine said glibly. "It's almost a reverse fairy tale with the handsome prince really being a beast in disguise."

It sounded a bit fanciful but Douglas could sort of see what she meant. "That still leaves the question, what shall we do now? There is no way we can get to the island before them. Michael speaks Greek; we know that from the messages on the mobile. They obviously have money, I would presume they will set off for Sigandros tonight."

"We could get a boat too," Catherine tried to protest. Even as she spoke she knew it was impossible. Michael and her father would go as passengers. She needed to pilot her own craft. She felt weary with travelling now. There was no way she was going to handle a yacht safely tonight. "No, we couldn't." She smiled before Douglas could say anything.

"Then let's find somewhere to stay and we can work out the details later," Douglas replied.

They pushed the trolley through the now nearly empty arrivals area. There were still a few hopeful taxis hanging about. Douglas helped the driver load their things in the boot and then they were off in a cloud of dust.

They rode in silence for a few minutes. Catherine looking idly out of the window at the scruffy shacks that were dotted along the road, and the light fading on the distant blue hills.

"You're wrong, you know," she said suddenly.

Douglas was wrapped in his own thoughts, remembering a very pleasant stay he had had on Milos a couple of years ago when he had spent nearly a week exploring the Minoan ruins at Filakopi. "I don't doubt it," he replied calmly. "But on what particular point?"

"Father and Michael, it's most unlikely they will go tonight. By the time they find a vessel and do all the paperwork it will be full dark. They are in a hurry but not to the extent of taking unnecessary risks. Sailing through these islands at night is not a picnic. Let's face it, they're also used to the good life. Sleeping in the cramped quarters of a small boat will not appeal when they could so easily stay in a good hotel tonight and get to their destination only a few hours later."

"That's true." Douglas was quiet for a moment, then shouted something in Greek to the driver, who did a spectacular handbrake turn.

"What's going on?" shouted Catherine in alarm.

"Your father and Michael will be going to the main port, Adamas. They are not tourists, it would not make sense for them to go anywhere else."

"We're not tourists either unless you plan some sightseeing on the way," Catherine said acidly.

"Trust me, a little please." Douglas was exasperated. "Let me explain." He held out his left hand fingers together, thumb pointing outwards. "This is roughly the shape of the island. The capital and main ferry port of Adamas is here." He pointed to the pad under his index finger. "There is, however, another deep-water harbour here at Apollonia." He indicated the tip of his little finger. "When your father and Michael set out tomorrow they will have to sail all round the coast." The long finger circled his hand. "Whereas we could jump straight off."

"Will it not be a lot more difficult to hire a boat in some out-of-the-way village?" Catherine had not formed a very favourable impression of Milos so far. She thought it looked like a dump. Open cast mining had made the island look like a rodent-gnawed cheese.

"That's where a little local knowledge comes in useful. I have been here a couple of times before."

"Why?" Catherine thought once might be too often.

"There is an important Bronze Age town here." Douglas extended his hand again and pointed to his ring finger. As quite a bit of it is now underwater, I hired a fishing boat to take me to the farthest ruins. I got on quite well with the young man, Pandelís, who owned the boat. I visited the home of his parents several times. I have told the taxi driver to head for their house. They will help us get some decent accommodation for the night, and if anyone knows who has a boat for hire, they will."

Catherine smiled to herself. The guy was miraculous. Yet he did not seem to realise he was doing anything extraordinary.

Within the hour they had rooms over a bright little taverna on the sea front. They had showered in luke-warm water and changed into clean clothes. Over a bottle of the island's flinty white wine and a large bowl of shiny black olives, Douglas had negotiated with a guy who looked a bit like Long John Silver, only with two legs. They had hired a surprisingly trim little vessel complete with navigation aids and stores. Catherine had observed them from behind her large bottle of mineral water, nibbling on the occasional olive.

There had been a hiccup when Douglas had had to explain that the sailor would be Catherine. It had taken another bottle of wine, a plate of fried squid and another instalment of Euros before the old pirate condescended to agree. But even with the inflated hire charge, the costs were very reasonable, so that was not a problem. Catherine had made sure that included in the deal was a full set of charts for the area between Milos and Ios. She had taken these with her once she had inspected the boat, intending to put in some study after dinner.

Douglas, however, asked to look at them. Surprised, she spread the chart out over the table. The waters round Sigandros looked like a nightmare of rocks, tiny islets and the occasional deep-water passage. Catherine was not particularly worried about this; she had negotiated similar hazards whilst sailing round the Scottish islands. Only there she had had the additional disadvantage of the gales that blew in off the Atlantic or the North Sea.

"I think your father and Michael will have contacted Professor McKenzie by this time. He will be expecting them," Douglas began.

"Does that matter? You know the guy too."

"I had a brief acquaintance with him several years ago. Your father and Michael obviously have a much deeper involvement. Even if we are the first to arrive on Sigandros, we may not find a particularly warm welcome or very much co-operation."

"So what's your plan?"

"Since we started this mad escapade, I have been re-reading the letters of Philistophanes."

Bully for you, Catherine thought, just the thing for a little light entertainment. But Douglas had proved his worth too many times for Catherine to dismiss this remark out of hand. Aloud she said, "Okay and?"

"It's always been assumed that the temple to Athena the philosopher talks about was actually on Sigandros. When no one was able to find any trace of it then the old gossip was dismissed as a fraud."

"Why would he make up something like that, which could so easily be verified at the time?"

"Good girl!" Douglas was approving. "It could be that the temple was either on a headland, the causeway of which has been washed away or destroyed, or that it was on a separate little island and the girls were ferried across. If you think like that and then re-read the text, all Philistophanes tells us is that the girls come to Sigandros in order to visit the temple of Athena. Just as modern visitors who want to visit Delos have to go Myknos because no one is allowed to stay on the island overnight."

"I'm still not seeing the point you wish to make," Catherine insisted.

"If the temple was on another island then the priests and girls did not use the main harbour. If they had, the temple would not have been such a secret. On the other hand, there is no other place around that precipitous coast that looks anything like a harbour."

Catherine looked at the map with a seafarer's eye. "You could anchor quite a substantial ship quite close in here." She pointed. "How you would get delicately bred maidens up and down the cliff is another matter. There is a small island off the coast, although it is not blessed with a name even on a map of this scale. That suggests it's nothing more than a big rock."

"Well, I'm proposing that we find out. First of all, we try to gain access to this island via the back door. If we find it locked, we will just have to sail round to the harbour and throw ourselves on McKenzie's hospitality."

"It's worth a try," Catherine decided and put her maps away.

"Ready for something to eat?" Douglas asked.

Catherine was never very hungry. She would have been content with a bowl of fruit in her room. She realised, however, that this would have been churlish and unsociable in the extreme, so she agreed. They walked round the small harbour to look for the restaurant that belonged to Pandelís's parents. There were perhaps half a dozen places with tables and chairs spilling out onto the roadway. At one, Douglas was greeted by name and to Catherine's embarrassment a rather handsome Greek youth threw himself into Douglas's arms and kissed him on both cheeks. There was a great deal of laughter and exchange of rapid conversation before the pair of them were led to a table overlooking the sea.

Douglas looked neither exited nor discomforted. "I managed to get Pandelís into further education in Athens University. It took a bit of doing as he had only the most basic island education. Dionysious Solómos pulled some strings so that Pandelís could take a crammer course in the evenings whilst attending lectures during the day. He absorbed education like a sponge, but he always comes back home to help his parents during the summer vacation."

"Who paid for all the extra tuition?" Catherine asked.

"There was no need of extra fees," Douglas said lightly, "the Greeks have always been very keen on education."

Pull the other one, it hath bells upon it, thought Catherine but wisely said nothing.

A tiny old lady dressed entirely in black came to their table. Douglas immediately stood and made a little bow. It should have looked stupid; instead, it looked extremely dignified. There were a few moments of conversation then Douglas asked Catherine, "Would you like to go and see what's cooking in the kitchen? It's the correct thing to do."

Catherine shuddered. "No."

"Can you eat fish?" Douglas asked.

"Yes, but I would prefer a dish of lightly cooked vegetables if that's possible."

"My dear girl, the recipes for vegetable dishes in this part of the world start with 'take a half a litre of olive oil', and go on from there."

Catherine was beginning to look green. Douglas took the old lady's hand, kissed it lightly and then looking into her eyes made a long speech in Greek. The woman bridled and simpered like a young girl then almost raced up the path, shouting instructions to the kitchen.

"Who was that?" Catherine asked.

"Pandelís's mother," Douglas replied.

"She can't be! She's too old to have a son Pandelís's age!"

"She can be and she is. Island life is not easy on women. She was even more grateful than her husband was when Pandelís got the opportunity to better himself. Ordinarily she does not leave the kitchen. It's a great honour that she has come out to serve us herself."

Catherine was not sure about the honour but what sort of life made a woman age like that? Then her instincts took over and she asked, "What are we going to have for diner?"

"I've ordered Greek salads, one without any dressing, a couple of grilled fish and one or two of the plainer vegetable dishes. It will all come at once but there should be enough for you to enjoy."

When the food came, Catherine was surprised at how hungry she really was. The fish had smooth, firm flesh and had apparently gone from sea, to grill, to plate without too much intervention by the chef. The salad was crisp, clean and cool. Another bottle of white wine had appeared. She had got used to the fact that Douglas could seemingly drink the stuff like soda. Privately she swore she would stick to mineral water but halfway through dissecting her fish she realised that the level of wine in her own glass had dropped and had been refilled.

Eventually the dishes were taken away and replaced by a bowl of fruit and a slice of cheese. Catherine took a bunch of grapes and started stripping fruit from the stem. The bottle of wine was only half finished; she considered the problem then dismissed it. Two dead men had been taken away and replaced by fresh bottles, but Catherine had been too interested in her fish to notice.

"I've told you a lot about myself," she said to Douglas. "What about you, why are you without wife or partner? I've seen you with women, you like them, why don't you have anyone special?"

The restaurant was still quite busy. Waiters flitted in and out of tables, but they were no longer so attentive to the British pair. This was the time to relax and talk. Douglas looked out over the dark water. On the horizon, the lights of the night ferries dipped and twinkled. It had been a long day with perhaps an over sufficiency of wine.

"There was someone. Many years ago I fell in love with the wife of, if not my best friend, at least a decent acquaintance. We were members of the same photographic club. The husband, let's call him John, used to team up with me when we went away on courses and photographic weekends. He would invite me back to his house for drinks and meals because he knew I was on my own. Sandra was different. She was intelligent but trapped in a relationship that had become meaningless."

"She was pretty?" Catherine queried.

"Not especially." Douglas smiled. "She was slim, but with quite a prominent bosom for her size. She had long dark hair and very full dark lips even without makeup."

"Did John have to travel away from home on a regular basis?"

"He was an engineer on one of the oil rigs. He was away from home for weeks at a time."

"You went round to keep her company?"

"Yes."

"Things developed from there and you found yourself in her bed?"

"Yes. She said she was ready to make the break from, erm, John. I gave her quite a lot of money to set herself up in her own home. Then she said that she wanted to give her marriage another chance."

"She did not offer to return the money?"

"No."

Poor baby, thought Catherine, she really saw you coming. Aloud she said, "Was it really over for you both, did the marriage recover?"

"It was certainly over for me. John and Sandra did file for divorce quite soon after." Douglas hesitated for a moment then said, "There was apparently another man. Sandra left John and went to live with this other chap."

It explained so much. The single status, the discretion, so careful that even his colleagues at the library did not guess at the other woman. The inevitable double betrayal and the guilt at deceiving his friend and at his own foolishness. It would take a long time if ever for this damaged man to trust again.

Douglas, conscious of perhaps having said too much, made a show of ordering coffees and asking for the bill.

Eventually they walked back along the front to their rooms. Catherine asked Douglas about the cult of Athena Parthenos and how it would have affected the tiny island of Sigandros. Catherine, having had more food and wine than she was used to, really did not care about the goddess in any of her aspects but it was the easiest way of distracting Douglas from revelations he might very soon regret having made.

On reaching their bar, Douglas made a sort of half bow, reminded Catherine they would have an early start in the morning, then disappeared into his room without another word.

Alistair and Michael had ordered their taxi to take them directly to the harbour master's office. When they had paid off the ancient Mercedes, they stood for a moment in the sunshine, watching the battered stone carriers in a harbour that looked more like a lake.

"How do the ships get out?" Alistair asked.

"There's quite a wide entrance at the far side we just can't see it. This was the volcano in the ancient days." They stood for a few more minutes in silence, neither man very impressed with either the scruffy harbour or the dusty town that surrounded it.

"What was the text message from Marmaris?" Alistair asked at length.

"The *Herakles* is overdue. My contact is making enquiries. I suppose it's too much to hope that the whole boiling lot of them have gone to the bottom."

"If they have, then they've taken some good stuff with them," protested Alistair.

"Plenty more where that came from. Still, I'll contact Mohamed when we're finished here to see if he has found out anything more."

As Catherine had predicted, finding and hiring a yacht took the rest of the afternoon. Both men were happy to agree on an early morning start and booked into the Venus Village hotel on the harbour master's recommendation.

The following morning brought more bad news. The *Herakles* had berthed in Rhodes. The two islanders had reported the death by drowning of the former captain and mate. The two men had then disappeared, leaving the boat stranded to the fury of the authorities.

Michael had instructed Mohamed to send someone to collect the boat, pay what dues and fines were levied and get out as soon as possible. There was still no love for Turks on any of the Greek islands so maximum penalties would no doubt be imposed.

"What of the cargo?" Alistair asked anxiously.

"By this time the *Herakles* must have been searched from stem to stern. The fact that the authorities are bleating about harbour fees suggests the fishermen may have taken some souvenirs with them when they left."

"What do you think of this tale of Yánnis and Costas drowning?"

"It could be true but I, for one, don't believe it. Still, if they are supposed to be dead then they will have to lie low so they won't be making themselves inconvenient any time soon. Let's get to Sigandros and find out as much as we can. It would not surprise me if the Shadowman closed down this particular enterprise for a while. It's become a great deal too noisy."

"That's not going to suit McKenzie. He's got used to the extra income and I doubt he's saved a penny in his life."

"McKenzie's a fool for all his doctorates, but I doubt he's such a fool as to try to oppose the Shadowman."

The two men packed their kit and went down to the harbour to set off slightly later than they had originally intended.

Chapter Thirteen

Catherine had banged on Douglas's door shortly after first light. He had answered immediately and was already washed and dressed. Anticipating a dawn start, they had paid their bill the evening before. The early morning sun made the harbour of Apollonia shine golden, and the view was spectacular despite the signs of open cast mining eating away at the overlooking hillside.

Douglas felt very much a spare part as Catherine piloted them out of the narrow harbour and set course for Sigandros. When she was aboard ship she seemed a different person. The little girl lost who had talked about Mummy and Daddy seemed to exist in another world. The Sloane ranger who butterflied on the edge of the business world and divided her leisure hours between the shops and the gym had also been dismissed.

Yet Douglas still felt uncomfortable and he could not decide why. He had hired fishing boats in the past and been perfectly happy to leave the working of the ship to the owner and concentrate on his observations and notes without any desire to help steer or navigate. Why was he so edgy when it was Catherine in charge? Especially when she was so obviously competent.

Catherine seemed to be aware of, but not upset by, his discomfort. As Douglas began to relax and not clutch at the rail as if that were all that were between him and a watery grave, she said, "We will be sailing round the north side of Sigandros just before noon. We can anchor in the little cove I showed you on the map, but we will have to take the dinghy to get ashore. What's your master plan?"

Douglas was disconcerted. The whole trip had been focused on getting to the island but now he hadn't a clue what to do. Even if this was the secret departure point for the sacred isle in ancient times then there was no reason to suppose there would be any trace left for modern travellers. Then he mentally kicked himself. If McKenzie had discovered the secret of the temple, then he and his cronies would have left some traces.

"If this is the right place then there should be a path we can follow. They won't have let the girls down in baskets like the monks at Metèora."

Catherine laughed as much to give Douglas support as in appreciation of the weak joke.

"If we can get ashore then we will need to scramble up the hill. We can then walk across the island and observe what is going on. The original text message indicated your brother was with the students. I should be able to find their camp or at least where their camp used to be. From there we can make a few discrete enquiries.

"If we don't find your brother or hear news of him today then we might as well just sail into the harbour and knock at the door of McKenzie's villa. He has an excellent reputation with the islanders and nothing much happens on Sigandros without him finding out sooner rather than later."

They had an early lunch as soon as they were in sight of the island. Douglas had also put together a small pack of provisions in case they had to spend any amount of time on the island.

Catherine sailed in as close as was safe then made everything secure aboard the yacht. In silence they descended the ladder and set off in the tiny dingy belonging to the boat. A protected channel between two lines of sharp, dark rocks led to a set of marble steps set into the hillside. Douglas was entranced. Catherine, however, noted the modern stainless steel ring cemented into the rock. The priestesses of Athena didn't put that in place, she thought, but it was jolly handy nevertheless. Catherine had to haul on Douglas's shirt as he showed every inclination to spend the rest of the afternoon admiring the hidden steps. They pushed and slithered their way up the hillside with Douglas speculating that more marble steps were either hidden beneath the leaf mould or might have gone crashing into the harbour during ancient seismic disturbances. Despite all her hours in the gym, Catherine was too puffed to tell the academic to shut up.

Alistair and Michael finally got away from Milos in the late morning. The members of the crew could not understand why the grumpy pair of foreigners who had hired their boat seemed to take no pleasure in the cruise. Suggestions of a picnic in a secluded cove, a visit to an isolated monastery, a dive over a pirate wreck were vetoed in no uncertain manner.

This strange pair just wanted to get to Sigandros as fast as possible. Though what they wanted to do on that dump of a place they would not say. Yet the younger of the two spoke decent enough Greek when he wanted to. The pair of them spent the whole of the passage furiously flicking at their mobile phones. The crew's attempts at conversation or information on the passing scenery were rejected with bitter disdain. The seamen where not that interested in educating their passengers but how else would they secure the tip that made the difference between just getting along and affording some luxuries?

Michael eventually woke up from his worried preoccupation to promise a bonus for silent but rapid travel to the island. This is what they got. McKenzie was waiting for them on the harbour, and Michael told the crew they could relax for a couple of hours. He would send word if they were to sail further that day. The crew received this news in sullen silence.

McKenzie made 'good to see you' noises and social chat all the way up to the villa, ignoring the impatient looks from his guests until he was forced to hiss, "For Christ's sake, look happy and try to say something. Do you want the whole village to think I have had a visit from the Mafia?"

This made sense and both men made an effort to relax a little. They only maintained the charade until the door of the professor's study was locked behind them. McKenzie was wise enough not to offer refreshment but to start straight into the business that had brought his visitors so far.

"Robert is safe and co-operative," he said without preamble. "He's not here in the villa," the professor added quickly. "He's at the old prisoner of war camp we modified to take our visitors. It's basic up there but perfectly comfortable."

"When can we see him?" Alistair asked.

"Soon as you like. I'll take you up in the four-track as soon as I have brought you up to date."

"More bad news?" Michael asked.

"Not at all," the professor responded quickly. "The excavation at the temple of Poseidon has been closed down and probably will not reopen. The site is played out and is known to be exhausted. Using it any more would invite unwelcome speculation."

"What about your little harem?" Michael again. The man seemed to specialise in getting under a person's skin.

"If you mean the students," the professor said coldly. "They left this morning. Some were going home early, the rest have been taken by other digs for the remainder of the summer. I checked that all had destinations and the means of getting to them." In fact, Philip had done the checking. He was good at that sort of fussy administrative detail. He would probably end up working for the Civil Service. It would suit him.

"Where is Philip?" Michael asked.

"He is tidying up on the site. I have told him to stay in the village for the time being. He doesn't like it but he realises it's better for him to be kept out of things as much as possible.

"As you know, the islanders left the *Herakles* in Rhodes," the professor continued. "That has been tidied up and she is now on her way back to Marmaris. Death certificates have been issued for Yánnis and Costas. Our contact in Turkey is arranging compensation for the widows. Enough so, they will not start making a fuss, not so much that it looks more like a bribe to keep quiet."

"Are they dead?" Michael was sharp.

"The islanders have now returned and they assure me they saw both men go under."

"What about the cargo? Was that found?"

"No, the two Sigandros fishermen where bright enough to remove that and bring it back to the island. The delivery has only been delayed."

The professor had thought long and hard about whether to tell his partners about the loss of seven of the very best pieces. They were, by themselves, worth quarter of a million pounds on the black market. In the end he had decided against. The only detailed description lay in his own records, which were well hidden and written in ancient Greek. If he replaced them with similar items from his own collection, no one would know the difference. It was a sacrifice but one worth making if it helped this whole stupid incident achieve closure.

If Yánnis and Costas were not dead and tried to sell their ill-gotten gains, by the time the pieces reached the open market they would have probably gone through a number of expert hands and acquired perfectly respectable provenances.

Whilst keeping any secrets from such allies was dangerous, on the whole McKenzie had decided this was something about which they did not need to know. There was also the comforting thought that both fishermen and antiquities might very well be on the bottom of the sea.

"What about the other side of the business?" Alistair was beginning to recover.

"We have enough material to cover perhaps two more trips to Athens. There would have been little more even if I had kept the dig on to the end of the season. It's then up to the Shadowman if he wants to start again on another island or agree to the opening of the temple of Athena."

"What does Robert know?" asked Alistair.

"He knows everything. He saw the raw material up at the army camp. He put together most of it for himself and I told him the rest. He was interested and not overly bothered by its lack of legality."

"Let's go and see him. We can't move forward until we know if he's in or out," Alistair demanded.

Both of his companions wondered what the old man's reaction would be in the unlikely event of Robert being honest. Would he order the death of his own son?

They left the villa and climbed into the dusty four-track. The professor used it as little as possible because every drop of petrol had to be brought in on the ferry. He felt he did not dare to suggest to these pale office types that they walk up the hill. Nevertheless, he drove slowly and carefully, conserving his fuel and with respect for the steep terrain.

Catherine and Douglas eventually reached the road. By this time Douglas had ceased to lecture on the development of the cult of the virgin goddess and concentrated instead on the stitch in his side and the breath whooping in his lungs. He begged the young woman to slow down until he regained his wind. "We need to think if we follow this road up or down," he pleaded. Down, being by far the direction of choice in his own mind.

"Up," said Catherine succinctly and fitted action to her words.

After a moment, Douglas followed her, cursing quietly in classical Greek.

Robert was dozing on the camp bed when he heard them. At first he thought the voices might be part of a dream, then realised that he had been right all along. His little sister had come for him. He rushed out of the hut, yelling her name. For a moment Catherine, who had been frowning and shouting at the man with her, looked startled. Then she was in his arms, patting him as if to reassure herself he was real.

"Are you all right?" she said over and over again, not waiting for an answer.

Douglas wished that he could just leave them alone. But there was nowhere for him to go.

Robert stroked his sister's hair and eventually she calmed down enough for him to reassure her that he was fine.

"Father's coming," they said together then stopped, each as surprised as the other. Then they heard the wheeze and rumble of a vehicle on the mountain road.

"Come on," Catherine urged, "we've got a yacht at the foot of the cliff. You have to get away. Father's up to something and he'll kill you if you get in his way."

"It's all right," Robert soothed. "I know what it's all about. Everything's fine."

Then there was no more time because the four-track was rounding the last bend and Alistair and Michael were jumping out of the car even before it had come to a halt.

Alistair yelled "Robert!" then his brain caught up with his eyes and he realised there were two people standing with his son. "Who the hell," he started, then said, "Catherine, how did you get here? Who is this character?" Pointing at Douglas. "What in the bloody hell is going on?"

By this time McKenzie had brought the four-track to a stop and emerged from the driver's seat. "This I think is Douglas Grey."

"The fucking nosy librarian!" Alistair screamed.

"McFarlane!" the professor interrupted with his best classroom authority. Then with the smarm with which he had charmed the matrons in his university days, he attempted to diffuse the situation. "All this will take some explanation. Let us do it in the comfort of my villa. This old army camp is hardly the place for a conference. Douglas, will you ride back with Alistair and me? We'll let the young people walk back down the hill."

Michael was quick enough to understand. He caught Alistair by the sleeve and pushed him back towards the four-track. McKenzie held the passenger door open like a well-trained chauffeur. Douglas climbed in, not sorry to get away from the highly charged atmosphere.

The four-track turned and disappeared back down the hillside. The three who had been left behind began to walk down the hill. Michael turned to Catherine. "How much does he know?"

"Know about what? What's going on?"

Michael then asked Robert, "How much have you told these two?"

"Tell me who the hell you are and I might think about giving you an answer." Robert was belligerent.

"Catherine, tell him," Michael said shortly.

"This arsehole is Michael Buchanan, my former fiancé and Daddy's pet."

Michael looked at her in shock. This was a Catherine he had not previously encountered. Catherine, however, had not finished. "We have obviously walked into something. Douglas knows sod all because that's what I know. I want him treated well and sent on his way unharmed." Michael opened his mouth but Catherine talked over him. "Don't start to rage at me. This is entirely your own fault. If you had behaved like the respectable businessman you're supposed to be rather than the crook you are, none of this would have happened." Even Robert was looking at his little sister with something like awe.

"Let's hope McKenzie can keep the lid on things with Father. Now tell me what's going on."

Michael still had some bluster left. "What we should do is dump the bookworm into the sea and send you home with a slapped bum."

"You tried hitting me before," Catherine spat. "It didn't work then and won't work now. The so-called bookworm is on sherry-drinking terms with some of the best brains in Edinburgh University. If he goes missing there will be a hell of a stink. Robert, can you get through to this dickhead?"

Robert shot a warning glance at Michael, who looked ready to murder the girl. "Alistair and this character Michael had a sweet little scam going on this island. Drugs from Turkey relabelled as archaeological specimens get sent to Athens University with full customs clearance. There is some slight of hand in the university and the raw opium is sent to a soap works Father owns just outside the city. There the stuff is processed and refined then sent out with the legitimate washing powder."

Catherine was nodding to indicate she understood but she looked neither horrified nor upset.

"To sweeten the deal," Robert continued, "McKenzie and company are sending antiquities back to Turkey to be sold on the black market."

"So far, so good," commented Catherine, "so what's the big problem?"

"Father and Michael could not work something as big as this on their own. They have partners, some of whom are very dangerous indeed. These partners, or should I say bosses, don't like anything to go wrong, and above all, they don't like anything that attracts attention. I suspect anyone who invites these people's displeasure ends up dead very quickly.

"When I sent that text message to you I was creating unwanted noise. If I had been jolly Jack Tar, then undoubtedly I would be feeding the fish by this time. It was only because I'm Alistair's son that they have gone to such lengths to keep me alive and hush the matter up."

"I'm surprised Daddy didn't just order you silenced."

"He seems to have had a fit of the paternals. I don't know why, but I'm certainly glad of it."

Catherine turned to Michael. "You arrogant fool, one word, just one word of explanation and all this fuss could have been avoided."

Michael desperately wanted to slap her again. However, the grim expression on Robert's face and the well-defined muscles under the thin tee shirt kept Michael's hands by his sides.

They walked in silence for a few minutes. Then Catherine asked Michael, "How did you and Daddy get here?"

"We hired a boat in Milos."

"With crew?"

"Yes."

"Then here's a thought. We all have a big family reunion down at the professor's villa. All pals together and delighted to see each other. We thank Douglas nicely and send him back to Milos on your yacht. Daddy can give him enough Euros to cover his time and thank him for protecting his little girl. Hopefully we can play down that gaff about the nosy librarian. It was Daddy who set Douglas up for the muggers, wasn't it?"

Michael gave a grunt that could be interpreted as yes. "How

do we get off the island if this librarian chap takes our boat?"

"Michael, wake up please. How do you think Douglas and I got here, flew? I've got another boat anchored just off the secret harbour. We'll leave on that."

"How did you find out about the harbour?" Michael was suspicious.

"Elementary, my dear Michael, if you have a decent chart and a knowledge of the writings of Philistophanes."

"Who?" Michael was mystified but Catherine ignored him. She was enjoying herself as never before. It was so easy once you put your mind to it. She felt she owed Douglas for her newfound confidence if for nothing else. She would do her level best to ensure that he did not end up floating in the Aegean, victim of some sort of 'accident', if she could possibly help it.

When they reached the villa, they found Douglas and the professor on the terrace sharing the inevitable bottle of white wine. Alistair was nowhere to be seen.

"My dear young people," McKenzie greeted them.

"If he ever gets fed up of archaeology he could become a vicar," Robert whispered and Catherine giggled.

The professor must have heard but he carried on with relentless good humour. "Your father is waiting for you in my study. He asked that you join him there as soon as you arrive."

Michael led the way through. They found Alistair pacing the carpet. However, he did come forward to shake Robert's hand when he entered the room.

"You've caused us an awful lot of trouble, young man. What I need to know now is do you plan to cause us any more?"

"If you mean by that do I plan to run to the authorities the first chance I get, the answer is no."

"Then what do you plan to do?" Alistair's tone was suspicious.

"Well, nothing that involves staying on this God-forsaken island that's for sure. I've spent nearly a week here and I'd be quite happy if I never saw it again."

Alistair's frown deepened.

"So cards on the table." Robert sounded quite cheerful. "Option one, you give me a lift to somewhere I can get another berth and I sail off into the sunset for another ten years. I don't bother you, you don't worry about me."

"Robert, no!" Catherine sounded quite distressed.

Robert smiled at her. "There is of course option two. I have had quite a bit of time for thinking up in that dreary army camp. One of your current weaknesses is the transport of the stuff from Turkey to here. Mohamed at the Marmaris end is a weak link, even using Greek crews. Your answer is a neat little caique. It would take quite an initial outlay but it would soon pay for itself with legitimate charters. I know a few people who would be safe. A crew that was neither Turkish nor Greek would have less trouble calling in at both Turkish and Greek beauty spots. We could include Sigandros as a totally unspoiled island but preferably to see the newly discovered temple of Athena."

"That would please McKenzie," Michael commented.

Alistair then turned to Catherine as if noticing her for the first time. "Get out, girl. I haven't the time nor the patience to deal with you now. I'll see you regret bringing that over educated know-it-all to this island. You've given Michael and me just one more problem to clear up."

"No, Alistair, I won't be sent from the room like a naughty school girl. I have already proved I can be resourceful. After all, I got here before you and I don't have all the backup of a large organisation behind me. If you will only drop your blind prejudices I can be as useful to you as Robert or Michael."

Her father looked as if the cat had calmly refused to be sent out of the kitchen. "You'll do as I say," he blustered.

"Please try not to be so Victorian, you're making yourself look silly. If I'm in and working for the organisation then I am safe. If you insist on excluding me, then eventually the fact that I know about your little scam but am not involved will work it's way up the chain to your..." Catherine paused for a moment, "...partners. You need someone with people skills, especially if you accept Robert's idea of a little cruise boat. Your idea of management is to yell at people. It might have worked with my mother and with me for a while," she admitted, "but right now it's getting you deeper and deeper into the mire."

Alistair gave her a long appraising look. Eventually he said, "You have no problems with what we are doing?"

"A few. Whoever employed those two comedians Yánnis and Costas should be fired. They were always walking disaster areas." Michael went red. "You have been lucky there have not been more problems with the students before now. That side should have been more carefully considered." She smiled at her father. "If you mean the antiquities and drugs, then no. I realised quite some time ago that we could not have enjoyed our lifestyle in Edinburgh on the earnings of your legitimate business dealings."

Alistair looked again at his daughter and for the first time saw an attractive and competent young woman rather than a clingy child. He began to like what he saw. "We still have the problem of that librarian fellow," Alistair said.

"We should get rid of him, he knows too much." Michael was angry.

"I've already explained to Michael that the man knows nothing," Catherine appealed to her father. "He spends half his waking time with his mind in ancient Greece."

"He knows about the temple," countered Michael

"He's probably worked out where it is," Catherine conceded, "but it's not going to remain a secret for much longer anyway."

"We can arrange for him to fall off the yacht and drown. Very sad but it happens to someone every year," Michael said.

"This man's not a larger lout." Catherine had a momentary vision of the wine that never seemed far from Douglas's elbow. "Alive and back in his library he'll dream on about the ancient world and the most we'll hear is the occasional e-mail asking how the excavations are going. Dead, we'll have all sorts of trouble. He's not just popular with the academics in Edinburgh. He's best friends with Professor Solómos of Athens University. How much would your partners like an investigation with a man as important as him looking over the shoulders of the police?"

Alistair could see the sense in Catherine's arguments. He also wondered why she was so passionate about the long drink of water.

"You're going to have to inform your partners anyway, why not consult on this Douglas character as well?" Robert suggested.

Catherine said nothing but Alistair could see the tension leave her body. He suspected she would create no further difficulties. He was wrong.

"There is one piece of unfinished business before we move on," Catherine said. The three men looked at her. She walked over to Michael smiling and he stood to take her into his arms. With all the strength in her well-muscled arms, she hit him in the face. As he reeled from the blow, she hit him again, putting all her weight behind the punch. Michael went down on his knees and she kicked him in the stomach.

"Don't hit me again, Michael," she said pleasantly. Then she bent down and whispered, "And stay out of my bed until you're invited back in."

Turning to the room, she said, "I think we can move on now. Perhaps it's time to join the professor and Douglas." Without waiting for an answer, she walked onto the terrace.

Despite the force of Catherine's attack, Michael had been surprised rather than seriously hurt. As he got to his feet, he saw the other two men watching him with unfriendly eyes.

"I think honours are even now, Buchanan," Robert said in a neutral tone. "It would be a big mistake to retaliate." He followed his sister out of the room.

Alistair poured Michael a whisky. "I think we may have underestimated Catherine. I'd give her some space to settle down." The words were friendly enough but Michael caught the warning.

"It would be as well if you went to play grateful father for our librarian friend," Michael replied. "In one thing at least Robert is right. It's high time I reported in to the Shadowman. If you make sure they're all occupied, I'll make contact. We can take things from there."

"Very wise," Alistair said, then he too went out.

Michael rubbed his stinging face. Who would have thought the little cow could be so interesting? What did the Spanish say? Revenge is a dish best served cold. He removed his mobile from his briefcase. It was more than time to report in.

On the terrace Ekaterina had brought out a big dish of meze together with more wine and glasses. Alistair was formally introduced to Douglas and they laughed over their race to rescue a Robert who was obviously in no need of assistance after all.

Later Catherine asked Douglas to show her the old fort. As they walked through the olive trees, she said, "I did not think my father cared about Robert at all. Yet when I think back, all that business with the photographs and letters was just Daddy hiding his pain."

"You're probably right," Douglas soothed, although he was not convinced.

"It would do us all good to have a few days together away from the pressures of his business."

"Yes." Douglas was not sure where this was leading but he would not rush her.

"This can't be very comfortable for you. Stuck in the middle of a family reunion."

Douglas hadn't noticed but agreed anyway.

"I've spoken to my father. He says the best plan would be for you to go back with the boat he hired." She handed him two envelopes. "This is for the guy at Apollonia. It covers the hire of his boat for another two weeks. There is no way we will stay out here for that long, but the moncy should put the old pirate's mind at rest." She hesitated for a moment. "The other one is for you. It's to cover your own expenses getting back and to say thank you for looking after me. Daddy thinks you should go first thing in the morning."

Douglas took the envelopes automatically. Catherine kissed him on the cheek and ran lightly back down the path to the villa. He continued onwards towards the fort, feeling as if he had been kicked in the stomach. What had he expected, a holiday romance? Could he have possibly expected a wealthy, beautiful and athletic girl such as Catherine to be interested in a middle-aged scholar? As he passed a particularly fruitful olive tree, he tore off part of a branch. Eventually he reached the fort. He noticed the signs of recent occupation. Robert in his wanderings, he thought.

On the fortress wall he sat whilst the sky turned purple. The fort enjoyed the rising sun. He threw the olive branch into the sea, hoping that if the virgin goddess could not grant him love then she might bless him with contentment with his celibate life. It would be as well to return home as soon as possible. He looked in the envelopes. The fees for the boat were generous. The money that covered his own services surprised him. On impulse he took out one of the notes and let it flutter after the olive branch. Somewhere deep in the trees an owl hooted. Strangely comforted, Douglas got up and made his way back to the villa.

Chapter Fourteen

Rena wondered why she did not feel more cheerful as the ferry pulled away from the island. The thought of being at home and seeing her mother once more did give her some comfort. The weight on her soul that had turned her last days on Sigandros into a grey misery was still there.

Margaret had obviously noticed because she had carefully asked more than once if it was truly all right to come and stay. Rena had assured her friend with passion that she needed her to come home with her. The strange feelings that had made her want to leave Sigandros so badly had also told her that she wanted Margaret to accompany her to her home.

The journey seemed endless but eventually their ferry manoeuvred its way into the great harbour of Piraeus. They pushed out of the great belly of the ship with the other passengers, avoiding the trucks that seemed oblivious to the human tide around them. The two women ignored the long queues of taxi drivers shouting for trade and made their way towards the buses that would get them to their destination at a fraction of the cost.

Mrs Theoharous, Rena's mother, was tall, thin, white haired and dressed entirely in black. She embraced her daughter briefly, and Margaret could see the traces of bright tears in the muddy brown eyes. Rena's mother was not a well woman. Almost immediately, Mrs Theoharous turned to Margaret, shaking her hand and welcoming her in slow, carefully pronounced Greek.

Margaret was grateful for the courtesy. She replied in the same language, thanking her hostess for allowing her to stay. The flat was neat and sparkling clean. Most of the well-polished surfaces had hand-crocheted mats and runners in intricate patterns. Margaret glanced at the older woman's hands. They were knarled and twisted. She suspected it had been some time since Mrs Theoharous had whiled away the summer evenings with a crochet hook.

On every wall gleamed replicas of the famous icons, the late sun highlighting their elaborate metallic covers. Mrs Theoharous moved with deliberate slowness. Margaret suspected that the arthritis that had twisted the fingers was playing havoc with other joints as well. Discretely hidden in a corner was a heavy ebony cane. Margaret suspected it was used more frequently when Rena was away from home.

After the wonderful luxury of a bath, they changed into clean dresses. They were both a slim size twelve and Rena invited her friend to make free with her wardrobe. Margaret was beginning to feel like a new person. After an evening meal of a wonderful lemon-flavoured lamb casserole, they sat in comfortable armchairs and told tales of their adventures on the campsite.

"Your grandfather once helped on an archaeological dig," Mrs Theoharous reminisced. "He knew George Psychoundakis very well."

Margaret sat up on hearing the name of the famous historian. "How did they meet?" she asked. "How long did your father spend on Crete?"

"Peace, child, it was a long time ago and I have forgotten much. I think I still have some photographs from that time if you are interested."

"I would love to see your photographs." Margaret was enthusiastic. Then she gave an enormous yawn. "I'm dead on my feet tonight, but if I could see them some time before I go, I would be really grateful."

Later, when the two girls had settled between white lavender-scented sheets, Rena said, "You don't have to look at Mitera's old photos."

"I wasn't being polite, well, not just being polite," Margaret protested. "Photography is my speciality, you can learn so much from those old snaps. Some of the early photographers were artists their own right. Depending on what your mother has got, they could make an interesting chapter in my thesis."

"Mitera likes nothing better than to go through the old family albums," Rena told her. "What do you want to do tomorrow? I really should go into the university. Do you want to come with me? You could go into the library whilst I am with my tutor."

"Would you mind very much if I stayed here? I really meant it about those photos. Or do you think it would tire your mother too much?"

"My mother does not get enough company. I think it would do her good." There was more to say but the long day and wonderful comfort quickly brought the great dark wings of sleep.

In the morning, Rena left early. As she went thought the front door, she could hear her mother saying to Margaret, "This is my grandmother on her wedding day. My mother kept the wedding wreaths but I don't know what happened to them. I think my oldest brother's wife took them when our mother died."

Rena had no intention of consulting with her tutor. As far as she knew that lady was spending her summer on Samos and would not be back till the start of term. She felt a little guilty at deceiving her friend, but this was something she felt she had to do and that it was better not to involve anyone else. As she saw the familiar statue of the British Prime Minister Gladstone, Rena felt her heart give a small jump. It was not too late to go back and join in sorting through the family albums. Instead, she quickened her step and walked through the startling Danish-designed façade into the Panepistímio.

The porter knew her well and called a cheerful greeting as she passed his office. Rena waved but did not stop to chat. Instead, she made her way directly to the lifts. Professor Solómos's office was on the third floor at the back. Rena had not called ahead because she wanted to be sure of seeing her former mentor. The old man had a habit of disappearing if he thought that anyone was going to interrupt his work for too long. She had no fears that he would not be in. The students joked that the professor probably did not have a home but slept under his desk when he needed rest.

Rena eventually arrived at the glass-paneled door, knocked briefly and went in. The first room belonged to the secretary and was empty. Mrs. Elytis was also away on a well-deserved summer holiday. At the far side of the secretary's office was another door, solid and firmly shut. Rena did not understand why she felt so nervous. Professor Solómos had never shown her anything but kindness and courtesy. Perhaps it was because she brought him bad news that would disturb his studies and make him sad.

She knocked and entered again. Dionysious Solómos was about sixty. His long white hair and stooped shoulders made him look older than he actually was. On the other hand, his pale skin was clear and his eyes very dark and bright.

"Rena, what are you doing creeping about the campus? I thought you were with my old friend James McKenzie knocking lumps out of Sigandros."

"I was part of the dig at Sigandros, Professor. It has closed. I returned to Athens yesterday. I'm afraid I have some very bad news. I wanted to discuss the matter with you before going to the police."

"The police, that does indeed sound like bad news. Before you tell me anything else, is everyone all right, no illnesses, no accidents?"

"No, as far as I am aware, everyone is fine."

"Then whatever is troubling you is solvable." He turned to the percolator on its hot plate. "Sit down, have a cup of coffee and tell me what is wrong, slowly and carefully from the beginning."

Rena felt an enormous wave of relief. This is what she had longed for since the troubles on Sigandros started to build up. The professor would be able to lift the burden from her shoulders and everything would be dealt with by the proper authorities.

"The problems started when I first went out to Sigandros. Only little things at first but they built up to something very serious."

"Slowly and in order, Rena my dear. I know you would not burst in here for something trivial, so let the story tell itself."

Rena would hardly have called her gentle tap on the door bursting in. She schooled herself, however, and tried for a logical tale.

"I was disappointed from the moment I started work on Sigandros. The site was almost completely exposed and there were far too many of us for the little work there was left to do."

Rena went on to explain more about the site, the arrival of the *Herakles*, the claims and counter claims by Robert, the fishermen, Philip and the professor. She did not know why, because she was now convinced that Robert was as guilty as any of them, but she refrained from mentioning his name. Perhaps that last sunlit meal before all the trouble started still coloured her thoughts.

"There is certainly cigarette smuggling and McKenzie knows about it."

"Professor McKenzie, my dear," Solómos corrected gently.

"I am sure this English professor," Rena nearly spat the word, "has located the temple of Athena and is stripping the site. Then there were accusations of drug smuggling. It all needs investigating properly." Rena was on the edge of tears. "When it all comes out, the university will look so bad and it will not matter that it was all these foreigners who caused the trouble in the first place."

"Calm yourself," Solómos soothed. "You are right, it will not be pleasant, but there has been a seat of learning here in Athens for three thousand years. It will take more than a few greedy men to shake its foundations. Go home now. You can leave everything in my hands. You will be needed as a witness, of course, but I will try to keep your involvement to a minimum."

"That is very good of you, Professor."

"Not at all, I feel partially responsible. After all, it was I who recommended that you join the dig at Sigandros."

Rena picked up her bag and replaced her chair against the wall. With a last smile at her mentor she left the office, not quite closing the door as she left. Her heels clicked on the tiles covering the secretary's office. She opened and closed the outer door with moderate force. Then she slipped off her shoes and padded back to the inner sanctum. She listened at the crack.

The professor was already speaking on the telephone. His voice was almost unrecognizable. Always Solómos had addressed his students in a tone that was soft with an almost old-fashioned courtesy. Now his voice was harsh, hectoring, coarse.

"You bloody fool!" he was yelling. "You call yourself an administrator, you couldn't manage a mussel stall. You would do well to remember you're not the only thieving academic who can shuffle paper. One more mistake and I swear I'll have you and that half-arsed nephew off Sigandros for good."

There was silence for a few minutes then the professor's voice loud once more. "I'll do damage limitation here. You get everyone off that sodding island. If it comes to an inspection I want it looking as untouched as a nun's bum.

"Let Grey go back to Edinburgh, he would be more trouble dead than alive. I want to talk to Robert myself before I say if he's in or out. If anyone objects you can drop them off your famous cliff, him too, it would solve a lot of problems."

Rena had heard enough. Holding her breath, she slid back through the secretary's door. Holding the handle firmly she closed it behind her with only the faintest click.

Back in the office, Solómos had cut off the still squawking McKenzie. He waited a moment then impatiently pushed the buttons on his phone once more.

It was as if she could not feel her feet. Rena found her way back to the street without any memory of how she had got there. She sat on one of the public benches for some time, staring at the passing students without seeing any of them. Finally she got up and began walking swiftly in the direction of the archeological museum. It was a long walk and by the time she saw its neoclassical portals she was feeling calmer. The guardians on the ticket desk nodded her through when they saw her student's card. She walked forward as if going to see the Mycenaen antiquities then slipped down the stairs to the snack bar in the basement. A discrete door at the foot of the stairs locked with a number pad let her into the inner mysteries.

There were offices down here and storerooms. If she remembered correctly the post room and goods receipt section were at the back. It is true in any large organization that if you walk as if you know where you are going no one will ever challenge you. Rena stepped purposefully along the corridors, working at keeping a pleasant smile on her face when she would have preferred to weep.

It was Saturday afternoon and the post room was empty. There had been a dozen cases of artefacts loaded onto the ferry at the same time the students had embarked. Why had she not suspected sooner that there were far too many crates being shipped out for such a barren site? Because Philip and his uncle had dealt with that side of the administration, and she, like everyone else, had been glad to let them.

Goods inward should have received the cases this morning but they would not have had time to do more than log them in. It took more than ten minutes searching but she eventually spotted the red Sigandros stickers on two cases. They were firmly sealed with reinforced tape. She picked at them but succeeded in doing nothing more than breaking a couple of fingernails. She looked round for something to help her. On the posties desk lay a knife with a short sharp blade. A few seconds with the Stanley knife confirmed that they contained the assorted rubble that was currently coming from the site. Neatly labeled and encased in bubble wrap but essentially rubbish nevertheless. In the post book '12' cases had been carefully altered to read '2'. If the entry had not been so fresh no one would have been able to tell there had been an amendment. So where were the rest?

Rena thought for a moment then went to the dispatch area. Here were neat stacks of crates covered in plastic wrapping standing on wooden pallets awaiting pickup on Monday morning. Rena carefully examined each one. On the fourth stack she looked at, the new white Athens University label had not quite covered the original red sticker. She carefully weighed the Stanley knife in her hand. So far she had only done minor damage. A couple of lengths of packaging tape and no one would know that there had been an intruder. If she went further there would be no going back. There was no way she could work the packaging machines on her own.

She sliced through the swathe of plastic wrapping, then before her courage failed slashed open the suspect box. It contained bags of brown granules. She took one and put it in her bag. She thought she might need it to convince the police. They were happy to believe any accusation against students, but the involvement of an internationally respected figure like Professor Solómos was going to take a great deal of proof. It was time to leave. It would have been impossible to cover up her searches even if she wished to. It was better to leave it like this for the police to find. She wondered if she herself might be prosecuted? If she would be allowed to continue her studies when the trials were over? It was far, far too late to worry about any of that.

The post room was an eerie place. The crates and boxes on the steel racking cast odd shadows in the unrelenting sodium light. The great up and over doors were locked. Even the judas door was padlocked; she would have to go back the way she came. She turned towards the exit and felt unbelievable pain in the back of her skull. Then there was nothing but blackness and the echo of the barking of some enormous dog.

Margaret and Mrs. Theoharous were surprised when Rena did not return by lunchtime. They went out to eat barbecued lamb chops and giggled together that Rena was missing the treat. By five o'clock they were seriously worried. Margaret telephoned the university. She was answered by the night porter who assured her that there were no staff or students still in the building. At seven o'clock they telephoned the police, who tried to convince them they were worrying unnecessarily but asked them to keep in touch.

Mrs. Theoharous then started to telephone the hospitals. No woman called Rena Theoharous had been admitted and there were no unknown women victims in any of the casualty wards. At 10 o'clock they phoned the police again. A rather more harassed officer told them it was hardly unusual for a woman in her twenties to be out at this time of night without asking her mother's permission and rang off before they could explain further.

It was just after midnight when the doorbell rang. Margaret rushed to answer the summons, wondering if she would kiss Rena or slap her. On the step were two uniformed officers, a man and a woman. One look at their faces told Margaret all she needed to know. They asked for Mrs. Theoharous.

"We don't want you to worry," said the woman officer. What did they expect them to do? "A woman has been found dead in a hotel room." The officer continued as if reading from a script. "She had your daughter's handbag. From the looks of the woman and the, erm, location of the hotel, the bag could very well have been stolen. Was your daughter in the habit of carrying a great deal of money around with her?"

"I am a widow, my daughter is a student, we don't have a great deal of money," Mrs. Theoharous protested.

The two officers exchanged glances, but said nothing further. Margaret and Mrs. Theoharous were taken by police car to the hospital. Margaret snatched up her bag but Mrs. Theoharous allowed herself to be led out without even picking up her coat. They were taken to the mortuary. The body was lying on a trolley with a white sheet over it. The woman officer gently pulled the sheet away from the dead face. It was Rena.

Her face was bruised and cut. Mrs. Theoharous moaned and swayed. The officer dropped the sheet to catch her. In doing so more of the body was revealed. Margaret tugged the sheet down farther, ignoring the protests from the police. Rena was dressed in a red spandex bustier, black plastic waistcoat and a miniskirt that barely covered her crotch. Not just her face but her whole body seemed to be covered in bruises. There was blood on her legs below the skirt.

The male police officer snatched the sheet back, recovered the body and hustled them away. They were then taken to the police station. A detective in shirtsleeves, his stained tie at half-mast, took notes on a yellow legal pad. He might be taking notes but he was certainly not listening.

"For the tenth time," Margaret protested, "Rena did not own any clothes like the ones that were on her body."

"You knew the deceased well, did you?"

"We were friends for almost a year when she was living in Edinburgh and we have just spent ten weeks together on the island of Sigandros."

"Have you ever visited her home before?"

"No, this was the first time."

"Then you are not really in a position to know what clothes she owned."

"But her mother has told you."

"Well, in my experience, girls don't tell their mothers everything."

"We only returned from the dig yesterday or the day before or whatever the hell the time is."

"Then she would have needed money."

"Rena was a respectable hard-working student. She was not a prostitute."

"*Ne, i despinis*. Yes, miss," the detective said without conviction. "How do you account for the fact that she had 2000 Euros in her possession when she was found?"

"I can't account for it."

"There was also a sachet of cocaine."

"Rena didn't even drink very much, she never used drugs. Have you done a blood test?"

"That will be up to the magistrate, miss."

"At the moment it looks like a clear case of an illegal association that went wrong."

"Rena was a virgin."

"You know that for a fact, miss? How do you explain the hotel manager telling us she was one of his regulars?"

"It's not true, it can't be true."

"You don't want it to be true. Now look, miss, you've given your statement. It will all be taken into account. The old lady looks as if she's going to pass out. Why don't you take her home?"

"We came in a police car."

"We don't run a taxi service, miss. You'll have to see to that yourselves. There is a public telephone by the front desk."

Margaret searched in her bag. Her change purse was there with a few Euros but her wallet with all her cards and money was in her bedroom at the Theoharous's flat. To her horror she realised she probably did not have enough in her purse to pay for a taxi. She knew something about Athenian taxi charges.

She did what she should have done in the beginning and broke down in tears. Not the delicate crystal drops of a film actress but deep wracking sobs and floods of stinging tears that reddened her eyes and made her nose run. Satisfied by what he thought of as proper feminine behaviour, the detective thought a police car might be made available if they were prepared to wait. The uniformed officer on the front desk had more compassion for the grey-faced old woman who looked at death's door herself and the still-weeping girl. Within half an hour they were back home.

Margaret offered to help Mrs. Theoharous into bed.

"No, my dear, I could not sleep. I will stay here in my chair. It's easier for me. I need to think and pray."

Just before Margaret left the room, she heard the older woman whisper, "She was a good girl." Margaret also heard just a trace of doubt in the quavery voice. She went up to the room she had shared with Rena and lay down on her own bed, not bothering to take off her clothes. She saw again the battered face of her friend. In her mind she rehearsed the interview with the police. Trying to think what she should have said, could have said, how she might have convinced them.

Mrs. Theoharos turned off the lamp. In the darkness she could not see the photographs of her daughter or the small gifts Rena had sent home during her travels. Rena had been modest and religious. Her relatives in Edinburgh had sent back good reports of hard work and regular habits. Yet when a young girl went away there were temptations, and a cousin with a business and family of her own to take care of could not be expected to take a mother's care of her daughter.

In the silent small hours of the morning, small sounds are magnified. The endless round of unanswered questions in her brain was interrupted by a scratching sound and whispering at the front door.

Mrs. Theoharous reached for the heavy stick by her chair and painfully manoeuvred herself to her feet and shuffled silently across the carpet to stand by the door. Overpowering grief and anger left no room for fear in her mind. She had sat so long in the dark that she had perfect night vision. By the light from the street lamp she could see the handle to the sitting room turn slowly then the door begin to crack open. The minimal light in the room gleamed on the polished metal of a gun. The dark shape of a head cautiously peered into the opening.

The old woman brought her stick down on the skull with a sickening crack. Her victim screamed and the gun fell from his fingers. Mrs. Theoharos threw herself to the floor, the pain from her arthritic knees and ankles causing her to join their own screams to those of her victim. Despite her agony she scooped up the gun and fired it. There was a streak of fire and a loud popping sound. The unseen second man grabbed his friend and within seconds the hall was empty and the front door swinging on its hinges.

Margaret came down the stairs at a run and helped the groaning Mrs. Theoharous to her feet.

"We must call the police."

"*Ohi*, no more police. They can hardly stir themselves for murder, what do you think they will do about a damaged front door?"

"But they had guns, and what if they come back?"

"They will not come back tonight and by tomorrow night there will be so many people here they would trip over the bodies in the hall. Take that wretched thing and get rid of it. Then go to bed."

Mrs. Theoharous handed over the pistol, ugly with the heavy

silencer over the muzzle. The she freed herself from Margaret's grasp and hobbled to the bureau, where she poured herself a large glass of brandy.

"Go," she hissed.

Margaret could see the old woman's face was streaked with tears of pain. She went out. The street was empty. She walked for a couple of blocks then pushed the pistol into the heart of an overflowing rubbish bin.

On her return, Margaret called to ask if Mrs. Theoharous was all right, if she needed any help, but there was only silence.

Margaret returned to her room to wonder what she should do and rehearse again her memories of the night's events. It was not until around dawn that she began to wonder if the bizarre happenings of the night have something to do with the events on Sigandros.

Relatives started to arrive with the dawn. They had been summoned by Mrs. Theoharous's neighbours the night before when they saw her being taken away by police car. Very soon it became obvious to Margaret that she could no longer be of help to her friend's mother. In fact, she was now very much in the way. Sadly, she kissed the old lady goodbye.

"I am so very, very sorry," she said

Mrs. Theoharous hardly seemed to hear her

"Please let me know when the funeral will be. I would like to send flowers."

"*Ne, ne,* yes, yes." Mrs. Theoharous rocked to and fro, holding herself as if to contain her pain.

Margaret knew she would not be told. The old lady probably never wanted to see or hear from her again. She picked up her bags and headed for the bus stop. She desperately wanted to go home, but it was probably not a good idea to try to change her flight ticket on a Sunday when most of the offices would be closed. Now that she had retrieved her wallet with the rest of her things from Rena's flat she could afford to stay one night in a cheap hotel and head out for the airport in the morning.

The Olympia near the archaeological museum looked clean, quiet and had a tourist rate price within her budget. Margaret completed the formalities with the manager then went straight up to her room, intending to lie down for a while. Sleep, however, would not come to blot out her pain. She thought about her friend. They had promised one another they would go to the archaeological museum. Rena had said she would try to get permission to see some of the Sigandros artefacts that were not on show. Who was it she was going to ask, Solomon? No Solómos.

Margaret thought again about Rena's last day. She was going to see her tutor. What was the woman's name? Mrs. Paradissis, that was it. Keen woman to be in her office on a Saturday morning for students and in the vacation too. Why had Rena not come back to her mother's house? Had she mentioned where she was going next to her tutor? Margaret sat up on the bed. The porter's lodge might have a contact number for the tutors; it was worth a try.

Margaret made her way down to the reception desk and asked to borrow the telephone directory. There was something like a dozen different numbers for the university. She thanked the manager and on impulse decided to walk down to the university buildings. It might be better to try to get the information she needed in person. She ran back up to her room and took out of her case the photo she had of Rena taken in front of Edinburgh's Holyrood Palace. She had brought it as a gift for Mrs. Theoharous, then forgotten to give it to her. She had chosen it because it was the best of the snaps they had taken when Rena was in Scotland. It should jog a few memories even if they did not remember Rena by name.

The security guard at the university was bored. It was a lousy job at the best of times. Now he didn't know which was worse, being alone in the marble palace guarding nothing more than several tons of boring writing, or being at the beck and call of the useless wankers during the day. Both staff and students liked to have the porters running around like blue-arsed flies if they would let them. It made a nice change when the pretty little thing with the red hair came tapping on the booth window and asked politely in passable Greek if she could have a word.

"Excuse me, but were you on duty yesterday afternoon?"

"No, and I'm off duty tonight as well," he leered.

"I'm looking for my friend," Margaret improvised rapidly. The guard looked the type who would probably clam up if she said Rena had been murdered. "She told me she was coming to see her tutor, but we seem to have missed each other. I wondered if someone had seen her or you could let me have a telephone number for Mrs. Paradissis."

"There are very few of the staff about at this time of year. The lazy buggers are all on holiday, I wish I was. Your friend has probably given you the slip, darling."

Margaret fought down an urge to slap the moron. Instead she smiled and looked into his eyes. "I would be so grateful if you could help me." Margaret deliberately made her voice softer.

The guard had heard about foreign girls, he could be onto a good thing, and he had nothing else to do.

"*Endaksi*, what was the name of this tutor?"

"Mrs. Paradissis."

He made a show of looking through his records. "Mrs. Paradissis was not in yesterday. In fact, the contact number for her is in Samos."

"Does everyone have to sign in and out?"

"Well, they're supposed to, but if we know someone well we'll just wave them through."

"Is there a signature for Rena Theoharous, say between nine and ten yesterday?"

"No, there's just the cleaners and old Professor Solómos."

"Who was on duty yesterday?"

The guard looked up at the rota pinned to a corkboard. "Demos Christou."

"Do you think we could give him a ring, ask if he saw my friend?"

The guard pretended to think. Demos had been at a wedding party last night. It might be fun to wake him up and increase his hangover. "Don't see why not."

Demos, in fact, was no big drinker; he answered the phone cheerfully, much to the younger man's disappointment. Yes, he had seen Rena Theoharous. She had gone up to see that dry old stick Solómos and left about eleven o'clock.

Margaret urgently needed to think. She gave the guard another big smile but then turned on her heel and was out of the building before the randy character could put any moves on her.

The guard lit another cigarette and blew smoke at the photo of Miss August on the wall calendar.

Margaret chose the same bench to do her thinking as Rena had the previous day. Why had her friend told her she was going to see her tutor when the woman was apparently in Samos? Had she meant to go and see Solómos all along or was it just on impulse when she found her tutor was not in? Where had Rena gone after she had left the university? Why had she died?

Eventually, unable to answer her own questions and tense with sorrow and worry, Margaret got up and started walking. A street sign pointed to the archaeological museum. Margaret felt her throat close and tears start, thinking of the innocent plans that would now never be fulfilled. She walked slower; they were going to see the material from Sigandros. It was worth a try. Quickening her pace once more, Margaret headed for the museum.

The museum was busy. Free entry on a Sunday meant that it was a popular destination for family outings. Middle-class parents trying to drum some culture into their reluctant children. It was as if they thought that knowledge could be absorbed simply by proximity to the great artefacts without any attempt to explain their history or significance. The security staff on duty had no recollection of seeing Rena and were disinclined to be helpful. Margaret wandered aimlessly round the galleries for a while, then went to the basement for a cup of coffee.

She saw the door to the staff-only section of the building and wondered briefly where it led. She dismissed the thought. Even if she could get past the keypad she had no idea where to go or what to look for. She thought for the hundredth time, why had Rena not confided in her?

Margaret wondered what to do with herself for the rest of the day. She found a public telephone and tried to get in contact with the detective who had interviewed her on the previous night. He was not available. The colleague to whom she was eventually put through had an accent so thick she could hardly understand a word he said. She gathered that there was no further news on the case. She could tell from the tone, if not from the words, that the man was not particularly interested. As she was neither a witness nor a suspect there was no objection to her returning to England. Margaret found herself shouting 'Scotia' to the dialling tone.

It was Margaret's last day in Greece, possibly forever, certainly for a long time to come. She took the bus to the Acropolis and spent the rest of the afternoon amongst the ruins of the temples to Athena, making unformed prayers that the warrior goddess would guard the soul of Rena Theoharous and somehow bring her killers to justice.

Chapter Fifteen

Professor McKenzie tried very hard to make the evening a success. He instructed Ékaterina to work her magic in the kitchen and gave her money to buy whatever she needed from the village. He brought out the finest wines from his personal cellar. He told funny stories of academic life, but for all his efforts the dinner was a rather stilted affair.

Douglas excused himself early, saying he had had an exhausting few days and would need to be up early in the morning. No one tried to persuade him to stay. Once they were sure he had retired for the night, Michael signalled them all to go with him into the study.

"I have spoken to the Shadowman," he began.

"Who the hell is the Shadowman?" Robert interrupted him.

"It's the code name for the person who directs this operation," Michael said a little stiffly. He himself had always been uncomfortable with the pseudonym.

"Good God, it's a bit Boys Own Paper, isn't it?"

"If you don't like it, you can tell the man so yourself. We understand the Shadowman is a member of the elite in Athenian society. Those who get too nosy about his identity have all ended up dead, some extremely messily. This racket works and brings in a nice little earner for us all, as far I'm concerned he can call himself Monkey's Arse if he wants to." Michael's face was flushed.

"Okay, okay, keep your shorts on." Robert was surprised at

the outburst but said no more.

"The word is that Grey can go. We just have to ensure he gets the first plane back to Edinburgh. I suggest that Catherine goes with him."

"No, you're not getting rid of me as easily as that."

Michael ignored her. "The Shadowman wants to talk to you, Robert, before he agrees to you being in or out. We'll set up a secure link via the professor's computer tomorrow night. He also wants to talk to you, Professor, about opening the Athena site."

McKenzie looked pleased.

Michael added nastily, "The Shadowman says he has not yet decided if it will be opened or who will run the site if it is rediscovered." McKenzie looked as if Christmas had been cancelled.

"I think our Michael is doing a bit of editing," Catherine stated. "If Shadowfax or whoever wants to speak with Robert before he's made a member of the gang then he'll want to speak with me too. If I'm off babysitting Douglas it will be assumed I'm not interested and Michael gets rid of me. Well, not so fast, lover boy." She then turned to McKenzie. "Do you really think that it would be that easy to replace you? I've learned a lot from Douglas in these last few days. The archaeological world is not that large. Who do you know has sufficient eminence to run a site like the new Athena temple and keep the current scams going? You'll have to do quite a bit of work covering up the fact you have already been working the site. I think you're safe enough for the moment."

She did not add that if the mysterious boss did have a tame academic in mind then the best way to bring him in would be for the good professor to have a fatal accident. Well, he could work that one out for himself if he was as bright as he pretended to be. "I'm not going," Catherine finished.

No one seemed inclined to argue and shortly after they all drifted off to their own rooms. McKenzie and Catherine had rooms to themselves, but Alistair had to share with Michael, and Robert was in the room allocated to Douglas. When Robert carefully opened the door he was surprised to find Douglas still up. He was sitting in the dark by the open french windows, a glass of wine in his hand.

"It's very beautiful here," Douglas said without turning round. "I'll be sorry to leave in the morning."

"I'm sure Catherine will be sorry to see you go. You've been a good friend to her."

"I wonder," Douglas replied, but said no more.

In the early hours, Robert woke. He could just see the outline of Douglas still sitting by the window.

Next morning Douglas seemed bright enough. He thanked the professor for his hospitality, joked about being an uninvited guest yet again. Was given obviously false assurances that he was welcome back at any time and ushered onto the yacht in the harbour. He was waved away and Michael continued to watch until the little boat disappeared from view.

Douglas, too, stared back at the land until it was completely out of sight. Then he spoke to the crew. His polite manner and excellent Greek appealed to them. He offered a generous bonus if they would take a small deviation by way of the uninhabited island just north of Sigandros. This was more like it. They looked at the money in the envelope Douglas offered. If the crazy foreigner wanted to explore every rock from here to Milos he was free to do so. They consulted their charts. Douglas noted they were as up to date and as detailed as the ones Catherine had purchased, if a little more salt stained. They worked out together the most likely landing site.

In the end it was so easy. They anchored in a tiny sheltered cove and one of the crew rowed Douglas across in the dinghy. Promising not to be more than a couple of hours, Douglas set off up a faint track. The remains of the temple were on top of a small hill in the centre of the island. A group of green bushes marked the existence of a small spring of brackish water. The outlines of the temple and auxiliary buildings were clear. Years and the movement of the earth in this unstable part of the world had toppled most of the columns. They had been covered by layers of dust and flying sand. On the other hand this tiny island had never had a permanent population and the ruins had not been converted into barns nor the stones used to build houses.

Using a handkerchief, he gently brushed the dust off the corner of a block of marble. He had worked on enough archaeological sites to realise this was not the dust of antiquity but far more recently applied. He moistened the cotton square from the bottle of water he carried. The colours of a bright mosaic appeared as if by magic. Details of a warrior's helmet were followed by the wise and beautiful eyes of the goddess. Douglas stared at them and tears appeared in his own eyes. Such beauty as this should not be the subject of sordid trading. Scholars should have the opportunity to study it. More important even than that, it should be preserved for posterity and available to every citizen of the world to see freely.

Reluctantly Douglas recovered the beautiful face. "I swear to you, Pallas Athena Parthenos, that I will bring these vandals to justice and deliver your relics into worthier hands." Douglas turned and began to walk back towards the boat. His eyes were still full of the wonders he had seen when a strand of vine caught his boot and he fell headlong. The slope of the hill accelerated his fall and his outstretched arms ploughed into the sandy soil. Winded but not really hurt, Douglas remained still for a moment. Then rising to his knees his hand curled round a smooth stone. He looked briefly at the piece of marble, intending to toss it away. Then he saw that it was not perfectly smooth but had subtle carvings. The outline of a stylised owl looked solemnly back at him. In antiquity the owl had been the messenger of Athena. Douglas put the tiny trophy in his pocket, dusted himself down and returned to the boat. Within minutes the crew set sail and they were on their way to Milos.

Douglas stayed that night with Pandélis and his family. They were curious as to why Douglas had returned alone but were too well mannered to ask. They suspected a quarrel as their old friend was unusually quiet and ate and drank little. The boat owner grumbled about the unexpected extended hire, claiming he had important clients waiting. Douglas did not pay too much attention as he had seen the gleam in the old bandit's eyes when he counted the money.

Next day Douglas flew to Athens. As the small plane soared into the sun-filled sky he began to seriously consider what he would do next. He had a sudden longing to go home. To be amongst his own familiar things and in his own country. He would take the first available flight for the UK out of Athens. He had the return half of the open ticket Catherine had purchased from Edinburgh to Athens. If necessary he would upgrade it. Alistair McFarlane's money would take care of that. He reasoned it would be easier to start contacting the authorities from his own secure home base than as a foreigner in a city where he knew very few people of importance.

As soon as Douglas had collected his bags he walked over to the departure area, remembering the scramble he and Catherine had had when their great adventure was just beginning. There was a small queue at the BA ticket desk. A young woman with vivid ginger hair was arguing with the clerk. Her Greek was a little ungrammatical but perfectly understandable. The manicured attendant was pretending not to understand and replying in far less precise English that whatever was being requested was not possible.

Eventually the girl turned away from the desk. She seemed as if she was going to cry. Douglas looked at her again. He knew her, Ginger McDonald; no, she did not like to be addressed as Ginger although that's what most people called her. Margaret McDonald, that was it. She was taking an arts degree. He had seen her in the library and she had once consulted him on the draping of a peplos tunic for a photographic project.

Without giving much thought to his actions, Douglas awkwardly turned his luggage trolley and set off after her.

"Margaret, Margaret," he called.

She turned and he saw that she looked absolutely dreadful. The skin of her face was tight on her bones and her eyes puffy and red with prolonged weeping. Whatever the trouble, it had not been caused by the altercation at the ticket desk.

"Dr. Grey." She tried to smile. "What a small world."

Suddenly Douglas could not think what to say. Her problems, after all, were no business of his. He opened his mouth to make some equally commonplace remark that would allow them both to politely drift apart again. What he did say was, "Come and have a drink."

"It's only ten o'clock in the morning," she protested.

"Best time," he said shortly. He loaded all their luggage on to one trolley, pulled gently on her arm and headed for the bar. Suddenly everything seemed to be far too much for Margaret and she was glad to follow the tall figure of the librarian through the crowd and leave off thinking for herself at least for a little while. Douglas courteously seated her at a table by a window then went off to the counter. A few minutes later he returned with a bottle of the dry white wine of Santorini, a couple of glasses and a plate of olives. He seated himself and pulled from his pocket a couple of packets of salty biscuits that he proceeded to open.

As he poured the wine into the glasses, he said simply, "Tell me."

"Rena's dead, she's been murdered."

Whatever Douglas expected, it was not that. The irreverent thought drifted into his brain that he was glad he followed his instincts and purchased a bottle of wine. This was more than a one glass problem. "Rena, the little dark girl from Athens? How, why?"

"We had agreed to spend the summer together on the archaeological dig on Sigandros." Margaret told the whole unhappy story. "I traced her as far as the university but not where she went from there. There did not seem to be anything else I could do and so I decide to go home, the police said I could."

"So what was the problem at the ticket desk?"

"The bitch said I could not change my ticket. If I want to leave now I will have to pay full standard fare. I can't afford that much money. Neither can I afford to stay in a hotel in Greece for a month. I can't inflict myself on Mrs. Theoharous, not at a time like this. I don't know what to do."

Slow fat tears started to roll down her cheeks. Douglas automatically fished out his handkerchief. It was filthy with the dust he had cleaned off the mosaic. Margaret snatched at it with gratitude. Any port in a storm he presumed. Sigandros and Solómos, this was more than coincidence. Whilst Margaret cleaned herself up, Douglas sipped his wine and thought.

"Two problems here," he said at last

"Only two?" Margaret produced a watery smile.

"Unless you want to solve world poverty and international conflict here and now, two," Douglas replied gravely. "You said Professor McKenzie had found places for the other students?"

"Yes, but I had been invited to stay with Rena and didn't need a place."

"That was then, this is now. The professor still has a responsibility for your safety." Douglas pulled out his mobile phone and tapped in a number. He hoped Margaret would not realise he was simply selecting numbers at random. He told the number unobtainable signal of Margaret's problem. Said yes, no and of course, several times then put the phone away. "That's problem one settled. The dig will fund your stay in Athens for another week. The professor thinks, as I do, that you really ought to go and see the police again. Meanwhile, he has authorised me to help you with your ticket problem. There may well be a small fee for changing your flight date but to say you must purchase a standard ticket is rubbish. When the time comes I'll ask to see the manager at the BA offices in the city." Thank the goddess for Alistair's money, he thought privately.

Margaret looked at him astonished. "Professor McKenzie ran the dig on a shoestring. There was never any money to spare."

"The professor thinks he may have located the temple of Athena," Douglas improvised wildly. "He now has far more substantial backing from the university. Anyway, Rena was one of his students. He feels a personal interest in the matter."

Margaret could accept personal interest but she doubted that it was the professor's. Yet Dr. Grey had hardly known who Rena was and her own path had only briefly crossed that of the scholar. She could not believe this was an attempt at seduction. There were far less expensive chat-up lines.

"What's going on?" she demanded. "This is not making any sense."

"Perhaps I should try the truth. I've dealt in facts for so long fiction does not come easily."

Margaret nodded and reached for her own wine. Douglas

was right about one thing; it did go down well in the morning.

"I have just returned myself from the island of Sigandros."

Margaret nearly choked on her drink. Douglas went on to tell her about the chase to rescue Robert and the almost farcical outcome.

"If, however, you put our two stories together then it suddenly stops being funny and starts being very serious indeed. I also begin to wonder about the role of Professor Solómos. His name is cropping up rather too often."

"So what do you want to do?"

"Go back to the police. I've no desire to play Sherlock Holmes. I think that we may find the authorities are slightly more interested in our joint stories than they were in the mugging of one humble student."

Margaret bridled a bit at this statement then her shoulders slumped as she admitted its truth. "Do you mean to go to the police right now?"

Douglas looked at his watch. It was half past eleven. "Let's book into a hotel, a different one from the one where you spent last night. Alistair's money will stretch to something more upmarket. Then let's have some lunch and go over what we know one more time then we will try to get hold of the detective who first interviewed you. Do you remember his name?"

"Andros Pavlides. His name was on the door of his office in both Greek and European characters."

"Do you know his rank?" Douglas was curious. That seemed a bit excessive for a run-of-the-mill police officer.

"No, he never told us."

Douglas said no more but led the way to the taxi rank. There was some prolonged negotiation before a price was agreed to take them to the Electra Palace hotel. When Douglas demanded two single rooms the receptionist allocated them rooms not only on different floors but also in different wings of the building.

"Quick wash and brush up I think," Douglas stated cheerfully. "I'll meet you back here in reception in half an hour."

As they ate lunch in the charming garden restaurant, they

went over what they knew and the suppositions that arose from those facts. "Rena told me she was going to see her tutor," Margaret said. "But she must have known the woman was on holiday in Samos, so I think it was Professor Solómos she wanted to see all along."

"Why the secrecy?"

"She was very upset by what had happened on Sigandros. I think she wanted to consult privately before doing anything. It was Solómos who had arranged for her to spend the summer on the island."

"So she consults and according to the porter on duty leaves alone and as far as we know perfectly all right."

"Yes."

"You knew her well," mused Douglas.

At that point Margaret interrupted, "She was the most honest, well-behaved, modest young woman you could ever meet. We were close friends for the best part of a year in Edinburgh and lived side by side for six weeks on Sigandros. I know she was neither promiscuous nor took drugs." Margaret was shouting by the time she had finished and other diners turned to look at her.

Douglas said nothing, his gentle eyes hurt and concerned. Only when Margaret had finally fallen silent did he say, "I wondered if you had any feeling for where she might have gone next."

Margaret felt her eyes fill up with tears again. She muttered a muffled, "Excuse me," and fled for the ladies' room. It took her a long while to calm down. Eventually she had to emerge. When Douglas saw her, he signalled a waiter who immediately brought her a pot of tea.

The gesture nearly brought on a fresh flood of tears. Douglas, however, launched into a long rambling story about his time in Athens as a student. By the time both the story and the tea were finished, Margaret was once more in control of her emotions.

"Have you thought about where Rena might have gone after the university?"

"I did think of the archaeological museum. The attendants

there were too busy to bother with me, and the place is so huge the chances of Rena being seen and remembered are very small."

"Still, to make our case complete before we go to see Detective Pavlides it might be an idea to check out the museum once more."

They took a taxi to the museum. It was far less crowded than on the previous day. Douglas introduced himself to the attendants. They were far more polite to the distinguished scholar from Britain who was a friend of Professor Solómos than they had been to the scruffy student, but they still could not help. "So many people came and went," the attendant told them seriously. "No one could remember them all."

There was a further exchange of compliments and small talk then Douglas drifted off. He had been to the museum many times. He tried to make the opportunity for a visit every time he flew in or out of Athens. He had also studied the outlay of the place on his Greek language website. Unconsciously he followed the path Rena had taken, heading for the Mycenean Hall then descending to the coffee shop. Margaret followed, puzzled but trusting, at least for the time being.

Douglas stood in front of the keypad to the staff-only section of the basement. He tried a combination; nothing happened, though, for a moment then he tried a second set of numbers. The door yielded to his touch. They passed through.

Margaret started to ask how he had known the code but was silenced by a gentle finger on her lips. "Later," he mouthed. "Whatever I say, back me up, okay?"

Margaret nodded.

It was as if Douglas had an internal compass or an invisible thread of Theseus. Occasionally they met members of the legitimate staff. Douglas greeted them amiably and walked on, chatting to Margaret about some party he had attended and how drunk old Andreas had been, whoever he was. The sheer effrontery of the man got them through unchallenged.

Eventually they arrived in the storage rooms and goods received section of the building. A man in a brown coat was writing in a ledger. Douglas dodged behind one of the racks, pulling Margaret with him. "Keep him busy," Douglas hissed.

Margaret's mind went blank and she could feel her knees shaking, but she walked forward and approached the warehouseman. She smiled and said, "*Kalimera sas*, good afternoon." She was greeted by a frown. She was reminded of old Bob Jacks who was the mailman back at Edinburgh University. Perhaps storemen were the same the world over. She remembered some of the tricks that tutors who should have known better tried to play on students.

"I'm new here." Margaret tried another smile. It wasn't working. "I've just joined the art department. My supervisor has sent me down for a glass hammer."

She was rewarded with a torrent of Greek out of which she managed to understand that he was a busy man who did not have time for idiotic jokes. If she had the brains of a something or other she would have realised she was the butt of a joke. There came a much longer tirade on the stupidity of students in general, of women students in particular, and she suspected of herself above all others. The man was just running down and beginning to reach for the telephone when Douglas arrived on the scene.

He made a graceful apology to the still red-faced attendant, addressed a few harsh words to herself that had her gasping realistically, placed a large denomination Euro note under the ledger and propelled Margaret out of the side door and into the sunshine. They walked at top speed to the front of the building then jumped into a taxi, Douglas for once omitting to do the preliminary negotiations on the cost of the journey.

They were both trembling and near to tears. If this is how criminals feel it's a wonder there aren't more honest people in the world, Douglas thought.

He directed the taxi to the Plaka, the maze of streets at the foot of the Acropolis. Douglas paid the man without quibbling but also without a tip then led Margaret through the narrow alleyways to a pleasant-looking café. It was not until they were seated behind cups of Greek coffee and large glasses of brandy that Douglas consented to explain.

"You did remarkably well. My congratulations, Miss McDonald."

The old-fashioned formality seemed so ridiculously funny that Margaret genuinely smiled for the first time in days.

"As fellow conspirators I think you can call me Margaret, Dr. Grey."

"Then I am, of course, Douglas, my dear young lady." They both smiled.

"I was there but I'm damned if I know what went on. Why don't you explain it to me in words of one syllable, starting with how you got into the basement."

"When a lot of people have to use the same code, administrators tend to use a number everyone will remember. I first tried 1940. When the Greeks said *ohi* or no and repulsed the Italian invasion of Epiros. That did not work so I thought again about where we were and tried 490, the date the Persians were defeated at Marathon and presto we were in. I knew in theory were the stores were, so all I had to do was head in that general direction. If anyone had stopped me I had a story ready, but as you saw no one bothered about us." Douglas cradled his brandy glass, staring into the amber liquid as if it were a crystal ball. "I believe that if Rena had come to the museum then she, too, would have been headed for the stores and would have had no difficulty getting through the basement. In all probability she wanted to see if the delivery from Sigandros was still about."

"You did not believe that it would still be there for us to find?" Margaret was incredulous.

"No, it will be well secreted away by this time. I did think that if Rena had been attacked in the warehouse then there would still be traces. I could not believe these characters would be ace cleaners."

"So did you find anything?"

"Yes, I looked for a recently scrubbed piece of floor then looked for cracks or edges which might still contain traces of blood." Douglas produced his much-abused handkerchief, which now had a number of dark red flakes attached.

Douglas finished his brandy. "It's time to go to see the police again, my dear."

A uniformed officer ushered them into the detective's office.

Margaret immediately felt the change in atmosphere. They were treated with courtesy, politely requested to sit and asked if they wanted coffee. Was this just the presence of the eminent Dr. Grey or had something happened that made her more important than the grieving friend who would not immediately agree to their instant theories?

The policeman Margaret had seen on her last visit to the station was wearing a jacket and his spotless tie was carefully knotted. He approached with hand extended. "My name is Andros Pavlides," he said, then turned to Margaret. "Of course, you and I have met before."

"Yes," said Margaret, refusing to be charmed, "but this is the first time you have given me the courtesy of your name."

The smile didn't even flicker. "I am so glad to see you again, Miss McDonald." He actually looked pleased. "We sought for you at the airport but you seemed to have vanished."

"Looked for me?" Margaret was surprised. "I was told I could leave when I last contacted your office."

"Yes, that was an error."

Margaret saw the expression on the detective's face and felt sorry for the unknown officer.

"We have some further information for you, but you also seem to need to speak to Miss McDonald again. Would you care to go first?" Douglas was all charm.

"And you, sir, are?" The detective looked down his rather long nose. It was a practised expression.

"I am Dr. Douglas Marcus Antonius Grey, principal of the classical history section of the Scottish Library. I have recently been a guest of Professor McKenzie, the archaeologist on the island of Sigandros. The island lately vacated by Miss McDonald and the late Miss Rena Theoharous."

Part of Margaret wanted to laugh at the pomposity, but she was also impressed by the academic authority Douglas seemed to be able to put on like a cloak.

Douglas smiled and waved a negligent hand. "Please, Detective, go ahead."

"You were more persuasive than you thought, Miss McDonald." The detective smiled again at Margaret who remained stony faced. "I asked the pathologist to give the body of Miss Theoharos priority. The first thing the doctor noticed was that all the injuries except the blow to the back of the head that killed the young woman were inflicted post mortem. In the case of a frenzied attack, the murderer might go on hitting the victim after striking the fatal blow but this was too much." The detective began to look uncomfortable. "There was considerable damage to the vagina and sexual organs, but our doctor was able to establish that the rupture of the hymen was recent. In other words, Rena was indeed a virgin at the moment of death if not for very long afterwards. The magistrate then gave us permission to do blood tests.

"There was cocaine in the nostrils and traces of gin in the mouth." Margaret started to protest. Douglas put his hand on her arm. The detective nodded and continued. "There was no trace of either drug or alcohol in the victim's blood. That, too, had been applied after death. We were not dealing with the sadly common occurrence of the death of a prostitute during the course of her illegal activities, but the murder and callous disfigurement of an innocent girl."

Margaret felt enormous relief that Rena had been vindicated, then anger that the murder of a prostitute was considered almost a legitimate hazard of the profession.

"In the light of these findings we wished to interview you again. It was only then that we discovered that you had been given permission to return to England."

"Scotland," snapped Margaret.

"I am glad to see you changed your mind in any case," soothed the detective. "Now, please, what is this information you have for us?"

Douglas looked at Margaret who said, "Go ahead."

"The short story is that Rena Theoharous had become aware of illegal activities on the island of Sigandros. I have also found out about them by a quite different route. I believe Miss Theoharous went to confide in her mentor Professor Solómos of Athens University and that led directly to her death."

The detective looked bewildered. "Dr. Grey, I think this might make more sense if you told me the long story."

Douglas removed his coat, pulled his chair up to the desk and rested his head on his long sensitive fingers. "It all started the day I received notice to quit on my flat."

With the memory and logical mind of the scholar, Douglas went through his story, ending with his meeting with Margaret in the airport.

He then asked Margaret to tell her story, starting with the arrival of Robert on Sigandros. Margaret was more emotional. The thought of Rena in those relatively carefree days nearly broke her heart. Discrete questioning and Douglas's arm around her shoulder gave her the support she needed to get through the narrative.

Finally, Douglas took up the story once more. Skirting past the method he had used to get into the storage area of the museum, Douglas produced the dry brown flakes on his grubby hankie. Detective Pavlides thought privately that any DNA must be hopelessly compromised but he transferred the rag to a plastic evidence bag nevertheless. He wanted a big favour of the scholar and did not want to antagonise him.

"What you are telling me has Professor Solómos at the centre of the business, like a spider in a web."

Douglas and Margaret agreed.

"Unfortunately, there is no hard evidence, only conjecture and coincidence. To arrest and in particular to convict we need something a little more concrete." Detective Pavlides began to explain his plan.

Chapter Sixteen

Professor Solómos fiddled with the small statue of Pan that usually stood on the corner of his desk. Things were coming unravelled. Too many people were involved, too much attention being paid to what should have been an insignificant island so small and uninteresting that it would never even be listed in the guide books.

If he was honest he was not without blame himself. He had been too dependent on others. It was all very well being the mysterious Shadowman but there came a time when it was necessary for a leader to lead. It was not always possible to remain in the shadows and obscurity. What he needed was someone younger, active, with a keen mind. Someone who could take direction but also had initiative, a person for whom he could be the grey eminence.

He had almost drifted into a business that now had an annual turnover of millions. His wife had developed a particularly unpleasant type of cancer. He had needed a lot of money in a hurry for operations, a private nursing home and expensive chemotherapy. An academic salary is not generous and living a society life in Athens did not leave much for savings.

The storerooms of the university were stuffed with antiquities that had been catalogued and forgotten. They added little to the store of classical knowledge and were of minor artistic importance, yet collectors would pay a fortune for them. He had had a discrete enquiry some years before that he had rejected with scorn. It had been time to renew the connection.

By the time Maria had mercifully died, Solómos had developed a taste for intrigue. The money was no longer of primary importance. As the millions grew in his Swiss bank account, he thought vaguely about setting up an academic foundation or charitable trust. The real thrill had been the creation of the Shadowman empire and outwitting those fools in authority.

It was almost as if it had been meant. The venal McKenzie, whose appetites exceeded his income, had discovered the temple of Athena. With whom did he share his discovery? Why the eminent Professor Solómos. This had meant that Solómos could stop the risky plundering of his own university. There was a virgin field absolutely teeming with artefacts. Then when his contacts in Turkey had wanted to start to move drugs, he had met the greedy Michael at a civic function and knew this was a man he could use. Alistair with his soap factory had been an unexpected bonus. So it went on.

Then a couple of boozy fishermen had started a chain of events that threatened to bring the empire tumbling round his ears. Solómos looked again at the tiny god of chaos in his hands. He regretted the death of Rena Theoharos. It had been noisy and messy.

That was the penalty for dealing with the criminal classes. They had too little imagination, were too fond of the big vulgar display. A discrete traffic accident would have been so much better. He could have moved her to some remote site and arranged for a fall from a cliff or collapse of a trench. He had acted impetuously with too little thought. He was getting old. He thought again about the help of a younger man, the son that Maria had never been able to give him.

Solómos thought briefly about Michael Buchanan. He was not a possibility. The man was vicious, rapacious and had a strictly limited imagination. If you took Michael into your confidence you would spend the rest of your life watching out for a dagger in your back, either literally or metaphorically.

So what needed to be done? First break up that party on Sigandros. He had a conference call set up for later in the day with McKenzie. The foreigners must leave the island as soon as possible. Go back to their rain-drenched island and stay there at least for a while, until things calmed down a bit. Ideally, he would like to be rid of the lot of them. That gave him an idea.

Alistair and Michael stood in front of the blank computer screen. They could not believe what they had seen. No discussion, no consultation just a list of instructions.

> McKenzie remain on the island. Make sure all is secure at the temple site. Leave it alone until further instructions. Do not send or accept any further product until told to do so. Destroy any remaining product on the island.
>
> All foreigners to leave Sigandros and go back to England, keep a low profile.
>
> McFarlane and Buchanan are not to return to Greece unless it is for a provable business reason unconnected with the Sigandros enterprise.
>
> Due to this unavoidable break in operations there is no place for anyone else in the organisation.

"Who does the man think he is?" Michael blustered. "He can't even be bothered to remember where we come from. I've a good mind to set something up independently and show the bugger how it should be done."

"Calm down, Michael." Alistair sounded weary. "It's obvious things have escalated at the Athens end. He would not send an instruction to destroy the shit unless he thought this island was going to receive a visit from the police in the very near future." He turned on McKenzie with some of the old venom in his voice. "It's one of your fucking students. Why didn't you keep better control over them? We're losing money here and it's all your fault. I want to see you taking a smaller cut when all this is over."

This was too much and McKenzie raged back. "It was your bloody son that started it all. I should have cut his throat and sent him over the cliff the first night he arrived."

Alistair bunched his fist and made as if to punch the older man in the face. He stopped, however, when McKenzie pulled a gun from his desk drawer.

"Get out, get out all of you. Take your kit and leave."

Alistair was still scarlet and breathing heavily. It looked for a moment he might actually challenge the old man to fire.

"Come on, Dad," Catherine said, taking his arm. "Do you actually want to stay here? It's not exactly St. Tropez. Robert and I will bring the yacht round to the harbour. You get your stuff together and meet us down there. The sooner we leave this dump the better as far as I'm concerned."

Alistair gave one last glare at McKenzie and allowed himself to be led out of the office. Michael and Robert followed without a word. As soon as he was alone, the professor locked his study door and dialled a number on his mobile. It was some time before there was an answer and when there was the professor's ear was assaulted by a blast of bouzoúki music. "Phillip!" he yelled.

A voice said something unintelligible then the background noise level dropped considerably.

"Can you hear me?" the professor's voice was sharp.

Phillip's sulky tones agreed that he could.

"Listen and don't argue. The visitors are leaving. Get the four-track and take Catherine and Robert up to the old pathway. As soon as they are on their way, go back down to the harbour and watch until the yacht picks up McFarlane and Buchanan. When you are sure they are gone, come back here."

Phillip started to protest but stopped when he realised he was whining to the dialling tone. Some residual good sense or self-preservation told him he had better do as he was told and this time do it right. He caught up with Robert and Catherine as they were starting up the hill. Neither of them particularly liked Philip but on this occasion they were glad to see him. He tried to find out what was going on but all Robert and Catherine would say was that he had better ask his uncle. After a few more attempts at conversation, which his passengers ignored, they completed the journey in silence.

It was about an hour later when Catherine steered the boat round the headland, picked up Alistair and Michael from the harbour. Careful for once, Philip went back up to the headland. They sailed close to Athena's isle but did not stop. Eventually they disappeared into the blue haze. Only when he was certain they had truly gone did he return to his uncle's house. The old man looked ill.

"Who could think so much could go wrong in so short a time?" the professor asked. Philip had no answer. "I need your help to clear up. We may be getting a visit from the police in the near future."

Philip cursed under his breath. If he had known that earlier he would have begged a lift on the yacht, even if it meant being pleasant to that bastard Robert.

"I want you to leave on the next ferry. The dig is over for the year and there is no further reason for you to stay. However, between now and Friday morning, we need to get rid of the opium resin, box up all the remaining Poseidon site finds for despatch to Athens, and return all the Athena site finds to the island and rebury them as discretely as possible.

"Can I use help from the village?"

"Only for the Poseidon material. I believe the islanders are loyal to me but I don't want to put it to the test."

"It's going to be a lot of work."

"That is why I did not ask if you could have a place on Catherine's yacht."

The professor took a small brick of notes from his desk drawer. "You will need some money to cover your expenses during this next year at university. Your mother also wishes to change her car in the autumn, I believe the ashtrays are full." The professor locked the money away again. "If you oblige me in this I will be generous."

"We don't have much time. What do you want me to do first?" McKenzie smiled for the first time that day.

Philip drove the four-track back up the hill. Not knowing how much time they had before they got an official visit, the professor had instructed him to get rid of the resin first. "You can drop it over the cliff," he had been told. "The water is deep and no one fishes there because of the legends about the prisoners of war. Just make sure each case does go into the sea. The last thing we want is a case stuck halfway down the slope spoiling everything."

Philip stood in front of the cases of resin and tried to calculate how much money he was about to destroy. He couldn't do it. The scam would start up again as soon as things quietened down. He would be back next year and perhaps there might be the opportunity for some private enterprise. So if it didn't go into the haunted bay, where could it go? Haunted...of course, the old fort! The superstitious islanders gave that place a wide berth as well for fear of evil spirits of one kind or another. If he remembered correctly there were a couple of cisterns that would provide perfectly acceptable hiding places.

During the next few hours Philip worked harder than he had in his life. Speed was of the essence because he could not be away from the villa for much longer than it would have taken him to do the job he was supposed to have done. He loaded the crates into the four-track and wound his way through the olive trees across the island to the old fort. To his delight he found that he could manoeuvre the vehicle to within a hundred metres of the ruin. All he had to do then was manhandle the crates into the cistern and cover them with dead wood and bushes. When Philip finally did return to the villa, he was sweating, dirty and had dead olive leaves in his hair.

"Good God, boy, what have you been doing?"

"Just making sure that I did not leave any traces of my

activities at the top of the hill," Phillip improvised. The lie seemed to do the trick.

There was not a great deal of material to take back to Athena's isle. One trip in the professor's own small motor boat was all that was necessary to return the plundered artefacts. McKenzie had a pang of regret for the treasures that had gone to Turkey. He comforted himself, however, with the thought that he would not now have to give up some of his private material. Philip, who had the task of re-seeding the site, thought there was far too much as he scrabbled in the sand under the unforgiving sun.

Finally Philip was allowed to supervise a couple of the islanders into carting the Poseidon material down to the harbour. In Philip's case, this meant a great deal of shouting and hectoring and a calculated go slow by the unfortunate crew. However, when they were told that as part of their reward they could help themselves to the domestic fixtures and fittings, the huts were emptied as if by magic. When the professor finally locked the huts for the last time, the only thing left behind were dust motes quietly floating in the air.

Philip and the Poseidon material both left on the ferry. McKenzie wondered why he did not feel a greater degree of relief. It was if there was a storm brewing. The usually blue sky had a purple look to it. The air seemed heavy and the ever-present buzz of insects was silenced.

Ékaterina asked her employer if he wanted something to eat but he waved her away. He wandered into his study and poured himself a generous shot of single malt. He looked at the level in the bottle. It was time to order another case. He turned on his computer to report tasks accomplished. He was surprised to see the receiving mail icon.

> Special messenger arriving. Be at former prisoner of war camp at midnight to receive instructions.

It was the Shadowman's usual brand of abruptness and drama. McKenzie emptied the remains of the scotch into his glass.

Catherine insisted on steering the boat back to Milos, stating that she was the hirer and therefore only she was insured to do so. Robert suspected that she really wanted to show off her skills. Certainly she tucked the elegant craft back into its moorings as neat as you please.

They were met on the quayside by the owner, who made a great performance of searching the structure for dents and scratches. His heart was not really in it. The presence of three scowling male passengers made bullying the woman a less attractive proposition. He did, however, make some pointed references to the fact that Catherine had gone off with one man and returned with three others. Robert grabbed the man painfully by the biceps and informed him that if he wished to discuss his sister's honour they could do so privately.

That put an end to the comments but Robert was concerned to note that Michael had heard everything the boat owner had said but had done nothing to defend Catherine. In fact, he had begun to look even more sulky. There would be trouble there before long. What had possessed Catherine to hook up with the loser? Still, she was all grown up now and if things got too rough Robert supposed she could complain to her father.

They spent an uncomfortable night on Milos, the evening filled with long silences and meaningful looks. Catherine excused herself first and she did look tired. Robert could see Michael looking frequently at his watch. He waited about half an hour then stated he, too, would have an early night.

McFarlane had been drinking steadily all night, saying nothing much to anyone. He watched Michael leave then turned to Robert. "What do you plan to do now, son?"

"Fly to Athens with you and Catherine then look for another boat. There will be something for me in a harbour like Piraeus. I have a fancy to see something of Italy. Eventually I'll come home, but not yet."

"There's a place for you in the business, there's always been a place for you."

"I know that, Dad." Robert hoped the conversation would end there, that his father would accept that there were things he had to do on his own without enquiring into them too closely. It was never going to happen.

"Your place is at home. I'm not getting any younger and your mother needs you."

It was mostly the drink talking. Although his father would use mushy sentiment if he thought it would get him his own way. Robert did not doubt that his father did want him back. He also knew that if he became dependent on his father for a job and decent salary then the old man would revert to being a domestic tyrant. He tried to let his father down lightly.

"What about Michael? He thinks he's heir apparent. Catherine is a great deal more competent than you give her credit for. She would do well as a junior executive under your direction."

"Bugger Michael, Catherine too, it's you I want with me, son."

McFarlane's voice was rising; people were beginning to look at them. Robert needed to finish this quickly.

"Look, Dad, I'm not quite the bum I seemed to be on Sigandros. I have, let's say, one or two little deals going. I need to organise some things then we can talk about me buying a share in the business, okay? Remember whose son I am." Robert patted his father on the shoulder and made his escape before the whisky-sodden brain cells comprehended what he had said and the brilliant mind underneath started to ask questions he would not be able to answer.

Michael went straight to Catherine's room and tapped on the door. "It's me Michael. Let me in, we have to talk."

Catherine opened the door. The last thing she wanted was her personal life being shouted up and down a hotel corridor. Michael made a clumsy attempt at embracing her but she evaded him, pushing him onto the bed while she took the dressing table chair.

"We can't go on like this, you're driving me mad. Come to bed." He patted the mattress beside him.

"No, Michael, I'm not your plaything anymore."

"It's that weedy librarian. He's been putting ideas into your head and probably his dick up your cunt as well."

"For a so-called clever man you can be so stupid. I'm not going to go from being your doormat to being a hearthrug for Douglas. Good God, the man doesn't even have a home to call his own."

This seemed to make at least a kind of sense to Michael.

"Let's have a drink and see if we can talk this through." She handed Michael a glass containing amber liquid. There was an empty miniature of whisky from the minibar on the dressing table. Michael downed it in a couple of swallows.

"I don't want to talk, I want to teach you a lesson you will never forget." He half rose from the bed.

Catherine pushed him back while he was still off balance. "I need a pee. We can start my schooling when I come back." Catherine stepped quickly to one side, avoiding the clutching hands, and locked herself in the bathroom. She stayed in there for some time. When she came out, Michael had slipped off the bed and was lying on the floor. When she had packed for the trip she had included a bottle of her mother's sleeping pills. She had thought that Michael would try something tonight and the first thing she had done was dissolve three of the little dream makers in a glass of spirits. It would not have worked if he not been off guard and already half drunk. With any luck he would not remember anything after coming to her room.

There was another knock on her door. She went and opened it a crack. It was Robert.

"Are you okay? Michael looked a bit mean when he left the dining room."

Catherine let him in. "Will you help me to get him to his own room? He took a sleeping pill but it was one you should not take with alcohol and it seems to have affected him too quickly."

Robert looked at her, and Catherine blushed and grinned. He had been right when he told his father there was a great deal more to Catherine than he gave her credit for.

Between them they got the unconscious man to his own room, out of his shirt and trousers and into bed. Robert was careful to arrange Michael in the 'recovery position'. Not because he cared for the man, but if he choked to death it would be very inconvenient at this time.

Next morning, they all took the flight to Athens. Each for their own reasons was quiet and preoccupied with their own thoughts. Even by flying business class there were no connecting flights to the UK. The McFarlanes and Michael would have to stay another night in Greece. Robert shook hands with the men, kissed Catherine lightly on the cheek, then promising to stay in touch, headed for the exit. Alistair looked as if he wanted to call him back but by the time he had formulated the words the young man had disappeared.

Athens was a city both men knew well. They had no difficulty booking into a hotel with a decent level of comfort. Alistair went immediately to his room, telling Catherine and Michael that he would see them in the morning. If he wanted anything he would use room service.

Michael must have a head as hard as his heart because he showed very little effect from the previous night's excesses. He asked Catherine if she would like to see something of the city. She agreed willingly. He mentioned the previous evening a couple of times, but Catherine kept her answers light and neutral and eventually Michael let the subject drop.

They had one of the most pleasant afternoons Catherine could remember. They saw the Acropolis and the Plaka and then Michael took her shopping. As she tried on dresses and trouser suits in some of Athens's most exclusive shops, Catherine thought that if Michael came to her room that night her mother's sleeping pills would stay in their bottle.

Professor McKenzie looked at the clock. It was just after eleven. He briefly considered taking the four-track up to the prisoner of war camp. Then thought better of it. If the meeting was supposed to be so secret then taking the car would be like arriving with a brass band. Time to be going. He reached into the desk drawer and pulled out the gun, checked it, then put it in the pocket of his linen jacket, just to be on the safe side. He also took a torch. There would be very little moonlight tonight.

The wind from the promised storm raced through the dry branches, making them swish and crackle. The trunks of the trees creaked ominously. Occasionally he heard the rustle of a small animal or bird in the undergrowth, disturbed either by his presence or that of another predator. McKenzie was breathing heavily by the time he reached the flat top of the hill. He stood for a moment to regain his wind. The long low buildings of the camp were black against the sky. He walked over to the huts. They were locked and silent. The wind gusted, rattling some gravel. He could hear the crash of the waves on the rocks and a faint moaning sound. He told himself it was just the wind in the hollow of the hill that the peasants attributed to the shades of the murdered soldiers. It sounded human; it sounded infinitely sad. McKenzie shivered slightly, he was cold.

"McKenzie." The voice was harsh and accented.

The professor spun around. He could see no one.

"Turn off that damned torch and come over here."

The torch beam died and McKenzie slowly turned around. A figure emerged, a darker shadow amongst the bushes on the edge of the cliff. He walked over, stopping ten metres from the man.

"You McKenzie?"

"Who else would I be?" The answer held all the weariness in the world. He heard an exchange of conversation in Greek.

"Is this the guy?"

"Tall, white hair, white beard, belly on him, *malista*, he's the guy."

In English, the first speaker said, "We have a message for you from Professor Solómos." The two men walked towards him. "It's contract terminated."

The last thing the professor felt was incredible pain as a

weighted cosh slammed into his skull.

Working as a team, the two men lifted the old man by arms and feet then walked towards the cliff edge. When they were as close as they dared, they swung the body a couple of times to gain momentum then hurled it over the edge into the foaming cauldron below. Then, without another word, they melted into the darkness.

Chapter Seventeen

It took two days to obtain permission for the wiretap and almost that long to persuade Douglas to agree to the idea. There were endless fittings so that Douglas could move naturally. Finally Detective Pavlides coached the academic in the sort of questions to ask and how to phrase them. During this time Douglas slept badly. Part of his mind was excited by the thought of being a double agent and part was uncomfortable with planing to play a dirty trick on, if not an old friend, then at least a long-standing acquaintance.

Then the news broke about Professor McKenzie's suicide on Sigandros. It did not make headline news but in a country where archaeologists have the status of pop stars all the major dailies carried the news on one of the inside pages.

It was only natural for Douglas to telephone Professor Solómos to offer his condolences and express his shock and regret. When Douglas revealed that he was in Athens there was a distinct hesitation in the professor's voice.

Then the older man asked, "You are on holiday? I thought you had plans to come later in the year?"

This gave Douglas the opening to explain his visit to Sigandros and the adventure that never was.

"I intended to go straight back to Edinburgh from Milos but when I arrived here in Athens I decided to stay for a few days. I'm not due back at work until next week and if I still feel stressed about the mugging I'll take a few more days as annual leave."

"My dear chap, you must come and have dinner with me. There are one or two things I would like to discuss with you. Come to my apartment tomorrow night, it's more private than a restaurant, say 8 p.m.?"

Douglas agreed and in newly purchased shirt and slacks arrived at the professor's door with the obligatory bottle of Cretan wine. Douglas was aware from previous visits that one of the professor's older sisters acted as his housekeeper so he also brought a small bouquet of pink rose buds and a box of expensive chocolates. A tiny wizened woman in head to toe black opened the door.

"Kiría Anna," Douglas said in Greek, "you look lovelier than ever. Please accept these small tokens of my undying affection."

The old woman smiled toothless at him. "One day, Didáktor Grey, I will take you seriously then you will be in trouble."

She led him through to the sitting room where Dionysos Solómos rose to greet him. It was not until they were settled once more in armchairs with coffee and brandy after the meal that Professor Solómos turned the conversation to Sigandros.

"You have visited Sigandros twice now, Douglas. What do you think of the place?"

"The first time I was there, I must admit I was glad to leave. The second time it was more complicated. I began to think that whilst you would not want to go there for a holiday it might be a wonderful place to live. Especially if you had work to do there as McKenzie had."

"Why do you think McKenzie committed suicide? You must have been one of the last people to see him alive. Did he look depressed, worried?"

Douglas paused to think. "Not depressed, but yes, worried. On the other hand, with all the fuss over that Robert character and two different sets of rescuers turning up to try to save the day it would be disconcerting for anyone."

"Anything else?" Solómos was looking intently at Douglas.

Douglas avoided the question. "Look, the man is dead. He could have been depressed about any number of things, will it do any good to rake over them?"

"There are only the two of us here," Solómos insisted. "I have a very particular reason for asking."

"I suspect quite a bit, enough for the fact that McKenzie threw himself off a cliff not to be the shock to me as it must have been for everyone else. I can't prove anything; I don't want to prove anything. I suspect that James was playing with some very big boys indeed."

"I see you are a cautious man." Solómos did not look displeased. "Let me put this to you another way. The excavations on Sigandros need a new director."

"You're offering the directorship to me?"

"I am."

"I'm a historian not an archaeologist," Douglas protested. Internally he could feel the tug of temptation as fierce as the ebb tide of the Solway.

"Eager young people with a degree in archaeology are two a penny. Mature men who can balance the various shall we say 'requirements' of a dig such as Sigandros are far more rare. McKenzie, even before the Robert fiasco, was becoming both careless and visible."

Douglas could feel panic building. What if this had happened without half of the Athens CID listening in? Would he have given in? How should he play it? The answer came as a voice in his head. Play it straight. This is one of the cleverest men you know and you are not a trained actor. Try to be too clever and you're going to lose everything.

"Selling the artefacts has to stop. I hate it, hate it. The excavation of Athena's isle will have to be clean. Any pieces not already sold must come back."

Solómos looked surprised but not as surprised as Douglas felt.

"To be honest with you, I don't care about the drugs," Douglas continued. "If some stupid fools want to buy themselves an early grave then good riddance to bad rubbish, but I'll not have the site desecrated any further."

"You've made your point," Solómos said gently.

"I want to live in the McKenzie villa. Buy it off his heirs, do what you like, but that place must be my base."

"It already belongs to the university. McKenzie was in deep financial waters before he ever came to Sigandros. Eventually he offered the villa to the university at a bargain price in exchange for the post of directing the Poseidon excavation. He persuaded the then administrator that if he were allowed to live there rent-free he would use the rooms to accommodate the summer students. Whether my predecessor believed him or not I don't know, but of course it never happened."

"Young Robert promoted the idea of having a cruise ship move stuff from Turkey to Sigandros. That's a good idea. Using dodgy fishermen proved a liability in the end. I suspect Robert will not go back to Scotland with his father. Someone with your contacts might be able to find him in Piraeus. He's resourceful and already knows about the organisation. I don't know Michael's role in the organisation but I would want as little as possible to do with him. I don't like him and I think he's unstable." Douglas was red faced and breathing hard when he had finished as if he had performed actual physical labour. He longed to say he wanted Catherine kept out of the deal but knew that would give him away.

Professor Solómos looked at the younger man with some degree of shock on his countenance. "How do you know so much?"

"On that last night on Sigandros I went to bed early. They very nearly threw me out of the room they were so eager to get on with their plotting. So I went to the room allocated to me. I was not in the least sleepy so I sat on the balcony with a last glass of wine. I did not want to read, I just wanted to think, so I did not turn on any of the lights to avoid attracting the night insects. The room in which I was to sleep was directly over the study. It was a warm night. They had drawn a muslin curtain but the windows were wide open. I heard every word that was said."

"Were you not tempted to go to the police?"

"I was tempted to come and consult with you."

The irony hovered in the air between them.

"What about Catherine?" Solómos's voice was very gentle.

Douglas's heart lurched. Well, the truth had sufficed so far, he might as well try a little more. "I would like to buy the stars and give them to her for playthings. I would like to see her dressed in nothing but moonlight. I would like to read to her the most explicit love poetry in the original Greek and suit the actions to the words. The only thing that stops me asking her to marry me is that she would look at me with completely blank eyes and ask if I were joking."

"Oh my dear fellow, I wish I had not asked. We'll do what we can to keep the fair Catherine out of this."

Douglas remembered the policemen on the other end of the wire and felt a blush rising from his collar. Still, that would be attributed to his very natural emotional state.

"We will need to compromise." Solómos was all business now. "Our contacts in Turkey will not be pleased at the antiquities side of the business stopping so abruptly. It will need to be run down gradually."

"No, chose another director, do what you damned well please, but from the moment I am in, not one shard of pottery, not one amber bead goes anywhere but Athens." Douglas wondered what had come over him. His instructions had been to agree to anything and everything, reluctantly if necessary, but not to jeopardise the scam. Detective Pavlides would definitely not be pleased.

"Is that your last word?"

"It is." Douglas felt the whole operation going down the tubes.

"For a potential crook, you are an honest man. I like that. I mistrust those who agree to everything. I always have the feeling that they may eventually agree to nothing. I will, however, need to consult with my partners about when could you start."

"As I said, I still have some sick leave and some annual leave due. I could stay in Athens for a few more days and make a short visit to Sigandros. However, if your partners agree to my terms and wish me to take over as director then I would want to do it as officially as possible. That means returning to Edinburgh, giving the library management my written notice, arranging my affairs there and taking up my residence at the villa. It could be done in a month but it would be more compatible with the speed that things are done in the academic world if I took up my post on say 1 January 2006.

Good God, thought Douglas, I'm acting as if this was reality rather than fictional entrapment! Again that voice deep in his skull said, Dionysos will see through playacting. It has to be real for you here and now; otherwise, the reality may very well be your own death.

"There is one more thing." Douglas could feel himself going red again. "Mrs. Theoharous, I understand why you did what you did. Or at least I do now. I regret that young woman's death. Could you make some arrangement from the university or a benevolent fund or something to ensure she gets an annuity? Take it out of my cut if you have to."

"It will be arranged. I will contact you tomorrow. Telephone me here at noon. Use your mobile. If my partners agree to my proposal then I will want you to go out to Sigandros for about a week. Then if Robert is findable, he can take over as deputy whilst the mills of academia grind exceeding slow. In the past, business has not been so brisk outside the summer months. One of the things I shall want you to look at is increasing the opium trade, especially if we are to lose the antiquities business."

"I'll do that." Douglas tried to sound both sincere and committed.

The two men stood up and shook hands. It was time to go. Professor Solómos telephoned for a taxi, and when the horn sounded in the street outside, the professor ushered his visitor to the door. As Douglas crossed the pavement to the waiting cab, his stomach was churning and his knees acted like jelly. Douglas could not believe what he had just done. He wanted a glass of wine, hell, he wanted a bottle of wine.

The taxi deposited Douglas at his hotel. As soon as the legitimate transport was out of sight, a taxi belonging to the police department drew up to the curb. As the vehicle whisked him back to police headquarters, Douglas felt great tears start to flow from his eyes, down his face and into his beard, and if the police driver despised him then Douglas could not give a damn.

Andros Pavlides was very pleased indeed. There had been moments when he thought the stupid librarian was going to blow the whole thing wide open. Certainly the squad would be snickering about the love song to Catherine for a month, but all in all a very satisfactory conclusion. When Douglas walked into the interview room looking pale and exhausted, Detective Pavlides had the grace to feel some compassion. It could not have been easy for the civilian. They went through the interview. It was certainly enough for an arrest, although what an expensive lawyer would make of the tape in court was anybody's guess. It was a step, not the whole journey.

Eventually they finished. "I would like to go home tomorrow." Douglas sighed. "I'll come back for the trial, of course, but for now I need to get away. I'll take Margaret with me. If we can keep her out of it as much as possible I would be grateful."

Andros had been expecting something like this and would have to play his fish very carefully. He said nothing but let the silence lengthen between them.

Douglas groaned. "You want me to go back to Sigandros, don't you? You want me to help you net the whole barrel of stinking fish."

Quick on the uptake, our Douglas, thought the policeman. Aloud, he said, "We need the names of the contacts in Turkey and details of the distribution network in Britain. A classical scholar such as yourself should appreciate the fact that if you cut one head off the Hydra two more spring up in its place. We have to burn out the whole nest."

"I can't do it." Douglas sounded almost desperate. "I'm a scholar, not a commando. Use one of your own men." There was real fear on the scholar's face and that surprised Andros. However inept a conspirator he had been, he had never seemed to lack courage. Then it came to him and the detective chided himself for being slow. The man had been genuinely tempted.

He doubted it was the drug money, although there were few that could resist the lure of unlimited cash. It was the whole Sigandros setup, the villa, the legendary temple, an opportunity to become the next Schlieman. Dr. Grey had been playing it for real with the old professor. No wonder the scam had worked so well. Now the good doctor wanted to take himself out of harm's way.

"Don't worry, Douglas, you won't be on your own." The sudden lack of courtesy told Douglas that the detective had probably sussed out the real problem. Douglas felt a wave of fury, but he did not know if it was directed at the detective or at his own weak self. Andros lifted the telephone and said abruptly, "Wheel him in."

Whoever the angry Douglas had been expecting, it was not Robert McFarlane. "I think you two know each other." Andros was bubbling with amusement at the consternation on both their faces. "Castaway Robert here is actually a member of the Interpol department concerned with drug trafficking and associated crime. He was slowly gathering evidence on the Turkish end of the supply chain when the little contretemps aboard the Herakles changed the course of his investigations."

Andros then waved an expansive arm at Douglas. "Dougie here has kindly agreed to be our little Judas Goat."

Douglas had had enough and more than enough. Before the detective could react, Douglas sprang out of his chair, and with strength aided by absolute fury, he twisted his hand round the detective's tie and hauled him to his feet. Douglas was much the taller man and the detective was left scrabbling for balance on the tips of his toes.

"I allowed myself to be involved in this sordid deception because I wanted to rescue the temple of Athena for posterity and obtain justice for poor Rena Theoharous. I will not be spoken to as if I was one of the criminals. You, Detective Pavlides, and the whole of the Athens crime squad can go to hell as far as I'm concerned. I want no more of it, and that goes for Interpol as well," he spat at Robert. He then gave the detective a mighty push back onto his swivel chair. It toppled sideways, spilling the detective onto the floor. Douglas walked out of the office, slamming the door with a force that cracked one of the glass panels. By the time Andros had struggled to his feet, Douglas had gone.

"Do you think it was something I said?" he asked Robert a shade ruefully.

"I certainly think your famous tact may have let you down for once," Robert replied smiling then he became serious. "Do you think he really meant it?"

"Right now, yes he does. He wants the Sigandros job for real and is pissed that I know. I thought I would test him out a bit, see how much he would take. The guy has a shorter fuse than I suspected. I'll go round in the morning and eat humble pie. He'll do as we ask."

"What makes you so sure?"

"Think about what he yelled at me."

"Justice for the Theoharous woman and something about the temple of Athena."

"Just so, and what did he put first?"

"Ah!" Robert smiled.

Detective Andros was waiting for Douglas when he came down for breakfast next morning. He stood politely and said, "*Kalimera sas*, Dr. Grey, would you do me the favour of having breakfast with me?"

Douglas was surprised; he had been expecting threats of a gaol sentence and being banned from setting foot on Greek soil for the rest of his life. This man had more colours than a chameleon. Warning himself to be on his guard, Douglas sat and allowed the detective to pour orange juice.

"I have come to apologise for last night," the detective said with sincerity.

Douglas said nothing; this man was about as sincere as a cat.

"You must have realised by now that I was testing you. However, after all you had gone through and considering the lateness of the hour, it was excusable."

"It was, whether you mean your words or you do not."

"I have come not only to apologise but to beg you to go to Sigandros, if only for a few days."

"This is doing it rather too brown, Detective."

"Okay, Dr. Grey, here it is without either aggression or smarm. Professor Solómos was convinced by your performance last night. If, however, you leave this morning for the UK, he will smell a rat. One of the reasons we have had so much difficulty in getting into the organisation is that the various factions never meet. It's all co-ordinated by Dionysos like a spider at the centre of a web. We suspect that he sees you not just as a replacement for the unlamented McKenzie but as his successor. That means you are going to have to meet all the various elements at least once so they know with whom they are now going to do business.

"In the next couple of days we will see on Sigandros the top guys, the ones that pull the strings, the ones we have never had a line on before. The war on drugs is probably unwinable, but your co-operation will give us a major victory in the battle. It will also free Athena's island from the scam forever. If you don't help us then sooner or later the artefacts' trade will set up again and the temple of Athena will be utterly lost to scholarship. That's not fluff, Dr. Grey, that's bitter fact."

Douglas made a great show of smearing butter and jam on his croissant and pouring some coffee. Just when Andros was beginning to despair that his eloquence had not worked and that they had in fact lost this round, Douglas said, "My bags are ready at the porter's desk, my bill is paid. This morning a messenger arrived from Professor Solómos to say that he had found Robert and the two of us will return to Sigandros on a hired yacht. He also sent sufficient funds to cover my expenses. So I suggest you make a discrete exit through the rear of the hotel whist I take a chauffeur-driven limousine to the harbour."

Detective Pavlides, for once in his life, was too stunned to say anything. He stood as Douglas patted his mouth with a napkin and prepared to leave the dining room.

"I am trusting you to ensure that Margaret McDonald leaves Greece safely today and that there is no fuss either about the date of her flight or upgrading her ticket to business class. A small honorarium for helping the police with their enquiries would not go amiss."

"Now look here, Dr. Grey...."

"No, you look, Detective Pavlides, we have saved you weeks of work and hours of overtime. I, a civilian from another country, am putting my life at risk for Greece, with no thought of reward or courting the newspapers for publicity. The very least the police department can do is ensure the safety of my young and attractive female colleague." The librarian was being about as subtle as a sandbag, and Andros got the point.

"Certainly, Dr. Grey. I'll deal with the paperwork myself and ensure one of our female officers accompanies Miss McDonald until she gets on the plane."

"Excellent, my dear fellow." As Douglas passed round the back of the younger man's chair he bent down and whispered, "Andy, my son, if you ever call me Dougie again I shall personally ensure that the Furies with burning breath, blood in their eyes and snakes in their hair will fly away with your soul."

No police officer spends very long in the job without getting threats but Andros could not remember ever receiving one quite like that before.

Chapter Eighteen

Catherine was drinking coffee in the sunshine. She had taken one of the restaurant's garden tables. On the white cloth were the remains of her breakfast, crumbs from a sweet roll and the peel of an orange. She thought that whilst she would be glad to return to Scotland, there were things about Greece she would definitely miss. Her father and Michael had eventually decided to stay on in Athens for a few days rather than fly out immediately as was their original plan. They claimed they wanted to check on their business dealings in the city, so she had decided to stay with them and enjoy a short holiday.

When Robert had left them at the airport it had been hard. She believed he meant his promises to stay in touch but she did not know how well they would survive the rough and tumble of his life. Still, perhaps he might need rescuing again.

My God it had been fun, the dash to Greece, sailing Byron's wine dark seas. The corny poetic line reminded her of Douglas Grey and she gave an indulgent smile. The old bookworm had been quite fun. She signalled the waiter and asked him to bring her the English language newspaper. As usual she ignored the news and turned immediately to the arts and fashion sections. As she smoothed out the clumsy sheets, a familiar name caught her eye, Professor James McKenzie. Her eye skimmed the paragraph, then she read it again more carefully. Then dropping the rest of the newspaper onto the terrace, she ran back into the hotel.

Her father had not been pleased to be wakened at the unearthly hour of 8 a.m. Business was conducted both late and bibulously in Athens. His bad temper disappeared when he finally saw the article. He telephoned first to Michael's room then to room service. Within ten minutes they were eyeing one another over the coffee.

"What possessed the old fart to top himself now? We had everything sorted." Not for the first time Catherine thought her fiancé lacked sensitivity. "I'll have to go back to the island. He promised to clean up, but God knows what he's done." Michael paced up and down the hotel room. Then he turned. "It would be best if you go back to Scotland, Alistair, keep out of it if you can."

Alistair looked relieved.

"What about Spider Man?" Catherine asked, enjoying Michael's wince. "Do you need to contact The Boss? Why hasn't this all-knowing character been in touch?" Catherine was getting sharp enough to cut herself.

"You had better go home with your father." Michael looked furious.

"No, I'm going with you, lover boy. If you think about it really carefully you'll realise why." Catherine couldn't think of any reason other than the fact that she wanted to go, that she was not ready for the adventure to end. However, she knew Michael well enough to know that he would not call her bluff. "I'll meet you down in reception." She turned to her father. "I seem to have done quite a bit of shopping here in Athens. Not things I'll need on that lump of antique marble. Will you take them home for me, Daddy?" She bent down, kissed his cheek and without waiting for a reply she turned and left the room.

The taxi dropped them by the harbour master's office in Piraeus. Catherine was just beginning to start her arguments for hiring a boat that she could sail herself when she spotted a familiar face.

"Michael! There's Douglas and my brother." She was out of the taxi before it had stopped. She threw herself into Douglas's arms and got a painful crack on the thigh from the ever-present book bag.

Rubbing her leg gingerly, she asked, "What on earth are you doing here?"

Douglas detached himself and Robert said gently, "Something rather dreadful has happened. It looks like Professor McKenzie has committed suicide. Douglas has been asked to go back to the island to help sort things out. I was at a loose end as you know so I've been hired as general minder and dogsbody."

"Why you, Douglas?" Catherine still seemed merry. "What could you possibly do to help?"

The two men grimaced.

"Catherine, Douglas is an internationally recognised scholar, he knows Sigandros and he knew McKenzie. He is the obvious choice. Professor Solómos of Athens University asked him personally."

"Oh dear, foot in mouth again." Catherine did not seem particularly chastened. "Michael and I are also going back to Sigandros. Michael and the prof. have been buddies for years. He thinks he will be able to sort out some of McKenzie's business affairs. The poor old duck had no one else, unless you count that obnoxious nephew." Catherine clapped her hand to her mouth. "We can all go together! It will save money and will be fun. We can have a bit of a party on the way over."

"Catherine, we are all going to Sigandros because Professor McKenzie has died," Robert protested.

"So what?" Catherine was blasé. "None of us actually liked him very much."

Douglas was shocked. This was not the woman he thought he knew. He wondered if she was playing some sort of game, but there was no need to act out before Robert and himself. Still, it did make sense to share a boat if they were all headed for Sigandros anyway.

If Catherine truly expected a party, she was disappointed. Douglas buried himself in a book. Robert concerned himself with the running of the ship and Michael could not be parted from his laptop. Still, she remained cheerful enough. As they steered into the familiar harbour, Douglas took Robert on one side.

"We could be having company soon. Too many fancy boats in this little harbour could attract unwelcome attention. It might be as well to park this thing in Athena's harbour on the other side of the island."

"Douglas, you will never be a mariner, but I take your point. As soon as you, Catherine and Michael have landed, I will sail round and anchor off Dead Man's Drop."

It was as good a name as any for the little cove, but hearing it said so callously made Douglas shiver in the heat.

When they got to the villa, Ékaterina greeted them with floods of tears.

"I have worked here at the villa for ten years," she sobbed. "Kathighitís McKenzie was like part of my family."

Even stronger than her regrets for her dead employer were the worries about her job and her home. However, natural good manners made her reluctant to bring up the issue straight away. The money she earned and the steady supply of groceries she skimmed off the household budget had made her family one of the most prosperous on the island. It would be a blow if these stopped. The thought of leaving her comfortable room at the villa and trying to squeeze in with her daughter's family made the tears come even harder.

Douglas guided the weeping woman into McKenzie's study. "I need you to have courage, Kiría Parinou." He poured her a glass of brandy. "Your good sense and steady heart will be of great importance to me in the difficult days to come."

Ékaterina took a sip of the fiery spirit then blew her nose vigorously. This was beginning to sound hopeful.

"Professor Solómos has appointed me director of the Sigandros excavation until further notice. I have the university's permission to live here in the villa. I would be grateful if you would stay on and act as housekeeper for me."

Thanks be to our Lady, Ékaterina thought to herself. Aloud she said with dignity, "*Nai*, I would be prepared to stay, Didáktor Grey."

"It is inevitable that in the first few months there will be a lot of visitors and a great deal of the work will fall on you. I suggest that to compensate your salary should rise to." Douglas named a figure that had Ékaterina reaching for her brandy glass again.

"That would be most acceptable, Didáktor Grey." Ékaterina's voice was hoarse with both emotion and raw spirits.

"Please take all the time you need to calm yourself and then I would like you to prepare rooms for three guests and myself."

"Three? Didáktor Grey."

"Yes, another man, Robert McFarlane, will be coming later."

That wretched troublemaker! she thought. Nothing goes well when he is involved. Aloud she confined herself to asking, "Do you wish for something to eat now?"

"A few mezzo and wine on the terrace in an hour perhaps. I am expecting more visitors but I don't know how many or exactly when they will arrive. As and when they do come I would wish to offer them the hospitality of a meal. There should be no pork, no shell fish, no milk products."

"*Fisika*, of course, there will be no problems." Privately, Ékaterina thought, He's expecting some damned Turks, I should poison the stew. But the doctor has been fair with me, I'll not shame him in front of his guests, not even God-forgotten Turks. Ékaterina stood. "May I add my own congratulations on your appointment. I know you will be very happy here."

As the housekeeper left the room, Douglas felt his stomach churn. He could think of no better way of spending the next few years than living in this lovely house and directing the excavations on Athena's isle. Suddenly, Edinburgh and the library seemed very dismal and very far away. If only it was true and not just an act in a play orchestrated by Athens CID.

The yacht came into view just before sunset. One of Ékaterina's nephews came pelting up to the villa with the news. It was a beautiful craft—sleek, powerful and very, very expensive. Douglas asked Catherine to walk with him to the harbour to meet the unwelcome guests. A second yacht was spotted shortly after the first just as elegant and to Douglas's eyes just as sinister.

The men who disembarked were almost identical. The bosses, slender, dark-haired, silk suits and designer sunglasses. The minders, shaved skulls, jeans, plain white tee shirts and sculpted muscles. They walked up to the villa as if they not only owned it, but the whole island and everything on it. Douglas worries over food were needless. These hard men would accept nothing but black coffee and still mineral water.

Catherine and Robert were politely asked to leave with undertones that brooked no arguments. Bodyguards were told to stand outside the study door and window. Douglas began to think he had taken on more than he could cope with. Even Michael looked uncomfortable. There were a few preliminary trials of language but in the end English was used as the neutral option. None of the visitors gave a name.

"We are here because the Shadowman asked us to come. It has been inconvenient and expensive and we do not wish for it to occur again." The Athens contingent had taken the lead.

"No one could regret it more than we do," Michael burbled.

"Shut up." Athens again

The sunglasses swivelled towards Douglas. "We didn't like McKenzie and we don't like you. The Shadowman should have put a Greek in charge."

There was a rumble from the Marmaris faction. "Ingilz, Yunanli, we don't care. Millions of Euros worth of antiquities and shit are missing. What are you going to do about it?"

Michael tried again. "The professor was instructed to get rid of the opium. The island has been lousy with cops. The relics have gone back to the island."

"Shut up," this time with a Turkish accent.

"We've heard too much about what you like and don't like, picking and choosing what you will dirty your hands with and what's too much for you. We're here to tell you exactly what you will do."

"*Evet*, yes," from Marmaris

Douglas banged the table. "No, you shut up and listen." The suits looked shocked and the minders uneasy. "You had as sweet a setup as you could have asked for, and you fucked it up by being greedy. You have the nerve, the bloody brass neck, to say you want a Greek in charge when you are selling off your heritage to the Turks!" Douglas was shouting at the top of his voice. "What brings the most profit? The relics or the shit? If you had not been so short sighted you could have been turning over twice as much opium. It was the relics that made this operation noisy and brought a boat load of cops to an island that never saw a policeman from one year's end to the next. If you had been honest about the Athena site you would never have raised suspicions by packing up worthless gravel from the Poseidon temple to send to Athens."

"It was the McFarlane boy who started the trouble." Good, they were on the defensive.

Douglas banged the table again. They were not used to being spoken to like this, and Douglas needed to keep his advantage. He pictured them as the cheating students he had so despised in his library days.

"Don't be more stupid than you can help. Twenty gossiping students have gone home wondering why Athens supports this played-out island. You would have got an official visit long before the next season. Robert has done you a favour. We can get our act together before next spring. I assure you, gentlemen, that within the month this island will be so clean we could entertain the entire Athenian detective force."

And we surely will! thought Douglas.

"There is still stuff missing. We must be sure we are not being cheated." The Marmaris lot were not going to give up.

"It's at the bottom of the sea. We all lose out but it couldn't be helped. If you're worried, search the island, it's not exactly huge. Now get out of my house. We'll talk tomorrow when I've calmed down and hopefully you've found some common sense." Douglas stood up and pointed dramatically to the door. To his surprise, the bosses and their minders filed out. They gave him some very dirty looks as they passed through the door, but they went.

Douglas walked over to the booze cabinet, then thought his stomach couldn't take spirits. Instead, he turned to the small office fridge unit and brought out a bottle of white wine. He motioned to Michael with a glass, but the other man shook his head.

"You must be mad, they could have killed us both." Michael

looked terrified.

"Once you let yourself be bullied by rabble like that your relative positions are fixed for good. They say jump and you say how high. The only thing they respect is force. They were more likely to kill us if we offered to lick their boots." Douglas walked to the study door and shouted. "Ékaterina, dinner for four soon as you like."

Michael shook his head again and stumbled off looking green. The housekeeper appeared in the doorway. Douglas looked up. "Make that just for three, my dear. Kírios Buchanan seems to have lost his appetite."

Next morning at first light more than a dozen men left the two boats in the harbour and headed into the interior of the island. Two of the bosses with minders in tow walked up to the villa. With them was a wizened little man in baggy wool trousers and mismatched jacket. Douglas was having breakfast on the terrace with Robert and Catherine. Michael was sulking behind a newspaper but eating nothing.

Douglas greeted the intruders amicably enough and offered coffee.

"*Típote*, nothing, *efkaristó para polí*," the reply oozed. "If you have nothing to hide you will not object if we search your house."

"Search away." Douglas waved an expansive hand. "Robert, please go with these gentlemen and ensure they break nothing nor annoy the staff." The suits looked at Douglas with dislike but their companion did not seem to understand. They retreated into the house with Robert on their heels.

"Are you sure there is nothing to find?" Catherine whispered to Douglas.

"McKenzie was an old rogue, but even he would not have been so stupid as to try to fool these characters."

It took them half an hour. Suddenly, the terrace was full of people. One of the minders had Robert in an armlock. The scruffy individual cradled a tiny statue of Athena as if it were his first born.

"There was a wall safe in the professor's bedroom. This guy opened it in less than a minute," Robert gasped, indicating the bloke in the odd suit. "It was full of stuff. There was gold, glass and dozens of pieces of marble."

The minder tightened his grip and Robert howled then slumped. There was a moment's awful silence.

"McKenzie was that stupid," Douglas said to no one in particular.

Then the tone of a mobile phone shrilled into the silence. One of the bosses withdrew it from the inside of his jacket and answered it. There was a very rapid exchange in Greek. Then the mobile was away and its owner smiling. "They have found half a dozen cases of shit up at the old fort. It was apparently not very well hidden in one of the old cisterns. Now I find that when someone hides things there is always more to be found. Georges ask the delectable young lady to come over here."

The second minder grabbed Catherine and pulled her screaming over to his boss. Both Michael and Douglas stood, but the two bosses had both drawn small and deadly looking pistols.

"Sit down, gentlemen. This will go far easier if we don't get excited."

"Where is the rest of the professor's private stash?"

"We didn't know the old fart had this, let alone know where anything else is." Douglas was frantic. "Do you think we would have continued to eat breakfast without a care in the world if we had known there was anything for you to find? Christ, man, we have not been on the island ourselves for more than twenty-four hours. We had no idea the old fool had been salting stuff away."

"You academics always think others are wanting in logic. You had very little choice but to allow us to search. You may have only just arrived on the island this time, but you have all been here before, our dear Michael several times. Now, tell me what I want to know or the fair Catherine will be fair no longer." He looked at the minder who ground the pistol into her temple.

She screamed, "Tell him, tell him what he wants to know!"

Douglas and Michael shouted that there was nothing to tell.

"I detect a discrepancy in your stories." The man seemed almost amused. "Shall we say the traditional count of three?"

"Listen, you oily bastard, we don't know what the fucking professor was up to." Douglas was on his feet again.

There was a sudden crack and Catherine's head exploded, showering both boss and minder with blood and brains. There was one still moment. It was as if even the perpetrators were shocked at what had happened.

Then Douglas grabbed the table and hurled it with all his might at the suit. It was heavy and connected with his skull with an ominous crunching sound. Glass and pottery shattered on the paving. The other suit looked stunned. Then an iron chair leg took him in the midsection. Blood spread over his white shirt. The minder holding Robert loosened his grip, it was enough. Robert reversed the hold and rammed the man's head into the corner of the building. Stonework and bone both cracked. The minder holding Catherine's body did not seem to know what to do. His hesitation was fatal. Robert scooped up the dropped pistol and shot at close range.

Michael had vaulted over the terrace rail at the first distraction. He was now halfway to the forest. Robert grabbed the demented Douglas by the sleeve.

"She's dead, she's dead, there is nothing more you can do, come on." Robert was not sure if his words were getting through. He slapped Douglas once, hard, then pushed him towards the rail. Somehow he got the older man over and then they were running with all the speed that adrenaline could give them. As they reached the treeline, they could hear Ékaterina begin to scream.

"We have to make for the boat," Robert panted as they dodged through the olives.

"Catherine, Catherine," Douglas moaned almost semi-conscious, but Robert was able to keep him going.

They zig-zagged their way through the trees, heading for the priest's pathway. From time to time they saw evidence that Michael had barged through the undergrowth before them. Then over the sound of their own feet in the leaf mold Robert thought he heard shouting. He pulled Douglas into the dubious protection of some straggly bushes. He tried to quiet his breathing and concentrate on listening. He could detect

Michael's voice. Then the sound of jeering, a shot, a scream, another shot then silence.

"They know more about this island than we gave them credit for. They've got the priest's path covered. We need to go farther up."

Douglas said nothing but did not object when Robert pulled him up. They climbed steadily, making their way round rocky outcrops and clambering overexposed knotted roots. Every so often they would stop and listen. The shouts seemed to be louder, nearer.

He calculated that they needed to retain their freedom for about three hours minimum. When Detective Pavlides did not get his scheduled call then he would sail for the island with the cavalry. What bothered Robert was that Andros might wait until two messages had been missed and that even if the detective moved at once there would be an inevitable delay whilst the police launches sailed to the island. It had seemed logical when the plan was made that the good guys would have to stay out of sight. It did not seem quite such good planning now.

Eventually they arrived at the old prisoner of war camp. The islanders had taken literally the permission to strip the place. Now even the doors and window frames had gone. His plans for holding up here crumbled. He could hear the revving of the 4x4, the shouts of men in the woods. The wind whispered over the hilltop and made almost human moaning sounds in the hollow of the drop.

"Come on, brains, what do we do now?" Robert was frantic.

Douglas spoke slowly as if he were at a university dinner party. "How would they get gently bred maidens down that steep path to the cove?"

"Jesus help us he's flipped."

"There's another way down. That sound, the moaning of the dead soldiers, it's the sound of the wind in a cave. The cliff face has eroded since Philistophane's time. There was probably a small temple at the cliff edge. The girls would have made sacrifice at the altar of Athena then been led down stairs cut inside the cliff. The temple has gone. The cave is still extant, hence the echo of the wind and the ghost story. What we want to know is can we get to the cave without falling into Dead Man's Drop."

Robert heard the distinct sound of a 4x4 changing gear. A lot of Douglas's mumbling did not make sense, but he understood enough to comprehend. "Come on, let's find out because our chances here are nil."

They ran to the edge. There was a shallow slope then what looked like a sheer drop to the churning water below. Flinging himself to his stomach, Robert started to lower himself down, feet first, to the overhang, using every root and branch to support his weight. When the grass ran out, he was relieved to find that there was not a vertical drop but the scree formed a narrow pathway close the edge of the rock face. Slithering and sliding on his belly, he let himself down. Suddenly, his feet were no longer on the pebbles but overhanging the drop. Inch by inch, he moved farther down. There was a cave. He would have to throw himself to the right and hope to land in the cave's mouth and not a hundred feet below in the cauldron.

He heard Douglas slipping down the grass above him.

"They're coming," Douglas hissed.

No alternative, he let himself slither a little farther, twisting his legs into the cliff side. One sickening moment in the air then his heels hit rock. For a moment he teetered on the edge then he threw himself backward, fell hard and rolled down a couple of hip-bruising steps until he could fling out his arms and legs to break his fall. There was no time to congratulate himself. Douglas was just behind him. He shuffled to the edge of the rock just in time to grab Douglas's flailing legs. He guided the librarian backwards, holding onto his shirt and pants and jerking him back into the opening. They were on a narrow ledge between the sheer drop down the cliff and a flight of steps leading down into the heart of the mountain.

It took several minutes to regain their breath. They could hear their pursuers shouting that the bastards had gone over the edge.

"They won't come down after us, they would be mad." Robert did his best to sound confident.

Douglas's teeth were chattering and Robert suspected the man was weeping again. Robert wondered at the brief period of calm reason that had given them at least a chance of surviving. They sat for some time watching the sun cross the sky. There were no sounds of pursuit.

Douglas saw again and again in his mind's eye Catherine's head dissolving into a sphere of blood. She had been so young, so lovely, such a bitch. Douglas physically rocked with shock at the treacherous thought. He dug his hands deep into his trouser pockets. They clasped round the form of the tiny owl. He thought of Pallas Athena, strong, compassionate, virtuous. Ordinary women didn't compare well with goddesses. But then he was no Apollo in tweeds himself. Then he thought of the women who had touched his life in recent weeks. Perhaps there was one who had something of Athena's qualities.

Douglas crawled to the edge of the cave. "I don't think we are going to get back the way we came down."

Robert had been thinking something similar.

"If the mob think we have gone over the drop neither they nor Detective Pavlides are going to search for us. Death here in this cave could be more unpleasant than simply falling into the sea. Before the light fades let's do some exploration."

The steps were slippery and worn. They were also covered with the detritus from the fifty years or so since the landslip that exposed the staircase. Abandoning bravado, they twisted their shirts into a crude rope then Robert started the descent, shuffling backwards on hands and knees.

The stairway curved round inside the cliff face. A couple of turns and they were moving in the pitch blackness and progress was much slower. They moved downwards for what seemed like hours. The sound of water lapping on stone got louder. Suddenly, Robert found himself descending into water. Making sure that Douglas had a firm footing, he tried going down farther. There seemed to be no end. The steps and the sea began to suck at his body, and he would have been pulled off the stairs and into the unknown if it had not been for Douglas's strong hands. He scrambled back out of the water.

"What do we do now?"

They sat in silence for a while, listening to the sip and suck of the tide on the rocks.

"The water level is higher now than it was 2500 years ago."

"Do you know, Douglas," Robert was thoroughly exasperated, "just for once I could do without the academic frills."

"We swim through the flooded cave."

"What?"

"Explanations are not academic frills as you call them. They are the foundation stones that allow you to understand and accept my suggestion."

Robert was cold, wet and exhausted. For one brief moment he considered punching the old drone. Two things stopped him. In the stygian blackness, he could not be exactly sure where Douglas's chin might be. Second, he had noticed before that when Douglas went into scholar mode he came up with his best ideas. It would have to be done Douglas's way or not at all.

"Tell me."

"We assumed the temple at the top of the hill and a way down. Here it is. The maidens would have been led down. Torches or lanterns would have made the descent easier than ours. When they reached the bottom, they would have been handed into boats and out through a sea cave to be rowed across to the island. It would have been more in keeping with both dignity and secrecy than slithering down the hillside. The harbour stairs were probably used for the more mundane tasks of ferrying supplies to the priestesses on the island."

"So?"

"There is still an exit to the open sea. We can deduce that from the motion of the water on the steps. What we have to guess is how far we would have to swim under the cliff before we emerge on the other side."

"What do you guess?"

"That it's doable."

"Why?"

Douglas was tempted to say because there was no alternative, but dwelling on the possibility of failure would not increase Robert's chances. He was less sanguine about his own odds for making the dive successfully. He could do a couple of lengths of a hotel pool no problem, but he would hardly call himself a strong swimmer. Still, when the truth won't serve, lie.

"The current is strong. Given the weak tides in the Aegean, that means it is not travelling too far. We will have the ebb tide current to help us. This cave is excavated, not natural, so I would assume the builders would have gone as directly from top to bottom as the strata in the rock allowed."

"How do you know it's excavated? We can't see a thing."

"My dear boy, I have had my hands all over the rock face for the interminable hours it's taken us to get down here."

"So what do we do?"

"The tide must be ebbing because it pulled you off the steps, so we must go now. You go first because you are younger and faster. If I hold you up the likelihood of panic is increased. You can always pull me up when we get to the open water."

"Okay." Robert sounded cautious.

"Go back down the steps as far as you can. Wait until you have the rhythm of the water, then just as it pulls back go with the current. You will pop out into the harbour like a champagne cork."

There was silence in the cave except for the slap of water.

"Go, Robert. Thinking about it will not make it any easier. If we wait for the next tide we will be even more exhausted and thirsty. No one will come looking for us and there is no way we can get back up the cliff."

Robert slowly descended the steps one more, felt the force of the tide, then a terrific push on his back. With no other guide but the pull of the current, he set off kicking as strongly as he could.

Douglas knew he had to take his own advice. It was not going to be easy. He was not going to survive. He did not even think he wanted to, but like most men he would have preferred his passage into the next world to be pain free. He had never believed that drowning was an easy death.

"Poseidon, Enalius, Asphalius, of the sea and of safety guard me, Pallas Athena Parthenos, virgin unchanging, take my spirit." Douglas suddenly realized he had nothing to sacrifice. Then he thought of the tiny owl. Even on the brink of death he was reluctant to part with it. He took it out of his pocket, kissed it and threw it as far as he could into the blackness. He heard it faintly crack on the stone wall at the far side of the cave. Then he dived into the water.

The water was icy. Within seconds, Douglas did not know where he was or which way to go. The current dragged at him and he hit his head then his shoulder painfully on rocks. Seawater filled his mouth and nose, stinging his sinuses. He thrashed wildly trying to get back to the stairs but was once more hurled against rocks, scraping his hands across razor-sharp barnacles. The current caught him once more, pulling him under. He fought against it and cracked his head yet again. He opened his mouth and seawater flooded in. His ears were ringing and Douglas knew that he could not hold his breath any longer.

A strong hand grasped his wrist, tugging him away from the cave wall. Another hand forced his head down and then he felt the current take him. He was rushing through the water at the speed of an express train, bubbles bursting against his face. Then up, up and he was bobbing about on the surface, retching and gasping in the incredibly sweet air.

"God, Douglas, I thought you were never going to come up!" Robert was about twenty feet away. They must have been separated in that last rush to the surface. Yet Douglas was pretty sure that the hand had not left his wrist until he actually broke through the surface. Another bout of coughing took him and it took all his concentration to remain afloat. A few strong strokes brought Robert to his side.

"Look, man, look!"

Douglas tried to dash the water from his tearing eyes. They were in Athena's bay. Moored in the deep water some way away was their own hired vessel and also a short stubby vessel in battleship grey, bristling with radio antennae and with the words 'Astinomiko Police' on the side. It looked beautiful. A dinghy was already in the water and making its way over to them. Douglas was content to float on his back supported by

Robert until the strong arms of the law hoisted him on board.

Detective Pavlides welcomed them but allowed Douglas to be taken to the small surgery to be dried out and his various cuts and scratches treated by the doctor they had brought with them. In the way of medical men the world over, the giatros tutted over the cuts as if Douglas had inflicted them on himself, then instructed complete rest, no smoking and no alcohol.

An hour later he found himself in borrowed shirt and trousers in a smoke-filled cabin with a glass of brandy in his hand preparing for the debriefing. Detective Pavlides was in tearing spirits. Drugs had been found on both of the luxury yachts, which meant that both could be impounded. Several of the minders had been shot during the landing but none of his police officers had been hurt. Best of all, at least one of the suits was prepared to co-operate in return for freedom from prosecution.

Douglas let his thoughts drift. He stared out of the cabin window, first at Sigandros then at the tiny sacred isle. He wondered what treasures were still hidden under its thin soil. If Athena's temple could be reassembled it could be as big an attraction as Knossos on Crete or Delos, the sacred isle of Apollo off the coast of Myknos. It would bring prosperity to the little island and revenue to fund archaeological projects for years to come.

"Didáktor Grey, are you feeling well?"

Douglas realised that his inattention must be showing. "I'm sorry, Detective Pavlides. I'm a scholar not an adventurer. It has all been too much for me. What will happen to Catherine's, erm, body?"

"This is what we were discussing. We have informed her father and he is returning to Greece immediately. He will be arrested as soon as he lands, far more satisfactory than extradition procedures. We have enough evidence from his soap factory to ensure he does not go back to Scotland for a very long time."

Douglas was appalled. "But what about...." He stopped, unable to go on.

"We are not monsters, Didáktor Grey. The body of the young

woman will be sent back to her mother in the care of her brother."

"And Michael?"

"No one seems to want him. He will be buried here in Greece."

So the shots in the woods had been fatal. Well, he had never thought otherwise. "Not on Sigandros."

"No, we will take his body back to Athens. It will be decently interred in the British cemetery there."

"What about me, will I be needed as a witness?"

"No, that will not be necessary. The evidence we have, plus Kírios McFarlane's testimony, means we will not have to trouble you any further. You are free to go home as soon as you wish. We suggest tomorrow."

There was a hard edge behind the words. It was definitely more than a suggestion. Perhaps Detective Pavlides had bent the rules more than a little when he involved the foreign scholar and would now like the evidence safety back in Britain as soon as possible. Well, he would not be sorry.

"Thank you, Detective Pavlides. You are most kind. To stay in Greece for a long trial would be very inconvenient. If I could just recover my things from the villa, I would be happy to catch the first flight to the UK."

"I will have one of my men bring them to the main harbour."

So he was not even going to be allowed a last look at the villa. There was another question to be asked. Douglas thought he already knew the answer. "Professor Solómos?"

"I'm afraid the professor had a heart attack yesterday evening. He was taken directly from his office to the hospital but was found to be dead on arrival."

"That is sad news," Douglas said ambiguously. Oddly enough, he was sad. Whatever else the old man had been, he had also been a great scholar. "Who is going to take over?" Douglas tried to sound casual.

"For the present, his deputy Didáktor Vlahos is taking care of things, but there will doubtless be a great deal of in-fighting before a new director is appointed."

Detective Pavlides left the cabin to give instructions to his men to sail round to the main harbour. Douglas could hear him shouting other instructions but his mind began to drift once more, thinking of Catherine, her beauty, her enthusiasm, her stupidity. Again, it seemed as if his mind would not divert into completely sentimental mode where that young woman was concerned.

He turned to Robert. "I'm sorry about Catherine."

"So am I." The reply was curt.

"I don't know what we could have done."

"Made up some story, said there was a secret map tattooed on our backsides, anything to diffuse the situation. Hell, I'm a trained negotiator and I did less than you. Her death will always be on my conscience."

"It wasn't your fault."

"No?"

"You could not have stopped her coming to the island. If she had not come with us she and Michael would have hired their own boat. I think the suits wanted one of us dead, so that the rest would give in when we saw they meant business."

There was silence for a while, then Douglas said, "Thanks for coming back for me. I would never have made it without you. I was in a total funk."

Robert said nothing. He could hardly confess that nothing in the universe would have got him back into the cave even if he had been able to swim against the current. In extremis, men imagine all sorts of things.

Just then one of the sailors came into the cabin. "We were putting your kit in the washing machine. Tomas found this in the pocket of your pants. We thought you would want to have it back." In the man's callused hand was the tiny ivory owl.

Chapter Nineteen

Douglas made the trip back to Edinburgh like a man in a daze. He sat in the airport lounges and through the long flights with a book open on his lap. He looked through rather than at the text and an observer would have noticed he rarely turned a page. Eventually he arrived back in Edinburgh. When he let himself into the old building that had been his home and refuge for so long, the flat seemed claustrophobic and dark.

Next day he telephoned Margot at home. "Ring in sick to the library. I have something important to tell you."

To her eternal credit, Margot agreed without bombarding him with questions. She called for him at his flat and they walked down to Holyrood then took the road to Duddingston Loch. As they walked, Douglas told his friend about the journey to Greece, how it had developed and finally how Catherine had died.

Margot said nothing for a long time. Douglas turned towards her to see that she was walking blindly, tears rolling down her face and silent sobs shaking her body. He understood. There were no words. In the village he called for a taxi, paid the driver in advance and instructed him to take Margot home.

The following Monday they both returned to work at the library. To Douglas, the work now seemed dull and pointless. He did his job adequately, but the old enthusiasm was not there. Colleagues put it down to that twenty-first-century catchall, stress. September brought banks of smoke-coloured clouds and persistent drenching rain.

Margot and Douglas stood together at Catherine's funeral service. The death of her friend had hit Margot hard. A stiff black suit and ugly slate-coloured blouse had replaced her usual flouncy gypsy look. She looked older and worn. After the internment there was a reception in one of Edinburgh's smarter hotels. As they picked at the buffet, Margot confessed that this was the first funeral she had ever attended. Even her grandparents were still alive. It made death seem a great deal more real and near.

Douglas tried to say something to Catherine's mother but the woman was barely functioning. The pupils of her eyes were enormous and she smiled vaguely as people expressed their condolences. She said nothing at all and it looked as if very little of what was said to her actually registered. Robert hovered at his mother's elbow, guiding her through her duties.

Margaret McDonald was there, too, in a grey jumper and skirt. The few times that Robert could leave his mother in the care of one of his aunts, Douglas saw that he moved immediately to whisper in Margaret's ear. The looks the two of them exchanged said that there was definitely an attraction there. He wished them well. Although an affair with a man in Interpol might be even more difficult than one with a mate on a cargo boat.

Next day, Douglas slipped down to Margot's office. She was still wearing the black suit or rather it seemed to be wearing her. Her blouse was the colour of haar, the dismal fog that drifted in from the sea. In his lunch hour Douglas walked down to Princes St. He bought two long silk scarves, one with a swirly pattern in pink and cerise, the other a mixture of clear blue and jade. When Douglas returned to the library, Margo was no longer in her office. The jacket of the terrible suit was dangling from a coat hook. He twisted the scarves together and draped them over the collar. About half an hour later, Margot came up to thank him.

"How did you know it was me?" Douglas asked.

Margot gave him a rather watery smile but said nothing.

"Would you like to have dinner with me tonight?" Douglas asked. At Margot's slight look of alarm, he said, "I believe the Kweilin comes very highly recommended for Cantonese food." The smile became a little less watery.

During the autumn they went out frequently. They tried new restaurants, went to concerts in the Queen's and Usher Halls and took long Sunday drives into the countryside, usually ending up at a ruined castle or abbey. Margot asked several times what arrangements Douglas had made about his flat. The reply was always the same. "I have one or two plans in the pipeline but there's plenty of time." Beyond that he would say nothing more.

On 31 December, Douglas asked Margot to see the New Year in with him in his flat. He did his best to provide traditional Scottish fare, smoked salmon, haggis, Aberdeen angus steaks and the raspberry and oatmeal dessert known as cranachan. There was champagne, claret and a bottle of Edradour single malt to toast the coming year. When the bells and kisses of midnight were over, they settled in the squashy armchairs with refilled glasses of whisky.

"What are your plans for the New Year, Margot?"

"I've been unsettled since Catherine was killed. It suddenly dawned on me that my life was just dwindling away. I could be approaching seventy not twenty-seven. I'm going to give my notice in at the library when the holidays are over. I have some money saved. I am going to work at my art for twelve months. At the end of that time I should know if I have it in me to make it professionally in the artistic world or not."

Douglas was silent for a moment then said, "I have something remarkable to tell you."

Margot was aware that since his return from Greece Douglas had had something on his mind he had not wished to share. She encouraged him to continue.

"Just after I returned from Greece, I had a visitor here at my home. A very dapper-looking individual, sober suit, close-cropped hair and one of the most expensive briefcases it has been my pleasure to see. It was attached to his wrist by a chain that could have anchored the Royal Yacht. It was the first time

I had ever met a genuine Swiss banker. Before he would tell me anything I had to prove who I was. Passport, birth certificate, driving licence and confirmation from a neutral third party of some standing."

"Good Lord, who did you ask?"

"I was fortunate that Harry McIntire in the law department was at his desk. He seemed to be sufficiently eminent for my visitor."

"So, what did this character want?"

"It seems that just before his death Professor Solómos transferred his Swiss bank account to me."

"How much was in it? What about death duties, inheritance tax?"

"There was enough money to warrant a personal visit from one of the bank's directors. As the transfer was completed before the professor's death, taxes and levies don't apply. As the money is in Switzerland, it is not subject to UK law."

"But you've continued to work at the library!" Margo was incredulous.

"I did not want to do anything in a hurry."

"Now you have made up your mind?"

"Yes, I have bought the villa on Sigandros from Athens University at full market value. They were very pleased."

"I bet they were. Selling a property with that sort of reputation in the back of beyond would not have been easy."

"I am also going to take up a position as director of the excavation on Athena's isle."

"How did you wangle that?"

"Money. I offered to pay all the expenses of the excavation and the salary of a mutually acceptable archaeologist for at least five years. I also offered to build a small villa for this individual on the other side of the village."

"How much did Solómos give you?"

"Enough and more than enough."

"When are you going to go?"

"The excavation will commence at Easter, but I would like to be in place long before then."

"I wish you well, I really do." Margot seemed more choked with tears than happy for Douglas's good fortune.

"That only leaves one question."
"What's that?"
"How much do you want a big Scottish wedding?"

They were married on Athena's isle. Douglas in Prince Charles jacket and McClaren tartan kilt, Margot in a delectable creation of her own devising with lots of floaty bits. As they stood through the interminable Greek Orthodox ceremony, it seemed as if the entire population of Sigandros had turned out to watch the show. After it was finally over they returned to the villa. Ékaterina, with an army of helpers, served a banquet, including several whole roast lambs and all the traditional wedding trimmings. It looked as if the party would last long into the night.

At dusk, however, a sleek caique sailed smoothly into the harbour. Douglas had hired the vessel for their honeymoon, a two-week cruise round the islands. As their luggage was hoisted aboard, the captain came down to greet them.

"Didáktor, Kiría Grey, my felicitations on your marriage." The captain was a short man with a fine moustache and a prominent belly. On the other hand, his white uniform fit perfectly and was as crisp as if it had just come from the laundry. "My name is Yánnis Kapodistrias and this is my first mate Costas Sarakinos. Welcome to the *Herakles II*, the premiere vessel of the Agía Triáda line. We assure you that we will take every care of you. Now if I might show you to your stateroom?" The little man led the way on board.

THE END

Printed in the United States
31920LVS00005B/115-171